Seduction on Wheels

The Matchmaking Motor Coach

Book Two

BARBARA BARRETT

This book is dedicated to several people in my life who provided rich memories on which to base some of the plot points in this book.

- My mother, Evelyn, and my stepfather, Al Blocklinger, for treating me to a three-day trip in their twenty-six-foot-long RV along the Florida coast when they first retired. That experience provided me with the background I needed for imagining the cross-country trip Jenna and Gray make from Iowa to California.
- My piano teacher, Mrs. Murray, whose love of music and patience gave me enough knowledge of playing the piano to imagine Jenna's desire to return to the one thing she knows how to do after her former husband cleaned out their bank account. Included here are also my late aunt, Gerry Wickerham, and my cousins, Marilyn Lihs and Bonnie Trickler, whose piano was the first place I learned how to play.
- My sister, Peg Knobloch, for spending a fun week with me in Palm Springs, California. She went on the aerial tramway up the mountain with me, which set the scene for late in the book when Jenna, Gray, Mitch, Aubrey and Paige use that same tram as a diversion before ending their trip in Los Angeles.
- My husband, Veryl, for driving me from Iowa to Arizona, when we've typically flown there, so I could get a true feel

for the countryside, in particular, the trip on I-17 from Flagstaff to south of Sedona, Arizona, which he claims was no big thing but scared me to death.

- And finally, my daughter, Leslie Sloan, who served as the inspiration for Jenna's daughter, Paige. Even though she is a grown woman, my ongoing love for my firstborn was at the back of my mind as I wrote about the relationship between these two women.

One

"Help me!" the young female shrieked.

Crank call. Yet another interruption on this sultry July afternoon. "Who is this?" Graham McKenna asked.

"It's Paige. Jenna DiFranco's daughter. My mom's in trouble. I've got to talk to Mitch. Now!"

Were they never to be rid of Jenna DiFranco and her smart aleck kid? "Mitch isn't here. This is Graham, his brother. What's wrong with your mom?" Given the woman's pushy attitude, he wouldn't be surprised if she'd been arrested for ordering around some cop.

"She's in the car. Staring straight ahead. She won't talk to me. Or even move."

Quite a switch. All the woman had done since she'd arrived the day before was run her mouth, spouting one opinion after another. When she wasn't criticizing. "Where are you?"

"Some gas station." The girl supplied a name. "We aren't very far out of town."

"Are you still on the highway?"

"Uh-huh. But I don't know what it is."

Must be on U.S. 61, since they were headed north to the regional airport in Moline, Illinois, two hours from Burlington, Iowa.

Should call the sheriff's office. Let them handle it. But something in the kid's plaintive appeal for help kept him on the line. "Why didn't you call 9-1-1?"

"She's not hurt that I can tell."

"You said she's not moving."

"She's not bleeding or anything. Just sitting here. Please come, Gray, she needs help."

She'd called him by the name only his two brothers used. Better look into this. Of all times for Mitch to make himself scarce.

He shoved away from his desk and grabbed his keys from the hubcap on top as he made his way from his office. "I'm leaving now. Give me your cell phone number, so I can call if I can't locate the car." He jumped into his pickup and slammed the door. "Okay, I'm on the way. Stay with your mom. Keep the doors locked."

While he searched for the gas station in question, he asked himself yet again why he was getting involved. Jenna DiFranco was a virtual stranger. In all his thirty-eight years, he'd never encountered such a demanding woman until she became their client. Tough negotiator. Micro-manager. Nitpicker. When she showed up in person yesterday to claim her runaway daughter, she turned out to be quite a looker, too, with that long blonde hair and creamy complexion. But his libido took a nosedive when she questioned their work on her motor coach. He preferred his ladies agreeable, acquiescent and unencumbered with kids. Especially teenage kids. Why hadn't Mitch stuck around?

Within twenty minutes, Gray spotted the gas station in question and what he surmised was Jenna's rental car at one of the pumps. He parked the pickup off to the side and rushed to the other vehicle.

The girl, pale, eyes wide, opened the passenger door immediately. "She still hasn't spoken, although she seems to be breathing better."

"You did good, kid, calling for help. I'll take it from here." He rounded the car to the driver's door. "Ms. DiFranco? Jenna? What's going on?"

The woman remained perfectly still. Catatonic, though that probably wasn't the technical term for her condition. God, he'd never seen anyone act like this. "Jenna? Can you hear me? Are you paralyzed? Blink once, if you are."

Jenna didn't respond. He reached for her wrist. Her pulse rate was remarkably slow, but her skin felt clammy. He turned to the kid, who'd followed him. "Did the car hit anything, go over any bumps too fast?"

She shook her head. "Mom was in a hurry. But she drove carefully."

"Did she eat or drink anything before you left or on the way?"

"Diet soda."

"I meant, uh, medication of some sort." Drugs. During her brief stay to pick up the kid, she'd been so hyper, she might have popped a tranquilizer or two. Or more.

"Nuh-uh."

As unobtrusively as he could, he examined Jenna's arms. An unexpected wave of relief flooded him. No visible marks. She hadn't shot up with anything.

He didn't want to alarm the kid further, but he had no idea what was wrong with her mother. Time to turn to the experts. "She needs medical help. I'll drive us back to town." He reached across Jenna's chest to turn on the ignition, so he could check the gas gauge, ignoring the unexpected wave of heat that shot through his arm as it came in contact with her. As he suspected, she hadn't refilled the tank.

Though the woman's body readily folded into his arms when he lifted her out of the driver's seat, she remained otherwise inert. For such a tall woman, she was remarkably light. Smelled nice, too, even though her knit top was warm with perspiration. *Stop it! She's in no shape to be ogled. Even if alert and functioning, this one is off limits.* He maneuvered her into the backseat with little trouble other than having to tuck her long legs into the car without bumping them in the process.

The kid rode in the back, holding her mom's hand. "Don't worry, Mom. You're gonna be okay," she said every so often.

"Call your aunt. Tell her what's happened and ask her to meet us at the hospital."

"I'm not sure I'll get her. I tried before and she didn't pick up."

Probably off with Mitch doing … Never mind, better not to speculate. The lovebirds had just reunited following a misunderstanding about Mitch wanting to leave their family business and practice law. They were off somewhere *making up* properly. "Any luck?" he called over his shoulder.

"No. Maybe she forgot her phone."

Or conveniently turned it off. He handed her his cell. "Mitch is on speed dial. Try him."

"He's not answering either," she said a few seconds later.

He considered calling his other brother, Geoff, because he didn't like leaving his pickup behind. Needed someone to return it to town. But Geoff didn't do much driving these days with his MS, especially not outside town. The truck would have to remain where it was temporarily.

"Where are we? What happened?" a sensuous woman's voice asked from the backseat as they were pulling into the hospital emergency entrance.

"Mom, oh Mom, you're back!" Paige cried, her voice a squeal.

"Back? Where have I been?"

"You had me so scared. You just sat there, not saying a word. Like you were in a trance." What was Paige talking about? Her eyelids kept closing. Had to focus.

Heavy breathing thrummed her ears. Her breathing.

Jenna surveyed her surroundings. "This is our rental, right? Why are we in the backseat?"

"I put you there." From the front, a somewhat recognizable face twisted her way. The same attractive face that had frowned at her when she arrived to claim Paige and grimaced every time she demonstrated the least bit of concern about the level of care they'd shown her daughter. One implied accusation about her parenting skills after another emerged from those firm lips.

"Graham McKenna? Why are you here? And why are you driving my car?" Her brain was doing a slow thaw. Where was Aubrey? Or Mitch?

"Call him Gray, Mom, like his brothers do. He came to help when I couldn't get hold of Mitch."

Jenna eased back into the seat and massaged her forehead. Why did it ache so? And why was she so warm? Had they been in an accident? No, Paige seemed fine, thank God, and neither of them was bleeding. Maybe she'd hit her head.

Graham got out, opened her door, and stuck his head in. "Your daughter called the garage, trying to find Mitch or Aubrey. They weren't around, so I came. Found you behind the wheel, not saying or doing anything. What happened? Do you know?"

She attempted to fill in the blanks. "I remember pulling up to the pump, frustrated because I forgot to fill the tank. I was afraid we'd miss our flight if we didn't hurry. But after that? Nothing." She checked her watch. Twelve thirty. Nearly an hour had passed. "Oh, my God! We're really late now. We've got to get moving."

Gray placed a restraining hand on hers. "Not so fast. You've just experienced some kind of major episode. You need to find out why." He leaned in closer, apparently so Paige couldn't hear. A whiff of musk met her nostrils. "I know how anxious you've been about the kid's running away. Did you, uh, take something?"

Take something? Was he suggesting she'd been doing drugs? The nerve! The flash of heat generated by his touch disappeared. "I don't do drugs, if that's what you mean."

"Well, something sure got into you. You scared your kid sh—silly. Enough to ask me for help when she couldn't get your sister. You know how she feels about me."

She turned to Paige, the same child who'd scared *her* silly a few days back by traveling on her own to Iowa from California, ostensibly to help her Aunt Aubrey finish the interior of the motor coach the brothers had customized for Jenna's upcoming concert tour. "I'm sorry if I scared you, hon. But I'm fine now." She slid toward the door, but Graham refused to move. "I can't let you leave."

"What? Why? Who are you to stop me?" Her first impression of the guy still held. Despite the inexplicable physical vibes he set off, he was a sanctimonious, tight ass. Add bully to the list now. One who had no right to hold her here. She and Paige had to get on the road.

"Good Samaritan rights. I came to your rescue, and now I can't let you out of my sight until I know everything is okay."

Good Samaritan rights?"

"Before I let you back on the road, you're getting examined. Shut up and wait for the kid to get a wheelchair."

Though she opened her mouth to protest, she closed it again. She didn't appear to have much choice.

After her so-called Good Samaritan clued in the hospital staff about her supposed "episode," Jenna was forced to dress in one of those dreadful hospital gowns that looked like a dust rag. Everything from a tongue depressor to an EKG machine was called into play to check out her physical condition.

"Since you're from out of town, Ms. DiFranco, I need to establish a history," the young female doctor said. "You're a mother, right? That's your daughter out there who came in with you?"

"Yes."

"Only child?"

"Yes."

"Age?"

"Mine or hers?"

"You first. Then her."

"Thirty-five. Paige is fourteen."

"You were in town visiting?"

"Not exactly." She briefly explained how Paige had taken off.

"Married?"

"Divorced."

The doctor took a few seconds to input something on her tablet. "Where's the father?"

Jenna had no idea where that lowlife was at the moment, but he was probably somewhere expensive in the company of his new girl-friend. "Is that necessary?"

The young woman glanced up from her notes, lowered her eyeglasses slightly along the bridge of her nose and gazed back at her. "In case you experience any further problems, we might need to notify him to come take care of your daughter."

"No! Don't do that." Her hair-trigger response surprised her as well as the doctor, who jerked in her seat, pushed her glasses up her nose. *Further problems?* She gripped her thighs to keep them from shaking. Took a calming breath. "My sister is here. If something is that wrong with me, I'll assign her temporary guardianship."

"O-kay, then. I'll need your sister's contact information."

Jenna gave her Aubrey's cell number.

"You say your daughter came here without your permission? That must have given you quite a scare."

"Yes, it did."

"Did you argue?"

"She's a young girl, doctor. Barely into her teens. Extremely bright. Every other sentence she utters is argumentative. But no, she came here because she was worried about her aunt."

The doctor blinked but didn't pursue the statement.

Jenna felt fine. Now. Except for her head. It still hurt. And her hands continued to tremble against her legs, despite her efforts to steady them. "Will this take much longer? I have to get back home to rehearse."

"Rehearse?"

"I'm a concert pianist preparing for an upcoming tour, and every minute away from rehearsals could hurt my performance."

The doctor eyed Jenna's quivering hands but didn't comment on the incongruity. "Divorce. Runaway daughter. Concert tour. You've got quite a bit on your plate."

Jenna started to disagree, and then the tears she'd been holding back since the night she found another woman's panties under her bed pushed their way out of her eyes and down her cheeks. The waterworks overcame her defenses and fell relentlessly, no matter how many tissues the doc handed her.

"This isn't like me. I never cry. Not like this, anyhow."

"Maybe that's part of your problem."

"Huh?" Not the kind of response she'd been expecting.

"Recent events in your life—and I suspect there's more you haven't told me—may have become too much for your mind to handle."

"I have some kind of mental illness?" No way. She was totally in control. Well, mostly, when she wasn't … never mind that now. She couldn't afford to freak. Not when she had to get her life and Paige's back on course.

"More like a stress-related condition."

"Okay, yes, I'm under stress. Who wouldn't be? I just have to tough my way through. I have no explanation for today. If my daughter and the man who brought me here hadn't confirmed it, I wouldn't have believed it even happened. But I'm fine now."

"There's no guarantee this won't happen again, if you don't take it more seriously and start doing something about it. Or the next time it occurs, you could be in the middle of traffic instead of stopped to get gas."

"Are you suggesting I call off my tour?"

"Is that a possibility?"

"No."

"What about delaying it?"

Jenna considered the question. She was the one who'd set the start date, because at the time she planned to take Paige along with her until school started, when Paige would stay with her grandmother. But the time period, late summer, was proving difficult to book. Events like concerts seemed to shut down until fall. She hadn't signed any contracts yet. Plus, as the enormity of all she'd bitten off hit, she'd backed away from the idea of bringing Paige on the road—yet another cause of the friction between them these days.

"You're considering. Good. Because I'm prescribing at least two days' total bed rest. I'm not recommending hospitalization, as long as you've got someone who'll be there to care for you round the clock. Doesn't have to be a trained health care provider, just someone who'll make your meals, watch over your daughter and act as a buffer between you and any external influences vying for your attention."

"Two days? I'm already behind schedule."

"Two days is a lot shorter than a month-long stay in a rehab facility."

True. She could probably afford two days, although with each passing day, more of the small nest egg she still clung to slipped away. This sudden trip to Iowa was draining money she could ill afford to lose. "Is that it?"

"No. The following week, I want you to relax. Really relax. Read. Watch television. Take short walks. Go out with friends. Exercise. Gradually reinstate yourself into real life."

The doctor's recommendation sounded more like a vacation than a treatment plan. A vacation would be heaven, but not when she had so many responsibilities facing her.

"I want to see you in my office in three weeks," the other woman said, as if sensing her thoughts. We'll evaluate your readiness to go back to the grind then."

"Back here? Return to Iowa? If I have to take time off, I want to do it in L.A."

"I recommend you stay here."

"Here? Oh, no, we couldn't. We hardly know anyone here."

"What about the man who brought you to the hospital?"

"Graham? No. He was the only one available when my daughter called for help. We're not … he's not … I just met him yesterday." Yes, he'd made quite an impression. No, she hadn't missed his jaw-dropping good looks, even compared to his almost as handsome brothers. But men were off her radar for now and maybe forever.

"With your permission, I'd like to talk to him and your daughter about your case."

"I told you, I barely know the man." And didn't plan to become better acquainted, given his judgmental attitude.

"Patients who experience episodes like the one you underwent today sometimes can't take in everything they hear from medical personnel. You could use extra sets of ears."

"I heard what you said, doctor."

"Humor me." The woman would be a tough opponent in a stare down, but that didn't mean Jenna would cave.

"Excuse me. They said I could let you know I'm here." Aubrey, stood at the open door. "I'm sorry Paige couldn't reach me. Mitch and I—"

"You don't have to explain. You're here now."

"You're … " the doctor asked.

"Aubrey Carpenter, Ms. DiFranco's sister."

The doctor gave them what appeared to be a relieved smile. "You got here just in time. Your sister and I appear to see her treatment plan differently. You can break the tie."

NINETY MINUTES LATER, Jenna had moved from the frying pan to the fire. "Two days' bed rest in a trailer? I know I own it and it's been customized according to my specifications, but I'm not ready for it yet. I should be on my way back to California to make up the time I'm missing from rehearsals. "

"First off, it's a motor coach," Aubrey corrected as she tucked her into the coach's king-sized bed. "It's your best option, Jenna, unless you want to spend money you don't have on a hotel room and a nurse. One of us will be available at all hours to check on you."

"Just what I need, a pack of babysitters in a firehouse turned garage."

"Better you than me." Paige set a bottle of water next to the bed. "See how you like it."

A reply wasn't worth the effort. She'd save her energy for the real war games with her daughter.

Aubrey read from the instructions provided by the emergency room doctor. "Okay, you've taken the meds the doc prescribed. Check. You're in bed in your comfy jammies under a warm cotton blanket. Check. Room temp's at seventy-one degrees. Check. Aromatic room spray. Check. You're all set, so we'll leave you to your dreams."

Paige, who of late rarely demonstrated any signs of mother-daughter kinship, leaned over to drop a soft peck on Jenna's cheek. "Sleep tight, Mom." She must have really been frightened by the trip to the hospital.

"Now that we've taken care of Mom, what're we gonna do the rest of the day?" Jenna heard Paige ask Aubrey on their way out. Okay, not that frightened.

Great. No longer afraid she was in danger of losing a parent, the child was ready to celebrate her supposed newfound independence. Couldn't worry about that now. Couldn't worry about anything at the moment, as waves of drowsiness swept over her.

Jenna was just about to drift off when she sensed a new presence in the room. Breathed in the tantalizing aroma of musk. That same scent had greeted her when she came to in the back seat of her rental. It was the kind of scent that could overpower a woman's senses and make her do things she knew she shouldn't.

With great effort, she opened one eye a tad. Her gaze rested on a pair of men's khakis, package level. She didn't have the energy, or inclination, to either shut off the view or change her focus. She could have sworn she detected the slightest movement beneath the fabric. No, of course not. Probably the drugs affecting her vision.

"Jenna? You awake?" The question was the barest whisper.

"No."

"It's Graham. I have first watch. Didn't want to scare you if you woke up later and found me here."

"Thanks," she replied, eyes at half-mast.

"Just call if you need me."

"'Kay." Like she would ever need him. Although, she had earlier in the day, hadn't she? And he'd been there for her. Yet, thanks to him, she was ensconced in this bed, behind in rehearsals and helpless to prevent her daughter from doing exactly what she'd set off to do when she'd run away from home, spend time with her aunt.

Not much she could do about any of that now. Not even continue to react to the nearby Graham McKenna.

Jenna's eyes closed and her brain shut down.

Two

Two days later, Jenna declared rest time over. Had to admit, she felt worlds better letting everything go to give her body time to recharge. Of course, she'd never admit as much to Aubrey. Who was this person she called her little sister? Had falling in love given her the confidence she always seemed just shy of obtaining in the past? Not only had Aubrey done a terrific job finishing the motor coach, her sibling had become her caretaker.

Aubrey meant well. She had no idea how bad things had gotten the last several months. How far outside the lines her Big Sister had wandered, trying to find herself while she put her life back together. Aubrey, the family rebel and serial dater, would be shocked to learn about her antics of late. Antics that cost her desperately needed rehearsal time, which she now had to make up, as soon as she could get Paige and herself out of this town and back to their normal life, if anything was normal these days.

Leaving so soon wouldn't sit well with Aubrey, and for that, Jenna was sorry. Even though she was the one who'd given Aubrey the chance to escape her problems in California, she'd been a real pain to her younger sister ever since Aubrey started work on the motor coach, checking up on her almost every day by phone and questioning her design decisions. Jenna realized she was micromanaging, being a real bitch. But she couldn't help herself. She'd been one huge ball of nerves, nerves that she'd now successfully put to rest.

She took in her surroundings one last time until she went on tour. Aubrey had done a great job of creating a home away from home for her while she'd be on the road. Photos of Paige and herself and the two of them with Aubrey in front of the Getty Museum held place of honor in the niches on the facing wall. Paige had balked at the idea of soaking up so much "culture" that day until they'd agreed to have dinner at the beach afterwards.

There was even a shot of their mother and stepfather, Buddy Appleby, on the set of one of the TV shows on which Buddy guest-starred. Probably necessary to include the pair. The two of them did complete their little family circle, even though at times their mother could be a bit overpowering. Nonetheless, she'd been the one to steer Jenna toward a career on the concert circuit.

Now, though, relaxation time was over. Time to get back to real life.

She'd just finished dressing when Aubrey burst into the bedroom. "What do you think you're doing?"

Jenna glanced up from her carry-on bag, pulled the zipper. "Pretty obvious, I'd say."

"You're not supposed to return to L.A. for three weeks."

"Changed my mind."

Aubrey grabbed the bag, unzipped it and removed the contents. "Not your decision to make. We settled this before you left the emergency room the other day."

"You wouldn't let me leave until I agreed."

"You're going back on your word."

"I have to rehearse."

"Not for at least three weeks. We pushed the start of your tour back that much."

Jenna dropped the pair of slacks she'd just removed from the closet where Aubrey had taken them. "You what?"

"I called your promoter and explained the situation. He'd been having second thoughts about starting in August and lining up enough venues for you by then and was more than happy to defer your start date."

Jenna balled her fists. "You think you're helping, that you're doing this for my own good, but you really shouldn't have called him."

"Probably not, but it worked."

Aubrey rarely tangled with her older sister. But this time she'd assumed control. "We'll just see about that."

Jenna searched the room for her phone and purse. Unable to locate them, she rummaged through the closet, and when that netted nothing, she flung open drawers. "Where are the rest of my things?"

"I took your phone, purse and car keys. We returned the rental car yesterday."

Jenna's anger welled inside her stomach as a knotty ball and made her shake uncontrollably.

Aubrey reached inside the pocket of her slacks and brought out a small vial. She withdrew a tablet and poured a glass of water from the bottle on the bedside table. "Here. Take this. It will help calm you."

Jenna puffed out her chest, then expelled an irate breath. "I don't want to calm down. You've taken over my life. You just can't do that."

Aubrey shrugged. "On the contrary, sis, I can and I am." She unclenched Jenna's hand enough to jam the pill inside. "I don't like corralling you like this. But we were pretty sure you wouldn't follow the doctor's orders."

Jenna struggled to keep up with her sister's statement. She repeated the one word that registered. "We?"

"Paige and I at first. At the hospital, we convinced Graham to go along with us. Since then, Mitch and Geoff have joined in, as well as Mom's cousin, Peggy Summers, and her daughter, Eileen, Geoff's new girlfriend."

"All of you? It's a conspiracy."

"Were you aware of your daughter's reaction at the hospital? She was pale as a ghost. That's cliché, but it's the best description I've got. She's scared for you, Jenna. You may think she's still a little girl, but she's old enough to have noticed a major change in your behavior since Jerry left—more than just nerves about your tour. You've been drinking more, although attempting to hide it from her. You leave her alone for hours at a time, and you're not always at rehearsals ... because she checked."

Her little girl noticed such things? Jenna slid back against the bed, plopped down. Had she really become the woman her sister described? The last several months had been hell. But that was no reason for this group, most of whom were relative strangers, to intervene in her life. She could take care of herself and Paige.

She made a concerted effort to control her voice. "Whose behavior wouldn't change after they discovered their spouse had been unfaithful? Then cleaned out their bank account?"

Aubrey's expression softened. "No one blames you, Jenna. We're just concerned the pressures you've been under these last months have taken their toll."

"Appreciated but unwarranted. I'm strong. Paige's taking off by herself to come visit you without my knowledge threw me off, that's all. I've now slept round-the-clock for two days. I'm fine." She held out her hand. "Give me back my things."

"She can't do that, Mom," Paige said from the doorway. "Different people each took one and hid it and didn't tell the others where."

"Th-that's ridiculous! I'm fine."

"Paige knows what we did, but she didn't participate."

She'd been had, and she didn't like it one bit. Nor did she plan to go along with them a minute longer than necessary. But since obstinacy wasn't getting her anywhere, she needed to step back and consider the options, figure a way out of this. She slumped on the bed, swiped her hands across her face.

"Okay, now that we've established you're not leaving town for a bit," Aubrey said apparently sensing her retreat, "let's talk about getting away from the firehouse for a few hours. I'm glad you're dressed, because we're expected at the Summers' for a late morning meal."

"What? You'll actually let me out of this dungeon?"

Aubrey didn't debate her. "Peggy's big on entertaining. Especially relatives. And she's a great cook," she replied.

Jenna rose, sighed. "I don't need entertaining right now or a good meal, but I'll go, since it means I won't be cooped up here all day."

Brunch at Peggy Summers' turned out to be a girls-only affair— Peggy, her daughter Eileen, Aubrey, Paige and Jenna.

Peggy laid out an egg and sausage frittata, fruit compote and home-made cinnamon rolls then bustled around offering coffee, tea and juice. Jenna accepted the plate of goodies her hostess placed before her but merely picked at her food.

"I'm so pleased to see you in person again, Jenna, after all these years," Peggy told her.

"I was five when my mother divorced my father and took me to California. I never expected I'd be back." Jenna attempted to keep her tone friendly and control her temper. Their cousin meant well. They all meant well. But they'd overstepped their bounds. She'd tolerate their overkill a few more hours while she played the role of a completely sane, normal person. But if they didn't relax their guard— abandon it actually— she wasn't putting up with it.

"Anyway, now that you're here, do you and Paige plan to stay in your motor coach? I wish I could offer my spare room, but it's about to be repainted and renovated."

Peggy's house was nice enough, and Peggy seemed a decent person, but Jenna didn't need any more people watching over her. Aubrey and Paige were more than enough. "Not to worry. Might as well test out my new home on the road before it actually hits the asphalt." Sounded plausible, not that she actually intended to go through with it.

"Really, Mom?" Paige asked. "It'll be fun. Like a sleepover for three weeks."

There was that. When she was her daughter's age, her mother had actually made a list of the girls from the richest families at her school and set out to *woo* their mothers so they'd include Jenna in their circle. The harder her mother tried, the more Jenna was left out. As a result, she'd retreated into more progressively introverted activities, like the piano. Making friends hadn't come easily. So there'd been few sleepovers in her teenage years. "Uh, I guess." She stared intentionally at her sister. "Unless your aunt has a more secure confinement in mind?"

"Actually, I do. We're moving to the McKenna place. Geoff's been living there, but he relocated to the fire station garage before you arrived. The guys are still debating whether to put the old family homestead on the market, so they've offered it to us in the meantime."

"We can't—" Hold the phone. They were talking about a house. A house that could be blocks, if not miles, from McKenna Custom Coaches. A house that must boast at least two exterior doors, so her guards couldn't watch her every minute.

"We can't what, Jenna?" Aubrey asked.

"We can't possibly repay them enough for their hospitality." Good save.

The surprises didn't end there. Peggy brought out a box and lifted the stack of paper and photos about an inch to retrieve an old photo. "I showed Aubrey some of these items when she visited a few weeks ago, but we missed this one." She handed the picture to Jenna. "This is you, your mom and your dad in happier days. You must've been around three or four. Quite the young lady, as you can see, from your little hat and tiny white gloves."

Jenna accepted the photo. "This is me? I've never seen this shot. In fact, I don't know if I've ever seen all three of us together. Mother always told me she hadn't kept anything."

Peggy gave a sympathetic smile. "Your mother was eager to, uh, put that part of her life behind her when she left town. But I believed there might come a day like this when her little girl would be interested."

Jenna tried to speak, but her throat refused. Her early years were a huge black hole. She didn't remember much from the time she, her mother and father—now deceased—lived in this town. She'd been robbed of those memories, thanks to her mother's reluctance to share anything. Only recently had she begun to understand her mother's motivations once she'd found herself so protective of anything Paige learned about her own father's exploits. Not that Stanley DiFranco had been anything like Jerry Waller.

Aubrey put an arm around Jenna's shoulder. "I always thought you resembled Mom more than I, but seeing this photo, you've also got a lot of DiFranco in you."

"I do, don't I?" She turned to Peggy. "Mom didn't permit me to see my dad until I was in my teens. I was a little shy around him at first, but once we got past that awkward stage, it was … wonderful. I felt … whole … for the first time in my life."

"Your mom believed she was doing the right thing by taking you both off to a better life," Peggy said.

"I probably never would have stepped foot on a concert stage had we stayed here. It was Aubrey's dad, my stepfather, who detected my musical talent."

"Poor Dad. I couldn't carry a tune or count time." Aubrey added. "You got his attention where music was concerned."

"Your lives have been … interesting … to say the least," Peggy said.

"That's one way of putting it," Aubrey replied. "Exactly why I'm happy to settle here for the time being."

"I hope you also enjoy your stay, Jenna," Peggy said.

Jenna squeezed out a smile. "As nice as my hometown appears to be from what little I've seen of it, I've got a tour to start. I have to get back."

Peggy took Jenna's comment as a sign to put the photo box away, their family reunion at an end.

That afternoon, they moved into the McKenna house. Not much to "move," only Jenna's carry-on, Paige's backpack and a few things for Aubrey. "We should have stopped for groceries," Jenna said as they entered the kitchen. Surely there'd be an available pay phone near a grocery store. All she had to do was give Aubrey and Paige the slip, and she could get her promoter on the line in a…. No. No money. Couldn't do that. Yet.

"Already took care of food." Graham emerged from what looked like a closet next to the kitchen. "Dry stuff's back there in the pantry, and the fridge is already filled."

Aubrey tapped his shoulder. "Thanks, Graham."

"Yes, uh, thanks," Jenna murmured. For someone who seemed to have taken an immediate dislike to her, he'd sure been helpful the last few days. And around a lot. Memories of the last time she'd seen him, well, one part of him, came flooding back. She shifted her attention to the kitchen island so neither Aubrey nor Graham would see the pinkish color she was sure had shot up her neck.

"Mitch got tied up on some errand at the law office, so I got elected for grocery duty. Wasn't sure what you like to eat, so I just got healthy stuff."

"I took the liberty of augmenting your wardrobe with more slacks, shorts and tops," Aubrey added. "Also sleepwear and undies. Mitch brought them over earlier."

Jenna fixed a smile across her face and turned to face them again. "Sounds like you thought of everything."

Everyone had been so helpful. She should be grateful for their support. They meant well, but why couldn't they just leave her be so she could get her and Paige's lives back on track?

Gray watched Jenna struggle to contain her frustration. Tiny sparks flickered in her eyes and she kept flexing her fingers. Some part of him was sorry for her, for having this elaborate scheme to keep her in town sprung on her. But the other part of him was glad they'd anticipated her readiness to renege on her agreement with the doctor and head west.

Only he and the kid were aware how bad it had been back there in the car. He'd never witnessed anyone so motionless and out of it while still conscious. Scared the hell out of him. Which was the only reason he'd gone along with Aubrey and the kid's plan. Right? Sure wasn't some ridiculous need to keep her around.

This forced relaxation was best for Jenna, since she didn't appear to be following her doctor's orders on her own. Still, he empathized with her dislike of being held here against her will. He certainly wouldn't like it, if their positions were reversed, though there were times of late he felt his own kind of captivity. Not all prisons were physical structures. "There's something in the living room we'd like you to see. Paige told me you used to paint before this concert tour business arose."

"Some. Mainly dabbled."

He led her through the dining room and then into their man cave in the front of the house equipped with an enormous entertainment center, flat screen and dark brown leather sectional. In the middle of the room, appearing quite out of its element, stood an easel and wooden case. "They're mine, although I haven't done anything with them for some time. Thought you might like to use them while you're here." He waited, unsure how she'd react. Just so she didn't throw either object across the room. Maybe someday he'd want to use them again himself.

Jenna examined the easel. "Nice. What's in there?" She pointed to the box.

"Paintbrushes. There's acrylic paint in there too. May not be much good anymore, but that can be replaced as soon as we know what you want."

She didn't speak for a few beats. "That was ... very thoughtful of you."

"Could only find one clean canvas. But like the paint, just let us know what you need."

Finally, she turned her gaze on him, her gray eyes just a tad wider. Eyes that could penetrate a guy's defenses, if he let them. "Don't suppose you also play the piano?"

Aubrey had warned him Jenna might attempt to sneak under the radar to get herself back to what she considered "normal." Here it was. He hesitated just long enough to make sure his mouth remembered to smile. "No. Geoff's the musical McKenna, but even he doesn't play the piano."

A veil descended over her eyes, now absent whatever tiny bit of light he'd seen there just moments before. She swallowed. "Perhaps you could find one for me?"

"Sorry, sis, that's one thing we can't bring you," Aubrey said, coming to his rescue. "A piano equates with rehearsing, which is a no-no right now."

Jenna's lips tightened while her breathing increased. "You are so wrong. I relax when I play." She clenched her hands, which now quivered.

"I'm sorry, Jenna. For now, no piano. But we'll try to get you whatever else you need. As long as you don't overdo," Aubrey answered.

The color seemed to drain from Jenna's face. She pivoted from them and stalked to the front door, reached for the handle. "This is locked, right? Same as the back door."

"Please, Jenna—" Aubrey said.

"I don't believe this. If I were terribly ill or otherwise incapacitated, I could understand why you might try to take over my life. But I'm neither. I'm able-bodied and fully functioning, including my mind. You've gone too far to keep me a prisoner." Her voice wavered on the last part.

No one spoke while Jenna, white-faced, stood there, daring them to deny her accusation.

Gray looked to Aubrey for his cue, but he got nothing, because she was studying her hands.

"You're breaking the law, Aubrey!" Jenna's voice rose. "I have rights. You can't do this to me." The last came out as a wail. Her knees buckled and she collapsed into Gray's arms.

He lifted her and carried her into the bedroom that was to be hers. This was getting to be a habit, not entirely an unpleasant one. "Shhh. Just relax," he said as he smoothed away the hair that had fallen over her eyes. Despite his hesitancy to like her, she was a beautiful woman, even in this weakened state.

Aubrey and Paige followed. Paige removed the duvet and pulled down the blankets. Aubrey produced a capsule and water.

To his relief, Jenna took the pill and allowed him to lay her on the bed. "I'll stay with her until she's completely out," Aubrey whispered.

"I'm taking off, then." Suddenly, the house he'd grown up in became too confining. Gray's breathing had become almost as labored as Jenna's before she passed out.

GRAY STUDIED the specs for Jenna's coach. Now that he'd volunteered to assume the mechanic duties once Mitch joined Orville Drummond's law firm, it was time to figure out what that commitment meant.

Three days ago, his life had been more or less on track, though by no means perfect. He had a comfy home here in the refurbished firehouse he and the guys bought when they restructured their dad's failing RV business into its current identity. His brothers were close by for company, entertainment, and advice, when, on occasion, he allowed them into his private thoughts.

Not much going on in his social life other than the parade of ladies he graced with his presence at dinner, concerts and his bed. He liked it that way. No messy involvements, no complications. Been there, done that, and the results had been too painful to consider retracing that path again.

"How'd it go?" Mitch asked. The youngest of the McKenna brothers lounged in the doorway of Gray's office, as if debating whether it was safe to approach, since he himself had passed on being at the house when Jenna and company arrived.

Gray held out his arms for inspection. "No scrapes or scratches. Yet. Though when she discovered all the doors were locked, I did have to catch her before she hit the ground."

"Fainted?"

"Apparently the full realization finally registered. She started to shake, grew pale about the same time her frustration morphed into anger."

Mitch shook his head. "Poor Aubrey, suddenly finding herself caretaker for her sister and niece."

"How do you think Jenna feels? Husband cleans out her bank

account, kid runs away, and now when she feels she has to do the same, she's prevented from doing so by a group of well-meaning family and friends. And chumps like me."

"Chump?"

"I don't even like the woman. Or her kid. Yet there I was, buying groceries for her and now coming to her defense."

Mitch studied his brother's expression as if trying to find some hidden meaning in his words. "Yeah. Imagine. Wonder why."

Gray started to answer then stopped. He had no idea what had prompted this do-gooder thing. "You and Aubrey and the others can take over for a while."

Mitch screwed up his face. "Uh, not so fast. Aubrey has invited us all to dinner tonight. You, me, Geoff and Eileen. Misery loves company, I guess."

He'd had his fill of the woman. Needed a break. "No. I've completed my mission." He held up the specs for the coach. "Besides, if I take over your duties, I'd better start boning up on coach maintenance."

"Plenty of time for that, bro. I'm not leaving for some time yet."

"That's good, because I need you here to show me what's what, not off playing nursemaid to some neurotic concert pianist from L.A. or getting it on with her sister."

Mitch retreated a step. "What's with the attitude?"

Gray's shoulder slumped. "I don't know. Guess there's been so much change around here lately—you and Aubrey, Geoff moving in, Geoff dating Eileen, you going off to work for Orville—I'm just …" he raised his hands, "…trying to catch up. Figure out how I fit into the new order."

Mitch settled into the chair across from Geoff's desk. "Feeling like the odd man out?"

Gray rubbed his chin, aligned a stray pencil with the edge of his desktop. "I'm the oldest. In some societies, with Mom and Dad no longer here, I'd be considered the elder. The decision-maker. Instead, I'm the fifth wheel, the one you turn to when you need a babysitter for Jenna."

"Geez, man, I know things have been happening pretty fast lately. But I didn't realize you felt left out."

"Just trying to adjust. I'm glad I've been spared all the melodrama the women in your lives are generating. I deliberately avoid such entanglements, and I'm happy with my life just the way it is."

"Uh-huh. Who you trying to convince, me or yourself?"

"There's a lot I don't know yet about the mechanic's duties, and I don't like feeling uninformed."

Mitch chuckled. "Don't I know? You've always been the control freak of the family."

"I am not a control freak! I like things to be settled, to be on top of the details."

"You are a control freak," Geoff said, stepping into the room. "But we're both glad you are, so Mitch can do his thing with the law and I can do my schmoozing." Despite his MS, their middle brother, slightly shorter with lighter hair and brilliant blue eyes, was the glue of the family, the mediator and people person.

"Where've you been?" Mitch asked Geoff.

"Getting an earful from Eileen. Her mother, too, through Eileen's pipeline. After spending time with her this morning, they're worried about Jenna."

Mitch nodded. "Right. Eileen's mom hosted some sort of ladies-only get together. What happened—did Jenna lose it there, too?"

"Too?"

Gray related his encounter with their West Coast visitor.

"Actually, according to Eileen, it sounds like it was just the opposite. Jenna made small talk, laughed and smiled. But all the while, she seemed distant and disengaged."

"It was her first time awake after sleeping round the clock for two days," Gray said.

"True, but Eileen and her mom think there's more to it. Like Jenna was going through the motions to let everyone think she's fine with this enforced rest, but as soon as she gets a chance, she'll make a run for it."

"Can you blame her?" Gray asked. "Everyone's ganged up against her."

"For her own good." Mitch reminded them, defending Aubrey's plan.

"I agree with Eileen and her mom," Gray said. "All the woman has talked about since she arrived was getting back to California. If she can find a way to get out of the house, she will."

"She won't get far, unless she finds her phone or some money," Mitch said.

"Don't underestimate her," Gray replied. "She's resourceful and tenacious. She got all sorts of design concessions out of me before we ever started work on her coach."

"Have we clued in the neighbors?" Geoff asked. "All we need is for her to get out and go for help. We could all be in trouble if she claims we've kidnapped her."

"I don't think she'd turn on her own kid, and if push came to shove, she probably wouldn't report Aubrey, either. She's just not used to her little sister taking care of her."

He could identify. There were times when he resented Mitch taking the lead in getting the business on its feet. Well, not resented. Too strong. But it did bother him. "My read is she's biding her time until she can either convince Aubrey to let her go or she takes off on her own."

"You know this how?" Mitch asked.

"Just a feeling I got when I delivered the groceries." Feeling? Since when had he paid attention to *feelings*? Especially where this woman was concerned.

As the gravity of their predicament sank in, all three remained silent, immersed in private speculations. "Remember how when Aubrey first showed up we made her work environment as unpleasant as possible so she'd leave?" Geoff said at length, a hint of a smile tugging at his lips.

Gray recalled the experience all too well. "You referring to that list of conditions we made her accept?"

A slight cough emerged from Mitch. "Right, bro. That worked so well. She not only came up with her own list and proceeded to take over this place, I fell in love with her."

"Well, yeah, there's that," Geoff said, conceding the point. Nonetheless, his expression became even more animated. "What if, like we did with Aubrey, we let Jenna think she's getting what she wants?" He paused dramatically. "In other words, we let her go."

Three

Gray fell back in his seat. "Are you crazy? The woman needs help but not that kind."

Geoff raised a hand, held his ground. "Think about it. We can't keep her prisoner for three full weeks. Aubrey's plan is to help her relax by gradually getting her involved in various activities, but if Jenna repeats today's performance, she'll just act like she's going along. The first chance she gets, she's outta here. Rather than let the inevitable happen, we orchestrate it ourselves. Like a prescribed fire."

"You know how many of those so-called *controlled* burns get out of control?" Gray asked, still incredulous at his brother's wild idea.

Mitch ignored Gray's question. "Tell us more, Geoff."

Were they both losing it?

Geoff rubbed his chin. "I don't have a plan. Yet. Just an idea. We wouldn't let her do this on her own. We'd supply her with a protector. Someone she'd think she's convinced holding her captive won't work."

Mitch inclined his head. "She'd have to rely on them totally, because we'd make sure she still didn't get hold of her cell or any money. Those would give her too much opportunity to take off on her own."

"Right," Geoff agreed.

"It could work." Mitch said scratching his chin. "Although I don't see how we'd get her onto a plane without an ID."

Geoff leaned in closer. "Then we don't let her fly."

"Then how? We drive her back?" Mitch asked.

"That's one way, I guess. Or accompany her on a bus."

Gray shifted position. Was he really hearing this? The conditions they imposed on Aubrey were extreme, but what Geoff was suggesting was so much farther out there, it was almost like one of those caper movies. His brothers' imagination was on overdrive and had to be stopped. "Why not just give her the keys to her motor coach and let her drive it back to California herself?" he said facetiously.

Geoff and Mitch turned toward him, incredulous expressions on their faces. For a split second, everyone froze, and then Mitch exploded. "That's brilliant!"

Gray slammed away from his desk. "I was kidding! That was the most ridiculous idea I could summon."

"Maybe you think so," Mitch said, "but you hit on the perfect plan."

"If we can pull it off," Geoff added.

Gray fought to keep his cool. "Didn't you hear me? I wasn't serious. Everything about that idea is so wrong, so impossible, it would never work."

"Hear us out, Gray," Mitch said. "Before we dismiss this idea, let's list all the impossibilities and see if we can't somehow overcome them."

Here was his chance to bring them back to reality. "Then get your pad and paper ready. I'm loaded." He ticked off each objection on his fingers. "Jenna doesn't know how to drive a motor coach. That's not something she'd learn overnight or teach herself. Nor does she possess a commercial driver's license."

That stopped them. Momentarily. "Then her so-called ally would have to drive the coach," Geoff said. He gave a "so there" nod of his head.

"That's a huge job. And responsibility," Gray responded. "Where will they stay along the way? You don't just sail into a rest area or side street and pull up for the night. Motor coach overnights are planned well in advance." Surely the folly of this idea had dawned on them by now. He checked out Mitch, then Geoff.

"Done?" Mitch asked.

"Isn't that enough?" he asked, satisfied all the roadblocks he'd come up with couldn't possibly be met.

"They could probably stay anywhere," Geoff said. "The coach is self-contained with its own water tank and generator, and it can go a few days without dumping waste."

"We just need time to plan for the overnight stops," Mitch said.

"Time we don't have," Gray countered. "I'm telling you, escape is imminent. She doesn't tend to be a patient woman."

Geoff blew out a breath, as if he'd had enough of Gray's objections. Suddenly, he thumped the desk, apparently struck by some new bright idea. "We're members of a couple motor coach associations. We'll tap them for help."

"Make them party to this crime?" Gray's voice rose.

"There is no crime, bro," Mitch said. "Jenna would think it was her idea. She'd be a willing participant. Plus, she owns the vehicle."

Okay, one more point in their favor. But they were far from done discussing this.

Mitch and Geoff each claimed a visitor chair and the confab continued for several more minutes, Mitch and Geoff managing to rebut every argument Gray raised. "Okay. Let's say all this comes together," Gray said finally. "Jenna sets off on her cross-country adventure headed for home. What's to stop her from dumping her accomplice and enlisting some unsuspecting fellow traveler's help finding a faster way home, like hitchhiking or borrowing money to buy an airline ticket?"

"I wondered when you'd get to that," Mitch said. "Before you remind me how our plan with Aubrey blew up in our faces, remember what we did accomplish— we got her to agree to certain conditions to work here. If Jenna thinks she's conning one of us into helping her, said co-conspirator has to first make her agree to a list of requirements before they help her. Like no cutting out on them, no kidnapping claims, you get the drift."

"This woman just got dumped by her husband. She isn't trusting any guy these days," Gray said. "Maybe if Aubrey, or even Eileen, could handle Jenna's rig, she might turn to them. Although after the last few days, I doubt Jenna will trust her sister for a while either. And she hardly knows Eileen."

Mitch tilted his head, studied him. "Sounds like you're coming around to this idea, Gray."

"Where'd you get that impression? I've been advancing every reason why this won't work."

"Let's run this by Aubrey at dinner," Mitch said. "See what she thinks."

"Told you, I'm bowing out of the Jailhouse Jenna saga for a bit," Gray repeated.

"C'mon, bro," Geoff replied. "Eileen's mom is supplying the food. You know what a great cook she is."

Score one for Geoff. Their meals typically came from packages, cans, frozen dinners or delivery. Someone needed to keep a cool head and talk them out of the idea. He didn't want to tangle with Jenna DiFranco any more than he had, but he didn't see any way around it. He had to stop this craziness now before it got even further out of hand.

God, he hoped Aubrey opposed the scheme. "You're right, Geoff. I can't say no to one of Peggy's meals." He leaned over and patted Geoff's stomach. "Better watch out there, bud. You've already put on a few pounds since you've been hanging out with Eileen."

Geoff rose, pulled in his gut. "You're just jealous of my sudden meal bonanza."

Gray dragged himself from his chair, thumped Geoff on the back. "That's right. I'm so jealous of having a female checking on me every hour." They filed out of the firehouse. Gray and Geoff took Gray's pickup. Mitch headed off to his own truck, since he'd probably be returning later than them.

Aubrey allowed Jenna to sleep until a few minutes before dinner. As Gray learned later, she didn't tell her sister they had company until Jenna stumbled into the dining room to find Mitch, Geoff, Eileen and himself seated there along with Paige.

Jenna froze. "What's this? It now takes six of you to keep me under lock and key?"

Eileen answered. "Mom had to take my brother to a night game, but she sent a meal over with me and had me invite the McKennas."

"Thank you, Peggy." Mitch raised his water glass in salute to the absent cook.

Paige indicated the empty chair next to her. "Sit here, Mom."

Jenna didn't move. Was she disoriented, not quite tracking with what was happening, or was she about to protest? Gray couldn't tell.

Aubrey's tone was gentle, coaxing. "Jenna? C'mon, hon. Dinner's getting cold. Everyone's waiting."

After what seemed forever but was actually a few seconds, Jenna took the chair Paige offered. "How long have I been sleeping?"

"A few hours," Aubrey replied.

More like five. No wonder the woman was groggy.

"Hope you like green beans." Eileen passed the bowl Jenna's direction. "Mom said they'd be good for you."

Eileen ladled a healthy serving onto Jenna's plate.

Next came beef tips in gravy over egg noodles, homemade cranberry sauce and finally blueberry muffins.

Jenna kept her hands in her lap.

"You're not eating, Mom."

"I'm, uh, not hungry. Please thank your mother for Paige and me," she said to Eileen. "I'm sure this all tastes as good as the brunch she prepared this morning, but I don't feel like I could get anything down right now." Her little speech appeared to wind her.

Maybe the drugs were affecting her appetite. Or she wasn't used to eating this much at the evening meal, although the kid was certainly shoveling it in. Or maybe Jenna didn't appreciate being under everyone's close scrutiny. Bad enough to be confined to this house, but with all of them here, she couldn't even have privacy.

"How 'bout a sandwich instead?" he asked. "I brought some deli turkey earlier. Despite Peggy's good intentions, maybe this large a meal may be premature."

He rose and proceeded to pull out Jenna's chair. To his astonishment—and probably everyone else's as well—she let him. In the kitchen, he went to work assembling things. "Mayo?" he asked, having already stuck a few lettuce leaves and tomato slices on the bread.

"Huh?"

"Do you want mayonnaise on your sandwich? I like my turkey sandwiches slathered in the stuff, but not everyone does."

"Oh. Uh, sure."

He cut the sandwich in half and plopped it on a plate. Without asking, he grabbed a glass and filled it with milk. He set them on the small kitchen island and pulled out a stool for her. "Here you go."

Throughout this exchange, she rubbed her hands, didn't gaze at him. With the plate in front of her, she finally moved, took a bite of the sandwich. Just one bite. Then she put it down.

Was that to be polite, her small thanks for getting her away from the group in the other room? On the other hand, maybe she truly wasn't hungry.

While he pondered those questions, she took another bite. Then another. Soon, she was sipping her milk. "Got a napkin?" she asked at length.

He reached in a cabinet drawer and retrieved two.

"Are you part of that posse out there?"

Posse. He liked her sense of humor. Or was it just sarcasm? "Yeah, I guess. Wish it wasn't necessary. But you didn't leave Aubrey any choice."

"Choice?" Her voice rose. "Where I recuperate is supposed to be my decision. She's not my guardian, and she doesn't have my power of attorney. She simply disagrees with me returning to California."

"Your sister is a bit of a fixer. Meddler, if you want to go that far.

But if she hadn't stuck her nose into our family's business, Mitch would have given up the opportunity of a lifetime to practice law with his mentor and would have continued to be miserable working with us. She means well."

For the first time since coming into the kitchen, she looked him in the eyes. "I love my sister. Yes, she means well. But that doesn't justify keeping me here against my will. That's kidnapping. And you're all accessories."

"You think that's news to me?"

She blinked, as if his admission really was news. "Then why are you going along with them?"

"You scared the hell out me when I found you in a state comparable to the living dead. Since your doctor thinks this might happen again if you don't reduce your stress level, I'm going along with her assessment."

"Do you agree with keeping me here against my will?"

"I don't like you. You're demanding and high maintenance, but I'm not crazy about going to such an extreme to help you."

"You don't mince words, do you?"

"Geoff's the PR guy in the family. I tell it like it is."

"Then help me." Her voice, plaintive, was barely a whimper. "Help me convince my sister and the rest of them I can't take this captivity."

He started to turn her down. "How's the sandwich?" Geoff asked, apparently send by Aubrey to check on them.

"Just what I needed," Jenna returned. "Sorry about my outburst."

He leaned into Gray and delivered a brotherly nudge. "Yeah, well, I have an inkling of how your feel. When I was first diagnosed with MS, this guy and Mitch hovered like mother hens. For a while, it was like I couldn't breathe. All I wanted was my space."

She cocked her head. Geoff's words must have registered. "Did it get better?"

"Had to realize they were more scared than me but knew even less how to deal with my condition, because they were only experiencing it secondhand. Over time, it got easier to tolerate."

"But they didn't lock you in a stranger's house."

"True, but I also didn't threaten to leave town on my own."

Touché, lady.

She seemed to consider Geoff's words. "I'll give it some time, like you suggest," she replied after a few beats. "I just want everyone to back off and let me breathe."

Later, back at the firehouse, Mitch surprised Gray, Geoff, and Eileen by returning early. "Aubrey shooed me out. Said Jenna could use some mother-daughter-sister time."

Despite Peggy's hearty dinner, they all sat around the kitchen table munching snacks and downing a few beers. "I seem to have interrupted a heavy discussion between you and Jenna out there in the kitchen," Geoff said to Gray.

"As I recall, we were discussing the merits of mayo on her turkey sandwich," Gray replied.

"What I came in on was something like, 'help me'."

"Oh, that," he said, dismissing the question. "Just humoring her to get her to talk."

"Sounds like you succeeded," Geoff replied.

"Well—"

"So, we should build on that," Mitch added.

"Huh?"

Geoff stopped skimming his thumbnail through the label on his beer bottle and gazed at Gray. "While you were in the kitchen, Mitch and I ran our idea past Aubrey, Paige and Eileen."

Eileen, who'd remained silent up to now, added her two cents. "Though it's somewhat far-fetched, we all agree we should give it a try."

Damn! He hoped with a full meal in their gullets, the guys would have forgotten about Geoff's ill-conceived plan. His palms itched. Something was up. Something more than discussing how this crazy scheme could work. He had to put the brakes on this runaway train, or in their case, motor coach.

Gray banged his bottle so hard on the kitchen table, beer splashed across the surface. "You're kidding?" His eyes went from face to face. No kidding here. Just delusions of possibility.

Mitch assumed what Gray privately referred to as his *lawyer tone*. Patient. Calm. Confident. "Not only is it going to be difficult watching her 24/7, but she's also miserable with us watching her. Certainly evident tonight. So, we help her help herself. Though we've got a lot of planning to do to make this work, we still think it's viable. "

Gray pushed away from the table, the sound of his chair scraping against the floor pierced the mood. "You think? What is this—did you all drink the flavored water? This idea is riddled with impossibilities."

"Aubrey's working on every point you ticked off earlier, and Geoff and I can expedite the registration, licensing and insurance processes to be ready in a few days," Mitch said. "If we can reasonably address all your concerns, will you go along?"

Aubrey was ingenious at fixing things. But the cross-country trek they were now proposing was much more complicated. Just let her try to work her magic. "Okay. If Aubrey and the rest of you can clear away each and every one of the obstacles, I'll agree. Reluctantly." This ridiculous idea was so doomed.

"Let's tackle the first problem right now," Mitch said. "Who helps Jenna flee?"

"I'd love to see the West Coast, but I don't have much vacation time built up with my job," Eileen said, as if on cue.

"Besides, she doesn't know how to drive a motor coach. Nor Aubrey," Geoff added. "And, uh, we all know I can't be on the road."

"I promised Orville I'd start my part-time job with him next week," Mitch put in.

And there it was. The reason his palms itched. His brothers and their women must have rehearsed this setup while he was in the kitchen with Jenna. But Gray was on to them. They couldn't make him do something he didn't want to do. And he really didn't want to do this. No, running away with Jenna just wasn't in the cards.

Four

Geoff waved his hand before Gray's face. "Uh, you aren't saying anything."

"You got that right. Just so there's no confusion, my schedule's fuller than any of yours. Even if my workload was lighter, I still wouldn't agree to help Jenna break away."

He waited for one of them to dispute his statement, but the argument didn't come. "Did you think we were including you?" Eileen chuckled. We know how you feel about Jenna. You're the least likely person to come to her aid."

What was this? They'd already ruled him out?

"But we do want you in on the planning. You're way ahead of us listing all the things that could go wrong," Mitch added.

"Okay, I'll help with that part."

Geoff shoved his shoulder. "That's all we're asking, bro."

Gray flinched. "Watch the shoulder." The collarbone injury he'd received weeks ago when he collided with Mitch in a hard-fought ball game still ached.

"Oh, sorry."

"First complication, besides everything I've already mentioned,"

Gray said, "who's gonna be this *ally* for Jenna, if none of you can do it and I won't?"

Geoff cajoled him. "Think of yourself as Solomon, oh wise one. "We've each cited our reasons for not going. But which one or two of us, with the appropriate rearrangement of our life or redirection of our options, actually could?"

He needed to steer clear of this pickle. Whoever he suggested was bound to object. Okay. Go for the weakest link, the one who wasn't here to defend herself. "How about Aubrey? Jenna's her sister, her problem."

"How would she learn how to drive a coach overnight?"

"She won't. She'll concede to Jenna's desire to get back to L.A. on the condition she go with her and oversee her recuperation."

Mitch sprang from his chair. "Aubrey's tied up here. She doesn't have time to return to the Coast."

"And the rest of you do?" Gray asked.

"Try again," Geoff said.

"Okay. Aubrey gets a temporary restraining order keeping her sister here."

"You trying to get yourself booted from this confab, bro?" Mitch asked.

Gray shot to his feet. "Good idea. If it helps, I'll back off my no-fly notice when it comes to Jenna and take a shift or two watching her."

"You've got a deal," Mitch said. "Tomorrow night. Aubrey needs a break."

Aubrey. Aubrey couldn't take her sister back to California. Aubrey couldn't get a restraining order and legalize keeping her in town. Now poor Aubrey needed a break. When the woman first showed up at the firehouse, he had designs on her himself, and Mitch was the one who could barely tolerate her. Now, his brother was so smitten, Aubrey could do no wrong.

WITH NOTHING better to occupy her time the next afternoon, Jenna planted herself at the dining room table and flipped through one of the magazines Aubrey had provided. Once again, her sister's heart had been in the right place, but Jenna didn't need to be reminded of the change in her domestic situation with page after page of recipes, fashions and housekeeping advice.

Aubrey passed by carrying a stack of clean laundry. "Glad to see you're keeping your mind occupied."

"I'm turning pages."

"It's only been two days since you came out of your drug-induced slumber. Give your mind and body time to adjust. You shouldn't expect to return to your routine for some time."

"Piano was my routine. I don't know what to do with so much down time."

Aubrey put aside the pile of clothes and joined her sister at the table. "I hoped our little excursion this morning to see some of the town's sights would help. Next time, you decide where we go."

"Aren't there any places available to anyone who wants to play piano? Like churches or a hospital? You could stay with me the entire time to assure I wouldn't run off."

Aubrey closed her eyes briefly, like a suffering parent. "We've been through this, Jenna. The doctor said no piano. Maybe if you take things completely easy for this week, next week she'll relent."

A week. Could she hold herself together that long? She didn't have much choice. "Who's on guard duty tonight?"

"You'll be pretty much on your own tonight." Aubrey retrieved the pile of laundry and resumed her path to Paige's room.

"Pretty much?"

"With your permission, Geoff and Eileen are taking Paige and Eileen's brother, Tommy, to a movie, and Mitch and I are treating Orville to a jazz club. Graham will be back to keep you entertained."

"Graham? What are you trying to do, set me up while I'm here?"

"You seemed to prefer his company to ours last night," Aubrey called on her way down the hall.

Graham for company. Alone. In this big house. She hadn't been alone with a man since … *Don't go there, Jenna. You vowed it wouldn't happen again.*

On the other hand, this was Graham, the Ice Man. He'd told her last night he didn't like her. Given her recent explorations on the dark side of the male-female world, his declaration of negativity boded well for the evening. Last night, she'd asked him to help her. If Geoff hadn't interrupted, how would Graham have responded? Tonight she'd have a chance to find out.

He arrived the same time Mitch came to pick up Aubrey. Some communications system they all shared, as finely tuned as any law enforcement agency worth its salt. They didn't leave her on her own for even a minute. "Brought you a grilled chicken salad. The pizza's for me."

"Thanks for getting that. My appetite has been nil. Everyone else seems to think food is the panacea."

He held up a six-pack. "Drink beer?"

"Okay, you miscalculated there, but water's okay."

After Mitch and Aubrey left, she and Graham sat at the kitchen island and devoured their meals. "Not half bad," she said after a few bites. Actually, for the first time in days, she was famished and had to remind herself to slow down. When she came up for air, despite the heavy aroma of tomato sauce, pepperoni and pizza dough emanating from Graham's plate, she could still detect his aftershave. Something citrusy this time. Not as inhibition-defying as the musk but more friendly.

"Stopped by my go-to place for this. Probably have it more often than I should, but it's easier than fixing a meal and tastes pretty damned good."

Interesting admission. She'd keep him talking. Get him to relax. Then she'd bring up their conversation from the previous evening. The ends of the close-clipped hair around the back of his neck separated slightly. He'd recently taken a shower. Just for her? Then she noted how his brown hair was slightly lighter than Mitch's and his forehead narrower and just a little higher, although his eyes were just as dark blue and penetrating as his younger brother. *Stop staring.* "Busy day?"

One eyebrow rose. "Guess you could say so. I've been trying to do my own job plus learn what Mitch did as the mechanic."

"I remember some talk about you taking over mechanic duties the day I arrived. But I guess I was more intent on dealing with Paige's hijinks."

"Yeah, you were pretty scared, even though it came out as anger."

"I seem to be angry all the time these days. Not the real me. Even before I rushed here to pick up Paige, when you and I spoke on the phone, I was demanding, just like you said last night. I've got so much riding on this concert tour, it's turning me into a person I hardly recognize." It was a nice change of pace to talk to someone who wasn't telling her what to do.

"Aubrey told me about your husband leaving you and taking most of your money. I wasn't aware of your situation when you were negotiating for the coach. If you don't mind my asking, where did you find the money?"

"Before he passed away, my dad set up a trust fund for me which my husband couldn't touch. Paige will receive some for her college education, but I've staked the rest on resuscitating my concert career. It's the only way I know to support the two of us."

He finished the last slice of pizza. "Explains the rush to get back to California." She nodded.

He made a show of dumping the pizza box in the oversized wastebasket before they settled in the living room. "You play cribbage? It'd give us something to do. I'm pretty good, if you like the challenge."

"Sorry, no, I don't. How about TV?"

"We could catch a game. The Cards are playing the Cubbies tonight."

She had no idea if he was talking football, baseball, hockey or whatever, as little as she paid attention to sports. "Sure. Which is your team?"

"Both, when they're playing someone else. Guess when it comes right down to it, my heart's with the Cards."

"Okay, then I'll support the Cubbies."

"Yeah? You know something I don't?"

"What do you mean?"

"Been tracking their season? Read some sports writer's prediction?"

How on earth could she answer his question when she had no idea who or what they were discussing? When in doubt, let him assume. She widened her eyes in a coy, I-know-more-than-you gaze. "Maybe."

"Want to put a few bucks on your so-called inside knowledge?"

She couldn't resist batting her eyes a smidge and slid an inch or so closer to him on the couch. "Aren't you forgetting something? I've been *stripped*, so to speak, of any monetary resources at the moment." She'd only meant to tease, but in the blink of an eye, or in her case, flutter of an eyelash, her alter ego took over. Stripped. Had she actually used that word?

His eyes went wide.

She'd pulled the rip cord and she was now in free fall.

"Uh, that's right. Sorry. Didn't mean to rub it in."

She let her voice drop an octave. "No offense taken. Maybe we could find some other *tender* with which to bet."

"Some other tender?"

"You know," she said in her most suggestive tone, "if I win, you do something for me, if you win, I—""Got that part. But what?"

She shrugged. "I don't know. I suppose I could bake you something. Do you like chocolate chip cookies?" Inspiration hit. She went with it. Before he grasped what was happening, she rose on her knees and reached behind him. "Perhaps you'd like a massage?" The deep, hypnotizing effect of his aftershave hit her as she leaned toward one ear. "Or maybe something else?" She let her voice drop to a husky whisper.

Graham lunged forward, rose and evaded her hands and mouth. "I, uh, bet that talk wasn't me coming on to you, Jenna."

She remained poised in the same position, draped against the couch. "No? That's too bad. We have the house to ourselves for the next several hours." For better or worse, the other Jenna had emerged. How would Graham react?

He didn't move for what seemed like minutes, but his eyes slowly came into focus and took her in, top to bottom and back. "I know you're bored and pissed at your sister. Probably all of us. But getting back at her, us, like that—"

"Getting back at Aubrey was the farthest thing from my mind. But if you aren't interested—are you already taken? Or gay? That's okay. I'll just sit and watch the Cars and Crubbies with you."

His hands went to his hips. "You think I could watch a baseball game with you now, after that Mata Hari routine?" His voice had risen. She'd struck a nerve.

"If you're not interested, just say so. I won't be insulted."

"Who are you, lady? I've witnessed uptight, bitchy, exacting and spaced-out. But I wasn't expecting this."

She pushed off the couch and slithered from the room, stopped before she was completely out of sight. "I'm going to my bedroom. You're welcome to join me … or not."

GRAY SAT THERE DUMBFOUNDED as Jenna slinked across the room. His radar where the ladies were concerned was generally pretty sharp. He'd completely missed this one. What was Jenna up to? Had the guys been right about her seeking the weakest link—him—for her ally? She hadn't mentioned needing his help or escaping once tonight. Probably a warning bell.

Thing was, she didn't seem to be putting on an act to seduce him into helping her. Her attitude was the real deal. Not mutual attraction. Certainly not liking. Just pure, undisguised sexual interest. Like she said, they had a couple hours to kill. Why not have sex?

She was playing him, right? She'd go to her room and wait, just to see what he'd do. If he did follow her, he'd either find the door locked or her inside smirking that she'd bamboozled him.

Damn her! He'd grown hard watching her sashay across the room.

Her hip action outdistanced the sensuous come-hither grass rolling of their neighbor's Siamese cat when she was in heat. His brain said one thing, his libido something else. Despite the act he put on for Mitch and Geoff, he hadn't been with a woman in weeks, well past the schedule his body craved.

What was a guy to do? On the other hand, what could it hurt?

He knocked on her door. His old room, wouldn't you know?

"It's open." Her voice sounded far off, throaty.

This was such a bad idea. But every so often a guy had to pursue one bad idea. His other head was talking now.

He gripped the handle, turned it and entered. Though still bright outdoors on this summer evening, the room was fairly dark thanks to the blackout shades he'd installed a few years ago. Across the room, on the desk, one small light cast a soft glow.

He didn't see her at first, though instinct told him to check the bed. As his eyes adjusted to the near darkness, he made out her shapely form kneeling on the bed, then he caught her attire—what there was of it.

"Aubrey didn't think to include a negligee on her shopping trip for me, so my bra and panties will have to suffice."

"I'll thank her next time I see her," he said as he ogled the sight before him. If he had to guess what type of underwear she'd be wearing, sheer black, including a wisp of a thong—which required no imagination to discern what it covered—would not have occurred to him.

"Not what I would have selected, but my sister's been a young single in L.A. too long."

"You were really serious?" Dumb, dumb question, but he spoke before he had time to think of something more clever, more in control.

"Lock the door behind you, then come here and find out."

Before his conscience took over, he followed her orders, removed his knit shirt and unzipped his slacks as he approached.

Her semi-glazed over eyes fixed on his. "So? What's your pleasure?"

"Huh?"

"Do you want to do the honors, finish undressing me? Or should I do you?"

"Don't you want, you know, a little foreplay first?" The words emerged in a choke.

She took one of his hands and placed it on a breast. "Go for it. With this flimsy fabric, the nipple should spring to action in seconds." She watched him like one would study a lab rat. "That's what most men usually want to do first. Fondle the merchandise."

Though the contact with her breast shot molten lava through his veins, something was off. He leaned into her face, but she turned it aside. "Don't you want me to kiss you?" he asked.

"Kissing is lovemaking. I'm here for sex. Aren't you?"

He didn't answer but instead pushed her from her kneeling position to sprawl on the bed and climbed over her. "Okay, babe, you asked for it." As his mouth took one breast through the fabric, he let one hand roam down her arm, then down her thigh and up again to rub her private area. All the while, his other arm, which went around her back, drew her tight against him, his throbbing penis pushing into her stomach.

She moaned and moved her hips under him.

Just as hazy euphoria was about to overtake him, to his utter amazement, he released her, backed off the bed and grabbed his clothes. "I don't know what kind of game you're playing, but when I'm with a woman, I like to think there's mutual pleasure involved, not just rutting."

He didn't give her time for a response but pelted from the room still half-dressed. Once he'd redressed, he stormed out to the kitchen and grabbed a can of beer and downed it way too fast. He'd never walked out on a woman, especially one as desirable as Jenna. But something told him her seduction act was off kilter.

A few minutes later, Jenna joined him in the kitchen, clothed. "Should I feel relieved or rejected?" Her voice was like a child who'd been chastised by trusted parents.

"If I believed you really enjoyed getting it on with me, I would've stayed. But that was … well, frankly I don't know what that was."

She didn't reply for some time. Instead, she settled onto a stool by the island, folded her hands, and bent her head. Silence permeated the room. Finally, she lifted her head. "I don't know who that was either."

He cocked a brow. "Really? Could've fooled me."

"I'm, uh, still trying to get my bearings since Jerry left me. Sometimes, the shame of it gets to be too much. Especially when I'm trying to concentrate on my music. When I should be totally into each piece, my mind wanders."

"No piano in sight just now."

She glanced away, as if facing him was an effort. "Right. I'm sorry. You didn't ask to get caught up in my personal drama."

Was she playing him again, only in some new diabolical way? Damn her, why did she have to sound so sincere? He'd give her a chance to explain. Once. "You've done this before? Come on to other guys?"

She didn't answer at first, as if unsure whether to continue. "At singles bars," she said at length.

Her answer caught him off guard. "You don't seem the type."

She turned back to him, lifted a brow. "There's a *type?*"

"You know, women on the make, looking for a fast roll in the hay with no strings."

She gazed at him without flinching. "That would be me. I kept wondering why my husband found it necessary to have sex with other women. What I hadn't been giving him."

Something squeezed his gut. How could any man cause this woman, maddening as she was, to question her sexuality? He didn't know what to say, but his curiosity got the better of him. "So you, uh, sought out men who'd prove your husband wrong?" The picture of this suburban soccer mom hanging on some bar stool offering herself to the first comer surprised him, yet he'd just witnessed a similar performance.

Jenna studied her fingernails. "I was very selective. Careful. I didn't go off with just anyone." She seemed to think through her words. "Okay, no way around it. I became a slut. The very thing I don't want for Paige as she gets older. Some mother, huh?" She covered her face with her hands.

Gray was at a loss. How was he supposed to deal with her in this condition? Comfort her? He was afraid to touch her for fear he'd set another bedroom scene in motion. Counsel her? What did he know? He'd botched up his own personal life so bad years ago, he hadn't let himself get involved with the opposite sex since.

After a bit, removing her hands from her face, she spoke. "Please don't tell Aubrey, or she'll be more concerned about me than ever, and I'll never get back to my tour."

Without thinking, he reached for her hand and squeezed it. "I won't tell her, but Jenna, you can't go on doing stuff like tonight. It's dangerous. And you're worth more."

She didn't pull her hand away. "Thanks."

Though he wouldn't tell her sister about her bizarre behavior, something still troubled him. "Why tonight, why me?"

"Every so often, something comes over me. One minute I was trying to get to know you better, and the next, well ... you got to know me better. Only that wasn't the real me."

He attempted to lighten the mood. "Looked pretty *real* to me."

Both eyebrows went up now. "Oh."

"You're a beautiful, desirable woman, Jenna. Don't devalue yourself."

"You think I'm beautiful?"

Oh, brother. He'd been here before with other females. It was watch-your-step time. "Of course, you're beautiful. But that's not an invitation for you to get mixed up with me. I'm not looking for anything permanent. You shouldn't settle for anything else from the next guy in your life."

"You know what's best for me? What I want?"

"Wouldn't presume. I'm certainly not the poster boy for relationship sanity. Just stepping in as a friend to keep you from going a direction you don't want to go."

"You're the commitment-shy, love 'em and leave 'em type?"

Though they'd come miles toward getting to know each other in the last few minutes, he wasn't ready to share his private life. Easier to invent a reason. "Haven't taken time to get involved with anyone while we've been building the business."

One side of her mouth curled up. "Really? Your brothers have."

"Only recently. Until Aubrey came along, Mitch had been out of commission after his fiancée left him because she didn't agree with his giving up the law to come into business with Geoff and me. Geoff's been hesitant to get involved with anyone since he became aware of his condition. Eileen refused to let him use his MS as an excuse not to date."

"I get the picture. But in the meantime, I could use a friend." She offered him a tentative smile. "Care to enlist?"

Five

hat was she thinking, asking Graham McKenna, the McKenna brother who'd been least pleased with her visit, the one who'd prevented her from taking off for California, to be her friend? Surely she wasn't still turned on by the admittedly gorgeous body she'd enjoyed for all of two minutes before his conscience got the better of him?

She didn't give him a chance to answer. "Never mind. I shouldn't have put you on the spot." She glanced away, sought something to dispel the awkwardness.

Graham went to the fridge and came back with a beer and a bottle of water. He offered her the latter. "I'd make it a can of beer, but you said you don't go for the stuff. You're still on some of your meds anyhow."

She tapped the container in her hand against his can. "To friendship."

Graham settled back in his chair, sipped his brew, his eyes never leaving her while she drank. "Okay, friend," he emphasized the second word, "now that I've seen yours and you've seen mine, so to speak, and we've toasted our platonic relationship, why don't you tell me what's got you so hell-bent to leave town."

She needed someone in her corner. Someone who would release her from her imprisonment. Her best bet at the moment was this man, all grisly six-something feet of churlishness. He wasn't about to unlock the door for her, let alone return her phone and purse, unless she gave him a good reason. "You already know most of it. I was a teenage prodigy on the concert circuit. Once I married, I became a stay-at-home wife. Playing the piano is all I know. But times have changed. I'm worried audiences won't materialize. I've been practicing night and day. Until my darker side showed up."

"While the doc was examining you at the hospital, your daughter told me how she'd been unable to reach you several times when you were supposedly rehearsing. That when what you called your darker side emerged?"

She could only nod. She hated having to discuss this with Graham. He seemed like such a straight shooter. How could he even begin to understand how someone's life could deteriorate so much she'd risk destroying it further?

"Have you told anyone else about these, what should I call them, *wanderings?*"

"No! It's one thing to be the wronged spouse. People can under-stand and sympathize. But for anyone to find out I've been sleeping around just to prove to myself I've still got it is humiliating."

"Know how to bake a cake from scratch?"

Huh? "Yes, of course. I was Susie Homemaker while I was married. Why?"

"I'm still hungry. If we start now, we can catch the last half of the game while it bakes." He ambled over to a corner shelf holding cook-books. "Need a recipe?"

She scrambled to rearrange her focus from one-night stands to baking. Had she embarrassed him? Shared too much information? "I can remember most of what I need, but a recipe wouldn't hurt."

They spent the next five minutes locating ingredients, greasing and flouring a rectangular cake pan and setting the oven. "Chocolate or vanilla?" she asked.

"What do you think?"

"I think we should make what I want, chocolate."

He high-fived her. "Good first step. Know your own mind."

She cocked her head and studied him. "Are you trying to teach me something?"

"I don't know. Anything in particular you need to learn?"

She could play this answer-a-question-with-a question game also. "I don't *need* to learn anything, but I'd like to know what you're up to."

He studied her back, the straight line between his lips opening just a bit. "Why do you think I'm up to something?"

Graham McKenna didn't say or do anything without a reason. "Besides addressing your hunger, you want me to do something I'm familiar with, thinking that will help me relax."

"Is it working?"

She gave the mixture one final stir. "Yes," she had to concede. "Nice technique. Was I making you uneasy talking about the men I've—"

"How 'bout we continue to refer to your actions as wanderings? You don't need to vilify them or yourself to atone. I assume that's what you were doing earlier, using me as your Father Confessor?"

"You'd prefer we drop the topic of my erratic behavior?"

"I'd prefer we talk about how you're going to change your behavior. Until you're ready, there's not much I can do to help you."

She threw down her spoon, letting it clatter on the counter. "You don't think I'm ready?"

"Not if that strip tease earlier is any indicator."

She hung her head. "I hoped we'd closed that chapter."

He picked up the spoon, scooped a dollop of batter and tasted. "For now. But something triggered that episode. Something you couldn't control any more than I could." He offered her the spoon. "You need to get help, Jenna."

His words were those of a friend, not judgmental, a different Graham than she'd dealt with so far.

She didn't reply. Instead, she poured the batter into the cake pan and stuck it in the oven.

They returned to the living room and he turned the game on again. Baseball. Should have known. It was summer. Football and hockey weren't summer sports.

She tried to follow the progress. Wasn't like she didn't know anything about baseball, she'd actually played softball when she was a teen. But tonight her mind was elsewhere. He hadn't taken advantage of her earlier. He hadn't judged, only seemed concerned she get help to address her problem. When they had clinked their beverages to friendship earlier, he'd meant it.

"That help you suggested I get?"

"Yes?"

"I could get it in California."

"True, but Iowa boasts some pretty good professionals as well."

"You've seen how my sister and the rest of you hover. Imagine what they'd do if I remained here getting help."

He seemed to consider her words. At least he didn't try to refute her assessment. "Stay here two more weeks. I'll take as many shifts as I can work in, and I'll see to it that Mitch and Geoff aren't left here alone with you."

Damn. He'd actually offered a logical alternative. She needed a kicker. Something in addition to her nymphomaniac tendencies to gain his support. "This forced confinement isn't helping me relax. Just the opposite. I think that may be what prompted my, uh, coming on to you earlier." His eyes narrowed ever so slightly. Did he believe her?

"You're pretty relaxed now, thanks to your expertise in the kitchen. You need to do that more."

"What—bake?"

"No. Do things you enjoy."

"Like playing the piano?" Checkmate.

He breathed out a heavy sigh. "You know the answer to that."

What more could she tell him to gain his trust? She'd already laid her soul bare, as well as most of her body. What was left? Then it came to her. Follow up on her exploits. "The last guy I, uh, *wandered* with, turned out to be a musician as well. While I was, uh, cleaning up, he went through my purse and found the mock-up of a flyer about my tour I'd prepared for my promoter. He threatened to go to the media and expose me, if I didn't give him a slot on my program."

"Appear with you?"

"Right. Like I don't have enough problems with my own performance. I left in such a hurry to get here, he'll think I ran out on him and make good on his threat."

"Call him. Explain the delay."

She gave him a second to think through his suggestion. Surely he'd realize why his course of action wouldn't work.

"Okay, you don't have a phone at the moment. But I can fix that. In fact, I'll call him and tell him to lay off. Coming from another guy, it should scare him off."

So much for her clincher. *Think fast, Jenna.* "He won't believe you. He'll think I just got a brother or some other male friend to get me out of this jam."

"I'll tell him I'm your boyfriend."

"After he and I, you know? I wasn't exactly *baking* with him. There's no way he'll buy it." But then again, maybe he, her imaginary blackmailer, would if .... Pretty far-fetched, but hadn't this entire Midwestern melodrama been on the flaky side? Had to play this just right and hope she'd gained Graham's sympathy. "That story might be more credible if you staked your claim in person."

Graham bounded from the sofa, crossed the room before he turned back to gaze at her, incredulous. "Go with you to California? Wait, not just that, you want me to spring you from here. Be your accomplice."

She went to him, grabbed his hand. "I know it sounds preposterous. You just got through telling me how much you have to do here. But ..." she paused, attempted to channel her most dramatic vibes, "my career, the only thing I have going for me and Paige, is over before I start, if that guy tells some enterprising reporter about my loose morals."

He didn't pull his hand away. He opened his mouth to speak, twice, and then stopped. Finally, though, he spoke. "I want to help you, Jenna. Really, I do. But what you're proposing ... I just don't know."

He hadn't said no! He needed time to get used to the idea. Maybe a little more incentive too. "I'd have to leave Paige here for a while. I can't involve her in some crazy escape plan, and, truth be told, once I'm back in California, I'll need time to myself to rehearse. Please, Graham. Gray. Please say you'll help me. You're my best, my only, hope." She gripped his hand tighter. "Sorry. I shouldn't put you on the spot like this. It's just … I'm so … desperate."

He didn't respond immediately. Nor did he try to reassure her, despite her award-worthy performance and his apparent concern. She'd lost him.

"I'll think about it. Okay?"

Oh God, oh God, oh God! She might just be getting out of here.

Six

After Mitch and Aubrey returned along with Paige, Gray drove back to the fire station in a near trance.

He'd been right about her growing desire to flee, although he'd had no idea until tonight what all had been driving her. The others had correctly predicted she'd turn to an ally for help. Him. Could he really let himself be the bait?

He didn't get involved in others' lives except his brothers', especially not other women's lives. Even if he did let down his defenses and agree to escape with her, there was still the matter of the terrain between here and California. Certainly not rolling prairie all the way. Could he handle the mountains? Moreover, could his barely recovered collarbone tolerate the long hours in the driver's seat? No, he couldn't do this. *Sorry, Jenna.* He had enough on his plate without stopping his life to help her, delectable as she was.

"Well? How'd it go?" Geoff asked as soon as Gray hit the kitchen.

"She made a cake. It wasn't bad, not bad at all."

Mitch apparently had said goodnight to Aubrey and hightailed it back to the firehouse so he could hear the answer to Geoff's question as well. "Cake? How'd I miss that? Did you at least bring some home with you?"

"Dream on. It was my reward for giving up my night to babysit."

"Aubrey suggested you might be against this plan because you blame yourself for keeping Jenna here when you insisted she go to the emergency room instead of catch her flight west. So, consider yourself spared from any further discussion of her escape. We'll take it from here," Mitch said.

Since his head was in the fridge, the pizza and cake distant memories in his stomach, Gray's annoyed expression escaped his brothers' notice. Once again, Mitch had stepped up and made the decision, just like Mitch had decided the three of them would customize motor coaches a few years back. Mitch's leadership abilities were great when it came to lawyering, but why did he have to impose them on his life and Geoff's as well?

In the time it took Gray to stand and swivel around, his mind also did a one-eighty regarding the ridiculous plot he'd been opposing. Mitch couldn't continue to "handle" things for him. He was the big brother. Not Mitch.

Gray located a plate for the piece of fried chicken he'd retrieved from the fridge. He settled onto a chair, one leg straddling each side. "Thanks for the offer, but Jenna's way ahead of you."

Mitch set down his bottle of water. "Really? What'd she say?"

"She asked me to help spring her from the house and get her back to California."

Mitch placed a hand on Gray's good shoulder. "You turned her down, right? We know how you feel about this plan."

Decision time. Hell, he'd already made up his mind in front of the open fridge. "Told her I had to think about it. Couldn't make it too easy, or she'd suspect something. But yeah, I'm going to do it."

Geoff responded first. "That's terrific, bro."

Mitch was less excited, like he couldn't quite take in this shift in his brother's attitude. "Yeah, that's, uh, great."

"She's already decided not to travel with the kid. One thing we don't have to worry about. It hasn't occurred to her yet to take her own coach, I won't spring that on her until the last minute."

"You've been so dead-set against helping her escape," Mitch said, his eyes narrowed. "What changed your mind?"

He wouldn't mention the gorgeous blonde with long legs and next-to-nothing black lingerie sprawled across his old bed. Nor would he tell Mitch he'd decided to take the lead this one time. "It was pretty obvious none of you could do it or wanted to do it. You were just wearing me down. Figured I'd spare you and me more theatrics."

"We were kinda hoping you'd come around," Geoff replied. "But you made it easy for us."

"Yeah, well, figured this was one way to get a vacation, while you're still here part-time, Mitch."

Mitch returned a surprised expression. "Didn't know you needed one. But whatever it took to get you to sign on, I'm all for it."

"Still not convinced this is a good idea, but I'm in," Gray said.

Mitch's eyes flickered ever so slightly. "Then the rest of us had better get cracking on all those *complications* you cited. As well as the *conditions* you're going to impose on her."

"Already have the conditions in mind. I won't give her any money until I'm convinced she won't strand me, same for her phone. We can be on the road no more than ten hours a day, since I'm the only one who can drive the thing. We'll charge her for the gas after she gets back to California, and I determine the route. Those should do it." He smirked to himself. His list had come pouring out. Surprised him as much as Mitch.

Jenna's near striptease earlier in the evening still concerned him, though he wasn't sure if he was worried about a repeat performance or lack of one.

"You're being pretty easy on her. Won't she get suspicious?" Mitch seemed to be having a difficult time accepting the role of secondary player.

"Figured the no-money, no-phone part was pretty stiff."

Geoff turned to their younger brother. "You just want to have fun inventing some crazy, off-the-wall stipulations for her like we did with Aubrey."

Mitch folded his arms in front of him, but he didn't reply.

Later, as Gray lay in bed, sleep refusing to come, he stared at the dark ceiling above, wondering who was getting conned. Mitch, Geoff, Aubrey and Eileen? Jenna? Or most likely, himself. How had things gotten to this point?

JENNA SWEATED out the next two days wondering whether she'd convinced Gray to help her or scared him off by coming on to him. He didn't stop by or send any veiled messages through his brothers. Instead, the rest of them kept her *entertained*, whatever that meant. On the other hand, Paige was thrilled to be with her aunt and their cousins, especially spending time with Tommy, who was just a year younger.

Jenna had to hand it to her little group of caretakers. They all tried to engage her, do things she supposedly liked to do, as long as such activities were carried out in the house or within the confines of the car, Peggy's house or the firehouse. But Gray—she now used his nickname since the man had seen her nearly naked—was conspicuously absent, even though the other night he said he'd try to take more shifts.

As she played a game of Hearts with Aubrey and Mitch the evening following the night she'd asked Gray for help, she could contain her curiosity no longer. "I must have bored Graham to death last night, since he didn't come back tonight."

"He's putting in extra time finishing up our current project," Mitch said by way of explanation. "I can't start on the interior until he's done his magic with the conversion."

"Oh." Was he just being kind, making up a flimsy excuse not to hurt her feelings? Maybe Gray was actually out on a hot date with someone else.

Mitch went on, "He should be done in a day or so. I'll, uh, tell him you said hi, if you'd like."

She tensed, looked away. Wouldn't help her cause if it appeared she'd drafted Gray as an ally. "No need. Just curious."

Fortunately, she didn't have to explain her interest further, because Paige burst into the house, bubbling over with excitement. "I had such a fun day. Mom, you shoulda gone with us."

"Boats and fishing aren't my thing, hon." She surveyed her daughter's appearance. By the looks of her pink face, the girl had definitely gotten some sun, and her hair hung damp around her neck.

"Thanks for giving your permission to let her try her hand at water skiing," Eileen said.

"Aubrey reassured me you and Tommy were familiar with the river and you're certified in life saving."

Paige disappeared into the kitchen and returned shortly with a can of pop and a bag of chips. She flung herself into the chair next to her mother. "Can you believe it, Mom? I actually got up on those things. Only for fifteen seconds, but I did it! Tommy dared me. Said just because I'd been snow skiing didn't mean I could do it on water."

Jenna grasped Paige's chin, turned her one way, then the other. "Except for a tinge of sunburn, you look no worse for wear. How did you like being on the Mississippi?"

Paige shook loose from Jenna's grip and bobbed her head, her soggy curls shooting a tiny drop of water onto Jenna's face. "It wasn't busy or anything. We even took a break and picnicked on some sandbar upriver."

"You must mean O'Connell Island," Mitch supplied. "Great place to pull into and watch the barges."

"Barges?" A tiny flicker of fear shot up Jenna's spine. "You were out there in the middle of the river with those huge things coming at you?"

"Chillax, Mom. Only one went by, and that was while we were on the sandbar. I was perfectly safe. Eileen and Geoff made me wear a life vest the whole time, even when I was just sitting in the boat watching Tommy ski. He slaloms too. You know what those are, right? Both feet in one ski?"

Jenna hadn't seen her daughter so animated since before the divorce. Paige was actually coming alive being back here with relatives who'd readily included her in their plans. Perhaps leaving her behind for a few weeks wouldn't be so difficult. Might actually be good for her daughter. "What's that smell?" Jenna drew her daughter closer and took a deeper whiff. A nasty, sour smell greeted her nostrils. "Catfish." The odor from her childhood came throttling back to her olfactory memory. She hated catfish. "Eeuw! Go take a shower."

Once Paige headed to the bathroom, Jenna settled back in her chair and let her muscles relax. She might be struggling with this forced stay, but Paige was blossoming.

The following day, Jenna allowed her daughter to go bicycling with Aubrey and Mitch, while Peggy kept her company. "Where did you say they were going?" Jenna asked her babysitter.

"Aubrey wanted to show Paige some of the older homes on North Hill. I think she has her sights set on renovating some of them, if she can gain the owners' approval."

Apparently Aubrey was more serious about relocating to Iowa than Jenna realized. A few rehab projects should augment her income from finishing the coach interiors while McKennas continued to build the business. "Aubrey drove by a few of them when she showed me around town the other day. I hope Paige is a better listener. I'm not much into old houses."

"Me, either," Peggy chuckled, "unless you count my old rattletrap."

Before they could discuss the expedition any further, the cyclists showed up. The first to enter the house was Paige, who held the door for a battle-scarred Mitch as he limped in with Aubrey's support. "Before you start hyperventilating or yelling at Paige," Aubrey warned, "you should know, she was the heroine today."

Aubrey helped Mitch park himself in a chair in the dining area while she checked him out like a triage nurse. "Bump on the cheek, scrape under the chin, abrasions on both knees and what could be the start of a black eye. I still can't believe you tried that stunt."

Jenna and Peggy flocked around him to inspect his injuries for themselves. "What happened?" Jenna asked.

Aubrey glanced at Mitch, who hung his head. "I didn't realize I'd hooked up with such an over-aged jock." She scowled and shook her head. "I spied this incredible home overlooking the river and got to talking to the owner about some decorating changes she's considering. Mitch and Paige got bored and said they were going exploring on their own.

Jenna breathed in a deep sigh, anxious for Aubrey to proceed. "And?"

"I didn't know about this place called Snake Alley. It's this curvy, brick-lined street built on a hillside."

"I've heard of it." Then the words *brick-lined* sank in. "Tell me they didn't."

"According to Paige, Mitch stopped just to show her one of the town's claims to fame."

"Honestly, Mom," Paige added as she returned from the bathroom with a first aid kit. "I wasn't going down that street for anything. Those bricks looked fierce."

"But our hero here," Aubrey continued, "had to prove what a great cyclist he was after he made Paige promise not to follow."

"He did okay on the first curve, but then he sorta lost control of the bike, and he, uh, went flying."

Mitch attempted to defend his actions. "Hit a loose brick at the wrong angle, otherwise I could've made it down to the bottom, no sweat."

"Right," Aubrey said, her tone indicating she was unconvinced.

"Scared me to death, Mom," Paige added. "But I was afraid to go down those bricks. Had to go around this huge block to reach him. I called Aunt Aubrey on Mitch's phone as soon as I got there."

"I told you I was fine, Paige."

"The kid wouldn't let me get up until she was sure I hadn't broken anything. Even checked my eyes for concussion."

The girl beamed. "Learned that in my first aid class at school."

Jenna listened in amazement to the exchange. Her daughter, a heroine. She definitely was growing up.

"Nothing's broken," Aubrey said. "Well, perhaps the front wheel of Mitch's bike, but it's expendable. At least he wore his helmet. I wanted to take him to the Emergency Room, but he insisted he's fine."

Mitch groaned. "Just a little achy and a lot embarrassed."

The Emergency Room. Where all her current troubles started—the day she somehow went catatonic in her car. Ironic. Mitch begged off going when she couldn't. On the other hand, given how well Paige had done on her own, Jenna was less hesitant to leave her, if she could snag Gray's help. If.

"Jenna has a budding movie star on her hands," Mitch announced when he joined his two brothers at the dinner table a few hours later.

Geoff lifted a brow. "Went that well?"

"I was skeptical about bringing Paige in on our plans when Aubrey first suggested we help Jenna *decide* it's time to take off, but Paige has now put in two award-winning performances."

"The kid's okay with this whole plot?" Gray asked. "She was so anxious to go on tour with Jenna in the motor coach."

Mitch opened a longneck and took a swig before replying. "Aubrey told her we'd do an overnight on the road in one of the other coaches. Plus, she's having a great time while she's here. Especially since we all seem to have *adopted* her while Jenna recuperates. From what Aubrey's told me, her parents' break-up was pretty hard on Paige. This is the most normalcy she's experienced in months."

Geoff chuckled. "Us? Normal? Great indicator of how screwed up the DiFranco household has become."

"That's not fair to Jenna," Gray said, coming to her defense. "She didn't ask for her husband to desert them."

"Okay, okay." Mitch studied his brother. "Didn't figure you'd take that become-her-ally thing to heart."

"I'm not her ally. She's still a demanding, self-centered woman. But she doesn't deserve to have us pick on her."

Geoff saluted him with his beer bottle. "Whether that's the case or not, it sounds like Jenna's ready to trust us with her daughter's safety."

"And Paige showed her mom she could take care of herself too." Mitch rubbed a shoulder. "I hope you guys appreciate my contribution to this last part. I banged myself up royally when I deliberately let my bike go wild."

Both brothers turned their attention to Gray. "Our part's done," Geoff said. "Now it's your turn, bro. You ready?"

Was he ready? He'd be alone with the woman for several days. Could he be sure she wouldn't pull that flaunting-her-wares routine on him again? If she did, could he stop himself from falling for it?

GRAY WAS LATE. Jenna had expected him to be there by ten. It was now eleven. She'd even caught Aubrey checking her watch once or twice.

"He did say he was coming today, didn't he?" Jenna asked.

"Yes, but there's still plenty of time before the movie starts. Although I promised Paige we'd stop for a burger first. You're okay with burgers and a movie, right? No bicycles or river today, even though she did quite well with both?"

"One burger is fine. She'll try to ace you out of fries and a milkshake too. Don't give in too readily, but they're okay, as long as she doesn't overdo."

"Mitch promised to meet us at the mall for video games after the movie, so we won't be back for hours. Graham said he might bring some work with him this afternoon, but he's fine with sticking around that long."

Her sister's comments reminded her of the routine she used to go through with Paige's babysitters. Only now she was the one being *sat*. Did Paige ever feel like she did now, like a zoo animal requiring round-the-clock care?

Gray took his time getting to the old homestead. He wanted Jenna anxious for his arrival. She'd be more amenable to his demands and less suspicious of his motives. Besides, he had a million last-minute details to attend to before their exodus began. Had to get money for both of them to augment his credit cards. Lay in plenty of food. Gather his clothes. Tuck his secret list of overnight stays away in his duffle, so they'd appear to be spur-of-the-moment stops.

And condoms. Didn't plan to have sex, but he didn't trust himself around her. She got under his skin, the fact he'd changed his mind about helping her escape was all the proof he needed of that. If she took off her clothes for him again, he'd be ready. No more surprises. No more gentlemanly retreats.

He found her in the living room painting her toenails.

"There you are," she greeted him. "Paige and Aubrey have been chomping at the bit to leave. Don't know if they're anxious to get away from me or just hungry."

"We're off," Aubrey called from the kitchen.

"Okay. See you later," Jenna called back, her expression calm and angelic. She tilted her head, as if listening for something. As soon as she apparently heard what she'd been waiting for, she tightened the cap on her polish, pulled out the cotton separating her toes, and sprang from the couch. "Where have you been the last few days?"

"You're smudging your polish."

She shook her head. "Did them this morning before the other two were awake. Just wanted to look busy now. So?"

"I haven't been here because I've been finishing up a coach conversion so the guys can work on the interior while I'm gone."

It took her about five seconds before his statement clicked. "Does that mean …"

"Don't get excited yet. I've considered helping you get out of here." He held up a hand like a traffic cop, anticipating some sort of outburst. "First, hear me out. The terms may be too stiff."

She sank back on the davenport. "Okay?"

"We'll take your coach."

Her eyes flickered. "My coach, as in *my motor coach?*"

"That's right." He explained why other modes of transportation wouldn't work.

"I'd hoped you'd spring for airfare. Or take me in your pickup. This way will take forever."

"Five or six days. I injured my collarbone a few weeks ago, so I need to take it easy. My daily driving time will be limited. And I'll be the only one driving, since you've never driven one of these rigs, have you?"

"Uh, no."

"Those are the first two stipulations."

"Stipulations?"

He had her attention now. He went over the three requirements he'd shared with the others: no money, no phone, and she'd pay for the gas when she got back to L.A. "That's it? she asked when he finished.

"You want more?"

"No, it's clear you've given a lot of consideration to this trip. It's just that—"

"Yes?"

"I already have a driver lined up to take the coach back to California in a week."

"Once we're on the road, you can call and cancel."

"Oh. Okay. I guess I can do that." She appeared to think through his plan. "Six days on the road is a lot of time to spend together... alone," she said after a few beats. "What if something happens, like the other night?"

Yeah, what if? Should he cringe or start fantasizing?

A crease ran across her forehead as she contemplated his proposal. "You haven't said so, but your so-called *stipulations* shout that you don't trust me not to run off at the first chance. Also, you're probably afraid I could retaliate at some point by charging you with kidnapping. I get it."

"Good," he said. "Glad I don't have to explain further."

"But if we do this," she continued, apparently not done, "I've got my own concerns." She placed a hand on his cheek, then quickly removed it. "You're a nice guy, in a testy sort of way. You're not so bad to look at either. But I can't risk losing control again. Especially since we'll be on the road so long."

"Agreed." Those condoms in the bottom of his duffle would just have to wait for another woman, another time.

"I have my own stipulation."

God, shades of Aubrey. They truly were related. "Oh? What's that?"

"No matter what I do or say or how either one of us may feel at some point during this trip, no hanky panky. No cuddling, hugging, kissing and especially, no sex."

"You forgot handholding." He kept his expression bland, though it tickled his ego she was worried about resisting him.

She took a step back. "I'm serious, Gray."

"I get you. No sex. But for the sake of argument, what if I agree to your requirement and somewhere along the way west, one of us wants to drop it?"

She crossed her arms in front of her chest. "You've already told me how you feel about me, so that possibility is moot. Even if I got the hots for you— which won't happen—but say it did, if it's me and not my dark persona, I can't allow myself to get serious about any man right now. Don't know if I ever will again after what happened with Jerry."

She made a good case, so why was he hesitating? "You want to shake on it, or is that too much personal contact?" He grinned, so she'd know he was kidding. About the touching part, anyhow.

She held out her hand. Her lips turned up in probably the happiest smile he'd seen yet. "No problem. When soon do we go?"

"How soon can you pack? We need to hit the road right away."

"Now?" Her voice rose. "I haven't had a chance to say goodbye to Paige."

"Sorry. No time like the present to make our getaway, especially since all your guardians are otherwise engaged for several hours. By the time they discover you're gone, we'll be well on our way. Besides, you don't want to risk inadvertently giving away our plan by holding her too tight or tearing up."

A sigh escaped. "I guess you're right."

He waited while she gathered her things, deciding discretion was the better part of valor by avoiding her bedroom. It didn't take long to collect the limited wardrobe as well as her toiletries.

"You need to leave a note," he said as she headed for the door.

"Right." He'd already laid out a piece of paper and a pen on the kitchen island. She took pen in-hand but stopped. "What do I say?"

"Tell them you're with me, so you'll be safe, but don't say it was my idea. Keep me out of this as much as possible. Don't tell them how we're going. They'll figure that out soon enough. Tell Aubrey you'll call her later today, so she won't make herself crazy trying to call me. I'm turning my phone off for now."

She finished the note and then followed him out to his truck. "Do we have to stop at the firehouse for your things?"

"No. The coach is ready to go."

Just as he was about to start up, she placed a hand over his forearm. Apparently arm-touching was okay in terms of their pact, although heat still shot up his arm. "Will you be in much trouble with your brothers?"

He was tempted to let her think he was risking much more than he actually was. "They'll get over it," he said finally.

"I owe you. We've already dismissed the physical thing, but I'll find some way to pay you back."

"Let's get you to California before you consider payback." If she ever figured out how he and the rest of the gang were playing her, payback would be a whole different issue.

Seven

Jenna could hardly remain still as they rode toward the parking lot behind the firehouse, where her motor coach was parked. Numerous questions occurred to her, but she didn't speak for fear of jinxing her escape. For the moment, she simply enjoyed the anticipation of freedom.

She wanted to laugh, have Gray stop for an ice cream cone to celebrate. A rare treat. Later. First, she had to get out of town. "Are you sure no one's home?" If anyone was at the firehouse, their getaway could be thwarted before it began.

"Reasonably sure, unless Mitch or Geoff had a last-minute change of plans."

She gulped. "What are the chances?"

"About ninety-seven percent against. Even if by some off chance somebody returned, they won't pay attention to the back of the building. We can slip in under their noses and be on our way before anyone misses us."

"I hope you're right." This was no time to be anxious. Had to stay cool.

"When we get there, I'll drop you off behind the coach and park the truck near the gate, so my part in this won't be quite so obvious.

As soon as you see me walking toward the door of the coach, join me. It should only take a minute to stow your things and get underway."

Jenna did as he indicated. Within two minutes, they were inside her home on wheels. The rig took on a whole new aura when she wasn't sentenced to two days' rest in the bedroom. Her breathing came in spurts, but she felt like she was soaring above the world. She was no longer prevented from heading west. She and Gray were embarking on their very own caper. "Cool," as Paige would say.

"With a vehicle this large and this new, we'll stay on the main roads," Gray told her as they took their seats in the cab, "even though it might seem we could hide better on less-traveled routes."

Whatever. Since she had no sense of the geography in this part of the country, what did it matter as long as they got going?

They headed west, past signs indicating the community college and someplace called Westland Mall in West Burlington. "We'll take U.S. 34 across the state to I-35, then head south to Kansas City."

"Why south? Won't we be going out of our way?"

"Once we get to Oklahoma City, we'll turn west again."

The words didn't register. Did it matter? She was no longer a prisoner. She was headed home.

U.S. 34 took them near and through several small Iowa towns, even Eldon, where the house that inspired the famous "American Gothic" by Grant Wood was located. If she wasn't in a hurry to get as much distance between herself and Burlington, she might have asked Gray to stop. Would have been fun to pose in front of it.

"How you doin' over there?" Gray asked, taking his eyes off the road momentarily to check on her.

"Starting to relax. I kept expecting to see a sheriff's car pull alongside and flag us over."

"Could still happen, if we don't stop after a while and let them know you and the motor coach are safe."

She tightened her grip on her knees and sat forward slightly. "I suppose we have to, but could we hold off a little longer? I want to get more miles between us and them."

"We should make Kansas City by late afternoon. We'll stop before then for fuel. We can call from there."

"Sounds good." She settled deeper into her cushy passenger seat as the scenery sped by. Jenna had never been in this part of the state. At least she didn't remember being here as a small child. It was really kind of pretty, in a calm, pastoral sort of way. Green. So green. And rolling. Not flat like she'd always imagined. Cornfields or cattle in every direction.

Another half hour passed. She shook herself awake. For a brief moment, she had no idea where she was. Out of the corner of her eye, she spied Gray steering the wheel of ... oh, right, her motor coach. "Where are we?"

"Nearing the Interstate. Check the road signs. We turn south at Osceola."

"Oh, right."

Gray slid his sunglasses down his nose about a half-inch. "I sense anxiety. Haven't you relaxed yet? Maybe you should take one of your pills."

"Can't."

"Out?"

"Left them behind."

"You what?" His voice rose.

"I don't—won't need them anymore, since I'm headed back to L.A."

He didn't reply. Instead, he returned to concentrating on the road ahead.

He apparently didn't approve of her decision. It was a spur-of-the-moment thing. Maybe not the smartest move she'd ever made, but she was so tired of only being half there, she was ready to go cold turkey. Non-responsive Old Gray was back. But as long as he didn't convince New Gray to turn this rig around, she could put up with him.

"Try to relax, then. Drink some water. Take another nap. In fact, why not check out your bed? You're more likely to doze off longer there. I'll wake you when we get to KC."

Probably not a bad idea as long as she could trust him not to turn around while she was sleeping. She didn't have a choice. "Can I walk through here while we're traveling?"

"Of course. These babies travel as smooth as silk. Haven't you ever ridden in one of these?"

"Uh, no."

"Then why … never mind."

"Never mind what?"

"You invested a bundle in this thing, yet you had no idea whether you'd be able to travel in it?"

"What was there to know? It's a moving vehicle, like a car or a bus."

"Not everyone adapts to these things. Unless you plan to strap yourself to one of the seats all day, like you would on one of those, this is entirely different. A little like being on a ship. Some people experience motion sickness."

Motion sickness. Why hadn't that occurred to her *before* she bought the coach? About the same time she decided to undertake the tour, she read about some country western star's traveling coach and had gotten caught up in the glamour. With the rest of her life falling apart around her and every other exchange with her daughter a challenge, the idea of obtaining a motor coach for herself had taken shape. She wasn't thinking rationally. She was still raw emotion. The excitement of striking out on her own with the decision had been validating, energizing. Now, warily, and carefully, Jenna made her way back to her bedroom and climbed under the covers.

"Well? Did she buy it?" Mitch asked when Gray called, having assured himself Jenna was tucked away in her bedroom where she couldn't hear his conversation.

"So far, so good, though she's already exercised her newfound independence by leaving her meds behind. Any relaxing she does the next few days will have to be on her own ticket."

"The plan was to pressure her to get moving so her only option was to throw all her things into her bag and run."

"She surprised me. Go figure." He agreed with her about relying on as few drugs as possible, but he'd counted on her remaining just slightly out of it the first few days, so she wouldn't question how easy it had been to take off.

"Did she ask why you changed your mind about helping her?"

No point letting his little brother know he'd never really turned her down but instead had let her think she'd finally convinced him to help her. "Not yet. But she probably will, once she really starts to relax."

"We had a great time watching your escape. Looked like something from a spy flick."

"Had to convince her time was of the essence so she wouldn't stop to question why we were taking the coach."

"Sounds like so far, so good. Stay in touch."

Stay in touch. He didn't like how easy it had been for the rest of them to send him off on this *mission* so they could get back to their own lives. Didn't like this plan one bit. How long before she figured out she'd been had?

He'd inconspicuously observed his passenger while she took in the surrounding countryside and then slept. Jenna relaxed differently than he and the others. As mother and housewife, she was accustomed to being constantly occupied with one task or another. Perpetual activity was normal for her. She'd experienced very few of those tasks since her stay in his family homestead. No wonder she seemed so antsy.

Damn! Why hadn't he had this *epiphany* before they took off? He could've planned better. No time like the present, especially with three more hours of driving ahead before their first stop. How would he keep her occupied the rest of the trip?

THEY STOPPED at a fast food place north of Kansas City to check in with the gang back at the firehouse. "I don't see why I can't hold your phone. I won't run off with it," Jenna said.

"You agreed. No phones. I'll put it on speaker."

This was ridiculous. He didn't trust her to make unauthorized calls. Okay, once she figured out who to call and the number, he was probably right to take this precaution. But at the moment, all she wanted to do was reassure her sister and daughter she was fine. Plus, a small part of her wanted to thumb her nose at the gang she'd left behind. But she'd behave. For now. They hadn't yet put enough miles between them and her former captors to flaunt her newfound freedom.

When Aubrey came on the line, Gray explained what had happened. Her sister expressed relief and begged her to return. They'd drop guard duty. Jenna, who'd agreed to hold back and let Gray do the talking, apologized for taking off like she had but refused to return. Gray agreed to check in from time to time, so they wouldn't worry. "Sure you don't want to turn around and go back?" he asked after he put his cell away. "We haven't gone that far yet."

"No." She'd made her decision. There was no going back.

"No regrets?"

"I have many regrets, but hitting the road like this isn't one of them."

He studied her as she carefully separated her grilled chicken from the bun and cut it in little pieces, then resumed eating his cheeseburger. But apparently his curiosity got the better of him. "What kind of regrets?"

"I didn't expect you to follow up."

"If you'd rather not go into them ..."

She considered. She'd been her own counsel for so long, it would be a relief to talk to someone else. But Gray? "You already know more about me than I ever intended to share with anyone—my husband dumping me, fear of going before an audience again, that I'm not ready."

Gray took a sip of coffee. "You had no control over the first item.

Your concert tour hasn't occurred yet. The only legitimate regret on your list might be not practicing enough, but you can still do something to remedy that."

"That's not it."

"Explain."

"Do we really want to go into all this now? We should be getting back on the road."

He finished his coffee, gathered their trash and stood. "Fine. Let's go."

"We've got two and half to three hours before we reach this place beyond Kansas City, tonight's stop. Spill," he said once he was back in the driver's seat in coach.

Why had she ever brought up this subject? On the other hand, she didn't have much else to do, why not? "I regret realizing too late I was losing my husband. I regret not being enough of a woman to satisfy him. I regret blindly trusting him and not preparing myself better to be on my own."

"Done?"

There was more. Should she go on? What the hell? "I regret not having a better relationship with Paige. And Aubrey. And my mother. I also regret … God, I'm absolutely mortified by my recent sexual encounters, including my little show for you."

He shot a quick glance at her. "Let's deal with the last one first. It's okay for you to regret your performance, but frankly, I rather enjoyed it. I only stopped because you didn't seem to be you." He shifted his gaze back to the windshield.

"Uh, thanks. I'm lucky you're a gentleman." That's how she felt, right? Even though some little part of her wondered what sex with Gray would have been like.

"You're not involved with anyone at the moment, right? How about since your husband, uh, took off?"

"No and no. Why do you ask?"

"Just wondering if this other you would've shown up if there was a man in your life."

"Are you recommending I find myself a boyfriend?" Surely he wasn't coming on to her? He'd told her he didn't like her.

He scraped his chin as if attempting to hide a smile. "Interesting new psychological concept, boyfriend therapy. 'Attention all gigolos and male escorts. Your career choice has just been upgraded.'"

"Glad I can add a little humor to your day."

"Hear me out. Your jerk of a husband has been gone for how long —six months?"

"About eight."

"Have you dated at all since?"

She studied the rearview mirror on her side. Huge. Probably had to be on a monster vehicle like this. "Let's not go there."

"Why not?"

Why was he goading her? "Because it was humiliating."

He didn't reply. Must be waiting for her to go on.

"I had no idea Jerry was cheating on me until I found a pair of women's underwear when I was cleaning under our bed. The sheerest purple thongs I'd ever seen. Definitely not my taste. I don't know how long I stared at them before I stuck them in a plastic bag, like a crime investigator would preserve evidence, and hid them away. My husband had been with another woman. At first, I couldn't believe it was true, but then, as I recalled his behavior and attitude in recent years, it all fell into place." She took a breath, then continued. "As my brain absorbed the shock and horror of my discovery, anger took over. It appeared he'd done it right there in our own home. The thought infuriated me."

"Appeared? You gave him the benefit of the doubt?"

She stared at the GPS on the monitor between them. "I take it no one has ever betrayed you? If they had, you wouldn't be asking. Sure, I was aware what he'd done, but I couldn't bring myself to believe the proof. I had no other explanation for how that lingerie found its way under my bed, but I let my imagination run loose, trying to find one."

"What finally convinced you?"

How much to reveal? "I started following him when Paige was off at the mall with friends or staying with my mother. Guess I could have hired a private investigator to check him out, but my emotions were in such tatters, taking action on my own seemed to make the hurt less painful. Saying it out loud now makes me sound so pathetic, but at the time, I became a woman obsessed."

She paused. She hadn't shared her attempts to trail her husband with anyone except Jerry the night she confronted him.

"You caught him?"

"Took a few times, because once he went into a motel room, he didn't come out for hours. Hours I didn't have time to spend waiting. But one night, he emerged within minutes of going in, his arm around this half-dressed woman. I didn't know her. She was much younger. Barely twenty. They didn't even make it inside the car. He pinned her against the door and took her right there."

At the time, she couldn't turn her eyes away, as much as the scene sickened her. The pain of confirmation of Jerry's infidelity ripped her apart. Though the tear had begun to mend in the intervening months, she was still far from healed.

Gray snorted. "Tacky as well as a jerk. What did you do?"

"I confronted him. Gave me great pleasure to pull him away from that tramp, his business hanging out, decommissioned. We attracted a few onlookers, but I didn't care, and Jerry didn't realize how bad he looked. I called him every name I could think of. He took it for a while. 'I may be all those things, but you drove me to it, wifey. Who could blame a guy for getting it on the side when his wife is colder than a blizzard in January?' he said once I ran out of steam."

"Brutal."

She refocused her attention on the outside mirror again. "Until he accused me of driving him away, I never considered myself responsible for our marriage failing. But once he planted the idea in my head, I backed off to lick my wounds. I filed for divorce and threw him out of the house, but from then on, I carried this horrible guilt."

"But you'd literally caught him with his pants down."

"Yeah, well, my supposed frigidity became his theme song, although he only played his tune when no one else was around or for his cronies. I don't think Paige was ever aware how bad it got."

They approached an exit ramp and took it.

"Are we stopping already?"

"This topic is getting too heavy for me to drive and help you diagnose your problems at the same time. Let's stop for coffee."

"I—" What could she say? He was willing to hear this through. She wasn't used to a man actually listening to her. "Coffee. Sure."

"We have a coffeemaker with us, but I could stand to walk around a bit." He gave her a shy smile. "Not used to driving these long hours."

Late afternoon, few customers in the food court. Only one other couple, probably in their forties, occupied a table. Both Gray and Jenna chose plain coffee. Both kept it black.

"I don't get why you called your story humiliating. Angry I could understand. The same for hurt or disappointed. But humiliating?"

"We'll never get to California if we keep stopping to talk."

"Agreed. But you're revealing some pretty deep stuff. Needs more of my attention than I can give from behind the wheel."

She closed her eyes briefly. "About two weeks after Jerry moved out, the wife of one of his coworkers invited me to lunch. This was rare. I didn't have many friends. Once we'd gotten through the preliminaries, she told me Jerry was telling anyone who'd listen I'd disappointed him in bed. Said I'd come into the marriage sexually unaware and I'd never caught up. Afterwards, I realized she hadn't really told me as a friend but rather because she'd gotten some kind of perverse pleasure out of dropping her bomb."

"Ah."

"Not long after, one of Jerry's golf buddies asked me to dinner. He sounded so sympathetic on the phone, promised 'just dinner.' But as soon as dessert arrived, which I said I didn't want, he tried finding ways to extend the evening—going for a ride, stopping for coffee. Even though I begged off, he grew progressively more irate, until finally he threw down some bills and stalked off but not before grumbling about losing a bet with Jerry that he couldn't get his cold fish wife into bed."

The memory still made her cringe, feel so dirty she'd never get clean. Now here she was laying her heart bare. How had Gray gotten her to disclose so much?

Gray didn't reply. Just shook his head.

"Jerry and his pal spared no effort getting the word of my so-called frigidity out to anyone who'd listen. Even after Jerry left town, he still worked behind the scenes to degrade me. I think he was attempting to darken my name for the divorce proceedings, because I couldn't believe he'd otherwise be so hurtful and purposely mean."

"Hope you don't put all men in the same category as those two."

"I've got this terrible rep, thanks to Jerry."

"The guy has been playing mind games with you. So far, successfully."

Mind games? She'd been seeing Jerry's actions in terms of what he said *about* her to others. Gray was painting the damage in terms of what Jerry had said *to* her. "You mean he did a number on my self-confidence?"

"Just suggesting. Up to you to determine if I'm correct."

She mulled over his theory. After the incident with Jerry's friend, she turned down the few other men who had asked her out, thinking they must be competing to see which one could warm up the cold fish. She attended a few events at Paige's school until she overheard two women discussing her. Their cattiness and total insensitivity were worse than the men's jokes. That's when she began to question her sexuality. The anxiety over pinning her hopes on a concert tour comeback had sent her over the edge and on the prowl for men who'd reassure her she was one hot number.

Though his expression was soft, his eyes had narrowed. "Going back in time? Trying out my theory?"

"I've never really stepped away from my situation to name the problem and pinpoint the source. I've been reacting to each new complication in my life rather than avoiding or anticipating them."

"Easy to do. I've been in the same situation."

"Really? Should we analyze you next? All this self-reflection is tiring. Time to turn the tables."

He took what was apparently his last sip of coffee and tossed his container into the receptacle next to them. "Some other time."

"Not ready to talk?"

"Mentally exhausted. Plus, we need to get back on the road."

He was right. They'd been going over six hours. He shouldn't drive much longer today. But she wasn't letting him off this easy. She'd shared so much about herself. Before the trip was over, she intended to know all about him as well.

Eight

Coffee. Like he wasn't keyed up enough. Could he have come up with a worse idea?

Back on the road, Jenna seemed to dissolve into her seat and her own world. Gray attempted to get his mind around her revelations about her former husband. What a prick! The damage he'd done to Jenna's psyche was unforgivable. Even if the woman had disappointed him in bed, which Gray doubted given the feistiness he'd witnessed, the guy had no right to lay such a load of garbage on her.

They were half an hour behind schedule. No problem. They had a reservation at a place not too far past Kansas City in Kansas. The guys had come through. They had reservations for every night of the trip, although to Jenna it would have to seem like they were lucky. Maybe he could convince her he was calling ahead whenever they stopped.

He steered with his left hand while his right rubbed his thigh. His breathing was irregular. Coffee. Should've at least asked for decaf. Better yet, a bottle of water. What had he been thinking? At least Jenna seemed to have settled down. She'd been pretty agitated while they talked. Probably should've stopped her long before she went into so much detail, but she seemed to need closure. At least spit out the entire tale. The wound inflicted by Jerry Whatever-His-Name would take a long time to heal, if ever.

"Are you okay?" Jenna asked from what seemed like miles away.

"Huh?"

"You're massaging your leg like you've got a charley horse. You've been driving too long. We need to stop. Get you off the road."

"My leg's fine. Besides, we're almost there."

"Where?"

How to make this sound plausible? "Went online and found a place, an RV park, while you were in the restroom at our first stop. Even set the GPS. It says twenty more miles."

"Don't we just pull off the road and park?"

"Probably could, or use the parking lot of some super discount store overnight, but why beg for trouble?"

"If your leg doesn't hurt, what's going on?"

"Anxious to get there, I guess." Best she not know what an impact her disclosures about her private life were having on him. She might clam up in the future, and he sensed she still had more to say. She'd got him thinking about his own life. Not that his story was anything like hers, but he had his own regrets. Things that might have been, had others' poor judgment not interfered. Had his mother not died too young, had his father not piled up so many debts in his grief, had he enjoyed his job in Minneapolis, had he not gone into business with Geoff and Mitch.

Never mind. It had been a long day. His mind was wrung out from Jenna's story and concentrating on the road. His body wasn't used to so much time on the road.

They arrived at the RV park before dusk. Thank God for the GPS, or they might have driven past the small road sign denoting their destination. "Why don't you wait here while I register?" he suggested, just in case the registrar let slip who actually made the reservation.

"Is … is it safe here?"

"From two-legged or four-legged critters?"

"I've, uh, never been in one of these places."

"Me, either, but it looks safe enough. Keep the door locked for good measure. I won't be long." He could trust her not to run off here. She was already spooked by what lay outside, and he still had her phone and purse.

However, when he returned a few minutes later and didn't find her in the front of the vehicle, for a second he wondered if he'd judged her wrong. To his relief, she emerged from the back bedroom, clothed in a no-nonsense robe and slippers. Nonetheless, before he could stop himself, he remembered what lay beneath and his mouth went dry.

"I saw that look, mister," she said, apparently unaware of the impact her robe had made on him. "You presumed I'd taken off."

"Not really." He lied. "But since you were a tad nervous about being left alone when I went to register, I couldn't help wondering, for just a flash, if something spooked you."

"I got bored, so I figured why not get ready for bed? We're not leaving here the rest of the night, are we?"

"You're not. But I need to hook us up to the utilities and waste disposal. We could go a few days without such services, but why not take advantage of them while we can? Shouldn't take long. I'll put the slides out when I get back, so you'll have more room in your bedroom." He offered her the romance novel he'd signed out of the lodge bookcase. "Here. In case you can't fall asleep right away. Didn't know what you preferred to read. This was the only cover not sporting a guy's naked chest. Figured that might be a bad idea."

SHE ACCEPTED HIS UNEXPECTED GIFT. "Thanks, although I gravitate more to cozy mysteries."

"Best I could do. They told me television reception sucks."

Did he expect her to wait up for him? She wasn't really tired, but she needed some alone time. Time to prepare for her arrival in L.A. She'd been out of touch with the guy setting up her tour for days. And, of course, she'd have to call her mother. How had Aubrey been keeping her at bay, anyhow? "Well, uh, see you in the morning." She edged toward her bedroom.

"You know how the lights work. The bathroom functions like any other non-motorized bathroom." He swiveled for the door. "I plan to hit the road around seven in the morning. Feel free to sleep in until you're ready to join me. There's breakfast makings in the kitchenette."

It all seemed so civilized. So planned, since Gray had only recently agreed to help her. Oh, well, who was she to argue? A very comfortable bed was calling her name. She assumed Gray would sleep in one of the two bunk beds or maybe even camp out on the couch.

She retreated to her room and tackled the romance novel. To her surprise, it wasn't half bad. In fact, it was quite well written, the story of a female chef who found herself unemployable in New York City's best eateries and wound up co-hosting a local cooking show. But even a good book wasn't enough to keep her focused. After all, it had been one of the most unusual days of her life. She'd never staged a getaway or fled across country in a motor coach.

Nor had she spent much time with any man other than Jerry. She'd certainly never unloaded as much personal information on her former husband as she had in a couple hours' time with Gray.

Didn't mean she trusted Gray. How did she know he hadn't somehow turned the motor coach around and they were already headed back to Iowa? Should've gone with him to register, just to assure herself this was all legitimate.

The suspicion nagged at her for the next hour, then two, while she tried unsuccessfully to sleep. Maybe if she disconnected the nightlight Gray had installed and darkened the room completely, she could relax. Probably shouldn't have gone cold turkey on her meds.

She eased out of bed and turned off the light. Total darkness. Couldn't even see the end of the bed, although it wasn't more than a few feet away. After taking a couple tentative steps, she stood stock still, listened to the dark. Not quite total silence but almost. A wave of unmitigated fear swept through her, started at her fast-beating heart, worked its way out her arms, and down her torso to her legs. Was this what the end was like?

Jenna's bare feet cemented in place, though she experienced an overpowering desire to run.

Finally, she could move. The next few moments flew by in a blur as she stumbled into the main cabin toward the outside door. She almost made it, even down the steps before she crashed/collided/fell over a warm, hard cocoon.

"What the hell?" a male voice muttered.

What the hell, indeed! She struggled to sit up but was so entangled in hard body and blanket, her efforts were more a roll and squirm. Steel arms encased her, halted further movement.

"Tell me that's you, Jenna, and not some polecat that wandered in."

"Yes, it's me. What are you doing here on the floor by the door?"

"What are you doing here? The agreement was no taking off."

"Let me up first."

"Not yet. Explain. I've been battling this cubbyhole for a couple hours and just got to sleep. My body and brain don't take well to being wakened abruptly."

Her body wasn't cottoning well to such close proximity to his either. As best she could tell in the dark, she was sprawled over him, bare legs akimbo. Heavy fabric—a sleeping bag?—covered parts of him, but not all. The other part? Hairy, bare skin. In all her years with Jerry, mere contact with his body had never stirred her insides like this.

Was he in the buff inside his sleeping bag? Why was she even speculating? Had to get out of here before she found out. But without any light to guide her, each time she stuck an appendage somewhere to gain a grip or foothold, she touched Gray instead.

"Hey! That hurt."

"Sorry. Help me up, will you? I seem to be caught in whatever webbing is blanketing you."

His hands seemed to possess their own GPS as they moved up her hips to seize her waist and lift her. In an instant, those same hands locked around her back and drew her into him. Her lips met stiff, itchy chin stubble, but they didn't stay there long. He pulled her higher, her mouth now covered his, the short journey hauling her over his hard-on, which even under the sleeping bag she couldn't ignore.

For what seemed like an eternity but couldn't have been more than a second, her lips remained inert over his, as if waiting for her body to signal their next move. Her brain didn't get the chance to decide. Gray's lips made her decision for her, as one of his hands swept up her spine to cup the back of her skull and draw her into him. His kiss was powerful, insistent, compelling.

Her body welcomed him instants before her brain caught up. While her hands sought the back of his neck, her hips began to writhe and undulate with an urgency all their own.

The kiss lasted far too long to be considered mere instinct, reaction. Definite intent crushed her lips with no sign of ending. With each passing moment, the course of the hand still enfolding her back widened, finally reached her rear.

Despite the discomfort of the door well, neither seemed ready to pull away. Nor did either say anything other than to moan or mutter. Gray's hand slipped underneath her nightshirt and up the back of one thigh, his touch light, his destination unmistakable.

She shifted slightly so she could trace a hand down one of his pecs and enjoy the involuntary spasm. He gasped as her finger toyed with the area surrounding his nipple.

He slid his hand under her panties and caressed a buttock. She waited for his fingers to slide forward around her hip socket to seek her most intimate parts, but instead, he withdrew the hand and skimmed it up her back and around the front to fondle a breast.

The darkness gave tacit permission to explore, grasp and wriggle and heightened every sense but sight. Both took full advantage. Jenna licked his neck, the slightly salty taste stimulating further boldness. Her tongue sought his earlobe so her teeth could nibble the vulnerable flesh. Moisture pooled in her lower region as she scented soap, shampoo, and sweat. Man. A real man. Not an alcohol-encouraged one-night stand nor Jerry's formulaic approach to fulfilling his needs at the expense of her pleasure.

Gray's breathing assumed an erratic rhythm, punctuated by his groans and the slight swishing of the nylon-like fabric being pulled this way then that by their gyrations.

The heat coming from his naked chest fueled her own need. There was no before, no future, just now. Now meant feasting on this spectacular man. She traced her way down his front, stopped once or twice to coil his delicious chest hairs within her greedy fingertips. But her curiosity, unrestrained by normal convention, had to know—boxers, briefs or, oh, yes! Nothing. The man was completely available to her roaming, unsighted analysis.

Just as she was about to claim hold of his engorged penis, he moved beneath her, brought them both to sitting positions. "We've got to stop." He growled.

"We do? Why?"

His breath caught. "This … isn't … real."

"Felt pretty real to me. One more second and I would have known for sure."

"That's the point. Our no-sex pact, remember? Sorry. Guess I reacted instinctively."

Their pact? Her arousal had obscured her memory. Oh, right. The promise she'd extracted from him half for her own protection but also because she'd wanted to set up some kind of restriction for him, since she'd had to agree to his list of requirements.

"Flip on a light, will you? I would, but I'm somewhat out of commission."

She rose, used her hands to guide her up the side wall and fumbled around until she found the switch. They spent the next minute blinking to adjust to the light.

The sight of Gray sprawled in the stair well, long, muscular legs extended, chest exposed, and folds of navy fabric barely covering his private parts sent a pang of regret through her insides. She had no doubt how far she would have gone had he not cut off their rumble.

"What was all that?" she asked, putting him on the spot.

Gray raised hooded eyes toward her. "You tell me. I was sound asleep until you were on top of me."

"I woke in a panic. The walls were closing in. I don't remember anything after that except heading to the door. I had no idea you'd be there guarding it."

"Good call on my part."

"I wasn't trying to escape. Well, okay, I was, but not from you, from the coach."

He studied her, as if expecting her to say more. "What do you think would've happened if I hadn't been posted here to stop your flight?" he asked when she didn't go on.

"I don't know." Her voice was smaller than Jerry's heart.

"You're not even wearing shoes."

She checked her feet. What had she been thinking? She could have done considerable damage to them if he hadn't prevented her from leaving. "I would have stopped before I got far."

"There could've been an animal right outside the door just waiting for some stupid human to think city safety standards prevailed out here."

"And there it is."

"There what is?"

"You see me as *some stupid human*. Too dumb to take care of myself."

One eye opened slightly more than the other. "Let's review. Point 1: Just a few weeks ago you underwent some kind of catatonic episode. Point 2: Instead of following your doctor's orders to relax, you made ready to return to L.A. Point 3: You've balked at every effort made by your sister and daughter and others to make your stay in Burlington more pleasant."

"C'mon, anyone might act like that if they've gone through what I have the last several months."

"Perhaps. But there's more. Point 4: Rather than wait it out another week, you persuaded me to help you escape. Point 5: You left your meds behind. It's no wonder you couldn't sleep tonight. You came off them too soon."

"Nag, nag, nag."

"I'm trying to get you to take a long, serious look at your behavior. Don't you think you've been acting pretty much like a spoiled brat?"

"Spoiled brat? Me? Haven't you been listening to my tale of woe? I'm just trying to normalize my life as much as possible while setting off on a new path to support myself and Paige."

"Understood, but with the exception of my assistance, which you desperately needed to make your getaway, you've rejected everyone's offers of help. That's the same as saying you know better than anyone what you need. You're smarter than them. You don't trust them. If that's not brattiness, I don't know what is."

She started to reply, then stopped. Jenna hadn't thought about her reaction to everyone's wanting to help from that perspective. She'd just seen it as interfering, telling her what to do.

While she considered his words, he studied her. A bit too long.

"What are you staring at? Have I committed some other crime?"

"Did we not agree to no sex, no physical contact?" Leave it to him to throw her stipulation back at her. "I warned you I couldn't swear to keeping things platonic. You'd have to be the strong one. And you were." She attempted a smile. "You passed your first test, McKenna."

In a rough tone, he said, "Barely."

"Right. For a few seconds ..."

He ran a hand down his jawline. "Yeah. About those few seconds? I won't apologize, Jenna. I was thoroughly into it. Somehow, I managed to harness my unbridled libido, but if temptation recurs, I don't know if I'll be able to hold off again. Maybe we need to rethink this trip and head back to Iowa."

"No! I'll try harder to relax, so I won't feel claustrophobic again and go wandering in the middle of the night."

He chuckled. "Must run in the family."

"Huh? Oh. Aubrey told me how she and Mitch got trapped in the firehouse break room shortly after they met, which prompted her claustrophobia to reappear. No, until tonight, I've never experienced the condition."

"You needed those meds. If you can't relax for the next several days, this trek west will be hell for both of us."

She couldn't disagree. "I'll find some way to relax."

He seemed to consider her words. "Go back to bed. We'll brainstorm over breakfast. We both need our sleep now."

"Okay." She headed for her bedroom but stopped halfway. "You can't possibly be comfortable folded up in that stairwell. I promise I won't make another run for it tonight. At least move your bedroll onto the sofa."

"Go to sleep, Jenna."

"You, too." Within minutes, she was out for the night. On the Road, Day One, had come to an end.

Nine

By the time Jenna was up and dressed the next morning, they were already on the road. "What time is it?" she asked when she emerged from the bedroom. "Are we still in the Central Time Zone?"

"Nine fifteen. I headed out at eight. There's coffee back there in the galley, juice and milk in the fridge and cereal in the cabinet next to the sink. While you eat, we'll figure out how you're going to relax without your meds."

She poured a mug of coffee, assembled a bowl of cereal then joined him. "Where are we?"

"Headed south toward Wichita."

"Oh." She took a few sips of coffee, then switched to the cereal. "This is my brand of cereal. How did you know?"

"Checked out the kitchen the night you started talking about running away."

"Before you even agreed to help me?"

Foiled. By his own admission. "I was a Boy Scout. Wanted to be prepared." From his peripheral vision, he noted an eyebrow raise.

"You planned to agree long before you showed up yesterday. Were you deliberately making me sweat?"

"Of course not. I told you I needed time to think through the implications. Probably should've taken a little longer, given your midnight escapade last night."

"Regretting helping me already?"

Every single minute thus far. "I keep wondering if I'm enabling a very poor decision. Let's get back to the subject of helping you relax."

"I'm relaxed right now after a good night's sleep."

"Can't doze all day." Although if knockout pills would miraculously appear, he wouldn't object.

"Do you knit?"

"Never learned."

"How about beading or whatever they call that kind of jewelry making?"

"Seriously? One bump on the road and a hundred beads would be rolling around the floor just waiting to trip us. I did enough falling last night."

Was she deliberately sabotaging his suggestions? "What do you want to do?"

She went back to eating her cereal.

"Jenna, I have no idea what activities appeal to you. You did a great job baking a cake, but a steady diet of desserts wouldn't be healthy for either of us."

Cereal finished, she returned to her coffee. "I read occasionally. That romance novel you brought me wasn't half bad. But I'll have it finished in a few more hours."

"So we add reading to your list. Good start. What else?"

"For over a decade, I've spent my time being a homemaker and volunteer. I didn't pursue many hobbies." She sank into her chair and swiveled from side to side. "Maybe something to do with art, like you suggested the first day I moved into your family home? I've always wanted to sketch, although I have no idea where to begin."

"Great idea. Capture the scenery as we move west. Maybe we could find a how-to book to get you started."

"Where?"

"We can stop at some super discount store. Maybe some place in Oklahoma."

"What do I do in the meantime? Oh, God, that sounded so whiny. I guess I am a brat."

"Hey, self-recognition is a good first step. I'd say finish that novel or go back to bed, although you appear to be wide awake."

Taking his suggestion to heart, she retrieved the book from the bedroom and once again became engrossed. An hour later, she shut the cover and stretched. "That was actually a decent story."

Gray took his gaze off the road for a second. "You were pretty quiet. Didn't even hear you smacking your lips during the love scenes."

"I don't smack my lips for anything," she said with an indignant air.

Interesting observation. He'd file it away for future reference. "So noted."

She stuck the book in the side pocket of her chair, folded her hands in her lap, and stuck out her legs.

"What's the matter?" he asked, not sure he wanted to know.

"Nothing."

"We'll be shopping soon. Start making a list of the goodies you want. Probably a few more books, since you seem to read fast."

"I do. Comes naturally, like spelling or solving math problems for some people."

Once that conversational gambit came to an end, both clammed up for the next several minutes. Gray stared at the road, although they were on a fairly straight stretch. Every so often, he sneaked a peek at Jenna. For a bit, she swung her chair to the right to face the outside, supposedly watching the scenery. Then she pivoted back to sit straight ahead and stare at the horizon. One leg crossed over the other ankle. Shortly after, she switched positions. Within a minute, she uncrossed both ankles, jiggled up and down on the ball of her right foot. "I'm bored."

"Finish your list?"

"Long time ago. Want me to do a list for you?"

"Me? Packed everything I should need." *Including condoms. Which I won't need. Unless you go sleepwalking again tonight.* If she did, he couldn't guarantee he'd be able to maintain his gentlemanly demeanor. He'd just about given in to temptation last night. Now he was fidgeting, dammit! Had to think of something else before he went hard again.

Jenna's leg bouncing continued. Though she didn't make a sound, it irritated him. "Jenna! Please stop the leg thing."

She sat straighter, slapped a hand on her right knee, which stopped the bobbing. "Just when I was starting to tolerate you, Irritable Graham McKenna is back."

"Not to mention the return of Bitchy Jenna DiFranco."

Jenna shot him a killing look; he stared straight ahead. She rose and stomped back to the kitchen area.

She returned a minute later and flopped into her seat. Had she suddenly become her fourteen-year-old offspring? She'd retrieved a bottle of water. None for him apparently. A small amount of the liquid spilled on her slacks as she removed the cap.

Gray released a chuckle. So much for her tough girl act.

"You think that's funny?"

"I think you're funny, spoiling for a fight just because you're bored. Your act seems to have, uh, backfired."

"Barely got my slacks. But there's still a lot of wet stuff here."

"Drink up. Hollow threats don't frighten me."

"Hollow, huh?"

Before the ominous tone in her voice sank in, he found his right pants leg drenched. At the same time, from out of nowhere, a car passed and just as quickly cut in front of the coach. Though Gray was a good driver, Jenna's action cost him the few seconds he needed to comfortably respond to the other vehicle. Once ahead of them, the car sped off, but icicles shot up his spine as he considered what could have happened. "Jenna! Stop. We almost ran into that car because I was too busy reacting to your little stunt."

"Don't mess with the driver while we're on the road."

She slid to her right to check the side mirror once again. In a flash, she twisted around and flung more of the bottle's contents directly at him, soaking his right arm from the elbow up.

Although the rational part of his brain told him these were the actions of a woman coming off her meds, his irritation mounted. She was trying to goad him just to see what he'd do. He couldn't help himself. Her juvenile behavior deserved an appropriate response.

They approached an exit. He exited the highway and parked, then tucked two bottles of water under one arm, and with the other dragged her off the coach. "You fight dirty, lady, attacking while I'm at the wheel. Let's even the odds and see how you like the sudden shower." He flicked open one bottle and dumped the contents on her, which spilled down her front onto her slacks.

"You! You can't do that!"

"Just did."

In response, with one finger, she plugged the top of the bottle, shook it, and then released the contents over his shirt.

"Seems you're out of ammunition," he said then flung the contents of the second bottle over her head.

She backed off. "You … you ruined my hair."

"That got your attention? Your precious hair."

She pulled the wet strands from her eyes, brushed off her shirt. "I was just having fun. I didn't realize you'd go ballistic."

"Listen to you," he shouted. "What would you do to the kid, if she pulled something like that?"

She hung her head, her shoulders slumping. "Paige wouldn't do something like that."

Had he finally gotten through to her? "Why do you keep testing me?"

She swept a hand through her hair again, swiped at beads of water streaming down her cheeks. "Damned if I know. I'm sorry. I'm at loose ends, but I shouldn't have taken it out on you."

"No more games?"

"No more games. Leaving my meds behind was a bad idea."

Huge admission. Maybe they'd turned a corner. God, he hoped so. Her actions thus far kept catching him off guard.

Forty-five minutes later, dressed in dry clothes, they pulled into a major super discount store. Gray turned off the ignition and faced Jenna. "Here's how we do this. You stay in my sight the entire time. You don't talk to anyone. You don't gesture or communicate in any way."

"Got it. For all intents and purposes, I'm under house arrest."

A little overdramatic, but she appeared to understand. They rose to leave. "Show me your pockets."

"What?"

"I won't frisk you. Been there, not going there again. But I have to be sure you have no money, credit cards or phone on you."

"Really? I may have stepped over the line with the water, but I'm not going to run or pull anything to get you in trouble." Nonetheless, without further protest, she pulled out the lining.

Progress, of sorts. At least she'd acquiesced.

"Let's go." He took her arm and kept a hold on her until they were inside the store. He finally released her to grab a shopping cart. "Why don't you steer the cart?" To his relief, she grabbed the handle and set off.

Their first stop was in the office supplies section, where they picked up art paper and sketching pencils. Gray appropriated a couple of tablets, colored pencils and some ballpoint pens as well.

The store didn't have much of a crafts department, but they were able to find some child's play clay. "You're kidding, right?" Jenna asked.

"You need to keep your hands busy. This doesn't involve beads." He dropped the kit in the cart.

As they passed the sports section, he had her pull up long enough to grab another box and stick it in the cart.

"What's that?"

"Recreational therapy, in case we need it." He didn't explain further.

In the book section, she selected a current best seller, a mystery, another romance novel and a purported tell-all from a well-known celebrity. "That should do it."

"Not quite."

"Really, Gray, I have more than enough to entertain me the next few days."

"What kind of shoes do you have?"

"These sandals and the pair of ballerina flats I brought from California. Why?"

"Let's pick up some sports shoes and socks for the terrain out west. Aubrey didn't anticipate this junket we're on when she purchased your wardrobe."

"You planning on making me hike somewhere?"

Don't tempt me, lady. "You've been wanting your freedom. There might be a chance for you to do some running, get in some exercise."

She cocked her head to study him, as if she didn't believe his words. "Are you the same guy who kept his hand on my arm on the way in here? Or do you plan to run with me in tow on a leash?"

He ran a hand through his hair. "I deserve that. But these first two days on the road, your behavior has been so hard to predict, I didn't know what to expect when we got here."

"Fair enough."

No promise to behave the rest of the trip, but then, what did he expect? He could only hope these purchases would help her find the real Jenna. Only time would tell if his seventy-nine-dollar investment would reduce her boredom and eliminate further water fights.

W hat had she been thinking, soaking Gray with water? Granted, she'd needed something to occupy her mind, because she'd been about to lose it sitting there, gazing out on the countryside. The idea had just come to her. She hadn't been planning to do anything of the kind when a trickle of water fell on her slacks. Then Gray chuckled.

His laugh triggered a memory of times past with Jerry. Her former husband could take a pleasant chuckle and make it derogatory when aimed at her. Something inside her snapped on hearing Gray's little laugh, and she instinctively wanted to retaliate for all the times she'd not fought Jerry.

It hadn't been Gray's fault. He'd just wandered into her memory bank of miseries. The water thing had been great. Helped shake out many of the frustrations she'd stored up since landing in the Midwest.

Still, it was a stupid move on her part. What under other circumstances could have been fun, had only riled Gray. Here he was helping out, and she'd rewarded him with juvenile actions.

Time to face the music. Maybe she could win him back with a decent meal. "What do we have for lunch?"

Gray started the coach. "There's some frozen stuff you can microwave or sandwich makings," he called over his shoulder.

"Which would you prefer?" She kept her tone light, solicitous.

"Doesn't matter. Just get me something soon. I'm famished."

Sandwiches, then. Fruit. Was the celery pre-cut? Probably not. Better go with what was on hand for now. After she'd eaten, she'd chop some veggies for later. Within minutes, she handed Gray a paper plate stacked with food.

"Geez, I know I said I was famished, but this is overkill."

"Whatever you don't eat, we'll save for later."

He busied himself eating, and contrary to his earlier statement, ate it all. "Thanks," he said, handing her the plate.

No compliments. Still torqued off at her for the water fight, even though he'd gotten her worse than she'd soaked him. She needed to repair the damage.

She retreated to the kitchen area and began chopping celery.

"Uh, Jenna?"

"Yes?"

"Are you chopping something back there?"

"Yes. I wanted to fix celery at lunch but there wasn't time. I'm preparing it for later."

"I'd rather you wait until we're stopped. Don't want blood and fingers all over the place."

"Oh." Darn. She was a mother. Safety concerns should have occurred to her. "Okay." She cleaned up and soon joined him up front with one of her books.

She was well into the second chapter of the mystery when he spoke again. "Which are you reading first?"

"The mystery. Do you like them?"

"Haven't read much of anything the last few years. Too busy building the business."

"Same for me. Well, I wasn't building a business. At least until I started rehearsing. Before then, though, I was wrapped up in Paige's activities and being the good little housewife." *Stop, Jenna.* Too much information. She was rattling. Why was getting him back on her side again so important?

She read for the next hour, until her back end went to sleep. Time to switch activities, or she'd grow bored again. That had proved a mistake before. She rose and went off in search of another of her new goodies. Shortly, she was back in her seat next to Gray with one of the tablets and pen in hand. She didn't remember making a conscious choice to write. It just seemed to happen.

She began with the idea of recording her "adventures" since returning to the Midwest to claim Paige. But every time she started to describe her forced stay at the McKenna home, words eluded her. Maybe she should keep a journal of just this trip. It wasn't too late to record the territory they'd covered thus far. "Where are we?" she asked.

"Just about ready to leave I-35 and turn west on I-40. Not much longer to go today. We'll stop just west of Oklahoma City."

"What's on I-40? Anything I'd know?"

"I tucked a few maps in the console."

"Give me the headline version."

"Geography not your subject in school?"

"I was into the arts. Humor me."

"First major town on the way is Amarillo, Texas. We'll stay somewhere near there tomorrow night. Then Albuquerque, New Mexico and Flagstaff, Arizona."

"Amarillo. Doesn't that mean yellow in Spanish? Why would someone name a town for a color? Oh, right. 'The Yellow Rose of Texas.' Clever. I don't wear much yellow, except for an occasional very pale lemon."

Yellow. Always seemed like such a happy color. The sun was usually depicted as yellow. And butter. What was "happy" about butter? And yellow cabs. Were they still around? Forget those. Think about school buses. They carried children. Those were happy.

What did happy feel like? When had she last been happy? She'd felt an initial rush yesterday when she and Gray had first taken to the road. More relief than happiness, though. Time with her daughter was still the best part of her life, despite the challenging nature of their interactions these days. She came closest to happy when things went smoothly with Paige, but she worried so about being able to provide for them both and shielding her daughter from her father's peccadillos, total happiness had not been in the picture for some time.

She started a list and soon divided it into two columns: how did she feel when she was happy and what made her happy? In the first she wrote, "Hugs from Paige." No brainer. She added "finding the perfect bargain."

"Why are you laughing?"

"Just some ideas for a story."

"Better be careful. Not so long ago, I wound up drenched when I chuckled."

She glanced over to gauge his mood. Not exactly smiling. But thawing. She didn't push but returned to her lists.

How did she feel when she was happy? Content. Secure. At peace. When would she experience those feelings again?

A story about a young girl who searched for true happiness took shape in her mind. Sounded a bit like *The Wizard of Oz*. No, her girl was younger than Dorothy. And she wouldn't be blown away from Kansas and set down in the Emerald City. No, the main color in her story was … yellow. The girl would believe colors dictated her emotions, and she'd wander through lands of each color until she found her heart in Yellow.

For a brief time, Jenna forgot her tour and her recent escape as she listed on one page and wrote notes to herself on another. Eventually, a third page materialized on which she started a very general outline. At length, she noted they were turning off the Interstate. "Where are we?"

"About a mile or so from tonight's stay."

"Already?"

"Went online last night to line up this place. Made better time today than I estimated, despite our *stop*."

She would have totally missed spotting the turn-in save for the

GPS. The place didn't appear remarkable by any standards. Miles and miles of almost flat land covered with a scrub grass of some kind.

"Stay here while I go in and register."

"I could really use the air." How could she possibly take off out here? There didn't appear to be anything around for miles.

"Let's get settled, then you can stretch your legs as much as you want."

"I'll hold you to that." She went in search of her new sports shoes. Might as well be ready when he returned.

She tried to resume writing but couldn't focus. Not while she had this new location, temporary though it might be, to capture her attention. From what she could see from her seat, there were only a few other vehicles around. All RVs of sorts. Nothing like her motor coach. But it was early. Maybe RVers didn't come off the road until sunset, trying to get as far as they could in sunlight.

Gray reappeared within minutes. "We're all set. I need to hook to the utilities first, then you can explore to your heart's content."

She had no idea what getting hooked up entailed, but hopefully he'd be back soon. Meanwhile, she changed to her new sneakers and waited for Gray.

He wasn't gone long. When he returned, he pulled out a three-ring binder from one of the drawers and tucked some papers in it, then replacing it. "Okay. Here's the lowdown. The lodge is the main building. They've got vending machines with various snacks and sundries. Don't think we need any, but if you see something you want, let me know. There's a small library where you can borrow books, if you replace them with some of your own, but with your recent purchases, you probably don't need any."

"In other words, not much to see or do."

"There's a phone at the desk, and I imagine the clerk has his own cell. We may need to use one or the other if my cell doesn't work out here. I didn't impose many conditions on you, Jenna, in return for crossing my brothers and your sister, leaving behind a business that needs me and signing on to take you to California, but you agreed to no phone calls, no trying to escape. You've already blown one commitment. I expect you to keep your word about phones."

Long speech. The most he'd said in a while. He was laying a guilt trip on her. Still, he was right. He'd been the only one to come to her aid. She owed him. Besides, even if she could get through to someone, who would she call, and how could they help her while she was in the middle of nowhere? "Okay. Agreed." She kept her voice low, but he heard.

"The same goes for anyone else you might see out here, other staff, other guests. No recruiting collaborators. Okay?"

She nodded. He had a right to lecture, but she hated feeling like a chastised child. Did Paige feel like this when she went on ad nauseam reminding her of some minor offense? She started down the steps and opened the door. "Aren't you coming?"

"Got a few things to attend to first. If you go wandering around the park, stay in sight. There's a meadow off to the left. Don't know what kind of critters populate it, so watch your step."

She could hardly believe her ears. For the first time in a couple of weeks, she would be on her own.

HE WATCHED her take off for the lodge. Unless she headed straight through, he had a few minutes to put things away. Even if she did wander out back, he'd already checked the area, another lot for RVs. None there. Probably for overflow traffic. He went immediately to the drawer where he'd stored the trip binder. Probably innocuous where it was, but just in case she got curious, and he'd certainly witnessed enough of her unbridled energy when bored, he'd find a better place to hide it. Didn't want her reviewing his receipts in any great detail, or she might note the reservation numbers. Hadn't figured out a way to escape them, so he'd have to keep them out of sight in one of the secret caches located throughout the coach where he'd hidden her phone and purse.

Within two minutes, he was at the door. No sign of her. Time to move out.

She wasn't in the main room of the lodge, either.

"That your wife who came in?" the staff person at the desk asked.

"Traveling companion." No need to provide more information than necessary. This guy was probably just curious. "See where she went?"

"Checked out the vending machines in the rec room then headed to the back door. Don't know why. Right now it's a big empty field. Doesn't fill up 'til weekends or holidays."

Gray ambled toward said door. Didn't think she'd make a run for it. She'd have quite a hike on her hands, if she did. But he couldn't be sure.

There was no mistaking her when he got to the door. She was the only thing, human or otherwise, out there. She looked like she was measuring off the field on foot. She'd reached the roped-off boundary of one side and now turned to walk along it to the back boundary. What the hell was she up to?

He caught up with her. "Sightseeing?"

"You told me I was on my own."

"Right. Just wanted to make sure you were okay."

She pulled up, stuck her hands in her shorts pockets. "Unless a sinkhole opens up, what could possibly happen to me out here?"

"I got curious. Wanted to know what you'd do with your first alone time."

"Like you suggested, I'm getting some exercise. Haven't had much opportunity to work out the kinks lately."

"You got any problem with my sitting in one of the rockers out front? I like fresh air too."

She cocked her head in his direction. "Did you deliberately seek out some place with so few customers? Reduce my contact with the outside world."

"Have to admit, it's a pretty good idea, but I just happened onto it. It's still early. As heavily traveled as I-40 is, we'll probably find ourselves with a lot more company before much longer."

"How do you know I won't arrange with one of them to get me back to California?"

"To what advantage? Your coach is the most comfortable vehicle on the road. Unless it's me … You tired of me already?" He tried to sound non-threatening, but he couldn't keep the undertone of interest out of his voice. Was he starting to care what she thought of him?

She didn't answer.

"See ya." He strolled back to the lodge with forced nonchalance. Still wasn't convinced she'd stick with him, but he had to look the part.

On his way to the front porch and the rocking chairs, he picked up a paperback in the library. A bestselling suspense a few years back. Didn't intend to read it. But couldn't just sit there rocking once he'd made his call.

He hit Mitch's number. "It's me."

"How's it going?"

He debated whether to report the water incident and their unexpected stop to pick up items to give Jenna something to do. No. It was over and done with and would only concern those back home. Save the horror stories for when he really needed their help. So far, though she'd tested his patience more than once, he could handle her. "Main challenge is keeping her occupied. Too bad she doesn't know how to drive one of these. She could relieve me and keep herself busy at the same time."

"You stopped for the night already? At that place we set up?"

"Yeah. The road's pretty flat out here and less traffic than I anticipated. So far, she hasn't questioned my ease in finding stops. I've been hiding the registration receipts from her, in case she gets curious."

"About that? Aubrey wants to talk to you."

Aubrey came on the line. "Hi, Graham. I didn't get a chance to thank you personally for putting your life on hold to help Jenna get home."

"Yeah, well, I seemed to be the best option."

"Nonetheless, I really appreciate what you're doing. Jenna's had a tough year. She's been under a lot of pressure. Keeping her here against her wishes was a challenge, but I thought it was the best strategy. You knew before the rest of us it wasn't going to work."

"She told me as much when I took my turn watching her." Where was Aubrey going with this?

"She seems to trust you."

"More like she's dependent on me to get her to California."

Slight hesitation. "That's the thing. Now that she's gotten away, you might be tempted to tell her how it all happened. That we let her escape."

Would he? "I don't like the idea of putting one over on her. She's been 'handled' enough."

"Exactly my point. She already feels we took over her life. How do you think she'd feel if she learned we helped her get away?"

"Once she got over the surprise, she'd appreciate her family caring enough about her to let her go."

"Maybe. But more than anything, she needs to feel she's taken back control of her life. If she discovers that's not the case, it will hurt her self-confidence, and she really needs to get it back again."

Aubrey was asking a lot. "I want her to get her confidence back as well, but I don't want to lie to her. Whatever trust she has in me will be lost."

"Then don't lie. Just avoid the topic."

He shot a glance over his shoulder, just in case Jenna had tired of her exercise session. She could return any minute. "I'll steer clear of the topic, but if she asks ..."

"Got it."

"Look, I've got to get going. Need to check on her again." He regretted his words as soon as they were out. For some reason, he didn't want them to know she might still be a flight risk.

As a sort of penance, he held back. He'd give her a few more minutes. Meanwhile, he'd crack the book. Three pages in, he stopped reading as piano music reached his ears. No. It couldn't be. But the sound grew louder. He'd done a quick scan of the place before returning to the coach after checking in. How'd he missed a piano?

He threw the book down and raced inside. The clerk seemed to guess what he was seeking. "She's in there. Plays well, don't she?"

"Uh, yeah." Gray strode toward the door of what the clerk called the rec room but pulled up just outside and listened to the concert. God, she was good. Like a magician extracting a rabbit from a hat, she was pulling an incredible sound from an out-of-tune, upright piano. Why was she worried about her musical ability?

"Don't you want to go in?" the clerk asked, having come up behind him.

"Don't want to disturb her."

"Doubt you could. She's pretty much into what she's doing."

Yes, she was. She wasn't supposed to be playing yet. They'd gone to great lengths to assure she wouldn't meet up with a piano while she was recuperating. Probably should get her away from this one. But he held back. How could he deprive her of what appeared to make her so joyful?

"S'cuse me," an older woman in Bermuda shorts and sleeveless blouse breezed past him to take a seat near the back. Shortly, a man in baggy plaid shorts and a too-tight t-shirt joined her.

Within minutes, a dozen or more others slipped into the room as unobtrusively as possible so as not to disturb Jenna. Apparently she was unaware of her audience, because she kept on playing and didn't acknowledge them.

When she finished the piece, she was greeted by resounding applause. She jerked, then looked behind her, her hand coming to her mouth in surprise. "Th-thank you." She seemed to freeze in place momentarily before she rose.

"Please, don't stop," the first woman said. "You play beautifully."

"I, uh, haven't practiced in weeks."

"Who cares?" another audience member called. "I don't get to hear good stuff like that very often."

She started to reply, then her eyes fell on Gray standing in the back. He nodded for her to proceed. Back at his parents' house, she'd confessed to worrying about how audiences would relate to her. This was the perfect opportunity to find out.

She took her seat and played something light and fast. He was no expert on classical stuff, but the piece sounded like some kind of dance. Not quite a polka but something just as playful. By the time the piece ended, the crowd had almost doubled. Must be check-in time.

Jenna finished the piece to even greater applause than before. She gave the audience one more song before claiming she'd exhausted her memory. Despite several heartfelt requests to continue, she begged off. "I'm so out of practice. I wouldn't do justice to anything else. But thank you so much for your applause."

"You played so well. Even on that old pie-anno. Are you a professional?" one man said.

"I, uh, yes. But like I said, I haven't played enough recently to do it justice."

"Sure wish you'd change your mind," said the clerk, who'd been hustling in and out of the room throughout the little concert to check in new arrivals. "Don't get this much of a crowd in here except for Bingo."

Jenna quickly made her way to Gray at the door. "Maybe later. That's all I can handle for now," she called to them. She didn't say a word to Gray but made a beeline for the coach.

Gray followed, not sure what to expect. He'd no sooner closed the door behind him than she launched herself in his direction and planted a big one square on his lips.

He took a step back. "Whoa! Not that again." God, no. His resistance was declining with each passing hour.

She actually giggled. "No, no way. For the first time in days, I didn't feel closed in. I was completely alone when I walked that field out back. Thank you for giving me my space."

Why burst her bubble mentioning how few places there were behind the park to which she could escape? "You're welcome. We'll try to do something like that each day we're on the road, if it means so much to you."

"The exercise was just a warm-up. Getting to play the piano made my day."

And there it was. When she'd started talking about walking the field, he'd hoped they might get past the piano part. What a fool. "Even though it was off-key?"

"Better than nothing."

"Even with an audience present? That's the part you've been dreading."

She gave him a playful shove. "I was. You know why? I can't believe this never occurred to me. I need a manager. A manager would have told me. If I can find the wherewithal, I really need to look into finding someone when I get back to California. I could have avoided all this stress if I'd known."

"You're rambling. What never occurred to you?"

"I need a practice audience. Probably several. It surprised me today when people showed up. But once I got used to them, it was a real trip."

What could he do? "This is the most animated I've seen you since I met you. Was it the applause?"

She seemed to think through his question before responding. "Partially. But it was also being able to play again. Even a rickety old upright."

Guilt churned his stomach. Even though he'd promised Aubrey and Mitch he'd watch out for Jenna, how could he keep her from the very thing she seemed to love more than anything except the kid and her family? *Tread carefully, old man.* "Playing for your own enjoyment isn't the same as performing for a paying audience."

She angled her head, narrowed her eyes. "What are you trying to tell me, Gray?"

"Maybe your sister, Mitch and the others, including me, jumped to the wrong conclusion about your condition," he began, picking his way carefully. "When you were staying at my parents' house, you kept saying how all you wanted to do was play the piano, but you added how much rehearsal time you were missing. We got the two confused."

Her hands went to her hips. "I see. It was okay for you all to be *confused,* but not me?"

"C'mon, Jenna. We were in unknown territory with your condition.

We had no idea what caused that incident in your car, other than it had something to do with getting ready for your tour. You convinced me to spring you before we could convince you to see a professional accustomed to dealing with stress-related issues."

"I suppose." One eyebrow shot up. "But it's okay now for me to play whenever we run across a piano along the way?"

Rock and a hard place. No denying, her short time on the keys today had definitely energized her. But could more be too much? He needed outside help. In the meantime … "First, answer me this—will playing on less than perfect instruments hurt your technique? I had to borrow a buddy's baseball glove once when mine got locked in Mitch's car. Really threw me off the next time I had my own glove, because I'd had to adjust my ball handling to the other one."

She backed up a few steps, started flipping through the book he brought back with him. "Are you serious?"

So the idea had just hit him? Sounded legit to him. And the ball glove story was true. "Yeah. What would your coach tell you?"

"My coach?"

"Whatever you call the person who reviews your playing?"

"I, uh, don't have one."

Her admission shocked him almost as much as her seduction act had a few days earlier. Every pro had someone they turned to for advice, who helped them get back on track when their game lagged. "Don't need one?"

"One of the expenses I've put off."

He didn't know what to say. Okay, yeah, he did. Time to go for it. No more pussyfooting around. "Jenna! Don't you think maybe that's part of the reason for your emotional state?"

She collapsed into a nearby chair, hands covering her mouth. "I am so screwed. Worse, I did this to myself. Since I'd toured before, I was so smug about knowing all there was to know about putting one together. But I forgot about audience testing and needing a coach. What else have I skipped?"

Damn. He'd meant to help her see there might be reasons other than her own emotional state adding to her stress, not cause a further breakdown. In the course of a few minutes, she'd gone from elated to alarmed, not a good sign. He draped an arm around her shoulders. "Let's put that *skipped* question aside for now and just talk about this."

"We've been talking, Gray. What else do you want me to say? That I've totally messed up my life and my daughter's?"

"How about why you said that? What have you messed up?"

She sagged into the chair and studied him, like she couldn't believe he could ask such a question. "Let's start with you. I've dragged you away from your job. Caused you to turn against your brothers."

"You didn't drag me. So scratch that."

"I've totally mismanaged this tour. Rather than prepare smart, like hiring a coach and a manager who'd worry about technique and details, I spent my time and money on a fancy wardrobe and outfitting this motor coach. And when I've second-guessed those decisions, I made your life miserable second-guessing everything you were doing with this coach."

Was this a breakthrough? Couldn't tell. Might just be a pity party. He moved around to face her, bent. "That an apology?"

She blinked. "Huh? Guess so, although I was mainly talking to myself."

"But was it only talk?"

She shook her head as if suddenly becoming aware of him, even though she'd just responded to his question. "I, uh, don't know. I haven't considered my tour in these terms before. It's like shining a light on an enigma previously in shadow. It's overwhelming, you know? Unexpected comprehension."

Had she really turned a corner? Or was this just talk to get him to relax his vigilance? All the more reason to watch her carefully.

Eleven

"Ind"ow about we take a break? Ready to eat? There's a picnic table just outside, but I also noted a patio outside the lodge with other tables. Thought we could eat there once we heat our dinner."

She blinked, snapping out of her self-reflection. "Uh, sure."

Half an hour later and two trips each to the guest patio area, they were ready to chow down. "This casserole smells yummy. Did you make this?" she asked.

"Actually it came from Peggy Summers. Ever since Geoff's been seeing Eileen, Peggy sends goodies like this home with him. The freezer is almost full. Figured they wouldn't miss a few items, and this way, we could enjoy good home-cooked food without much effort."

"I like how you think. When I get back to California, I'll send her a thank you note for all the tasty food she's inadvertently provided. I wasn't very appreciative when she was sending it over to your parents' house."

"She realizes why."

"Still … Hey, look. We've got company."

Two young tykes, a boy and girl, sprinted toward them. Each held a food item.

The young girl reached them first. "Mama let me carry the bread tonight. Bobby gots to carry the 'bony.'"

"I see," Gray responded. "Important tasks, both of them."

"Sorry 'bout that," said a young woman in her late twenties, having arrived just after the children. "I hope they didn't disturb your meal."

"Of course not," Jenna returned. "Your little girl is quite proud of her assignment."

The young woman's face went blank for a second, then blossomed into a smile. "Oh, right. They're still young enough to love helping Mama."

A man about the same age as the woman came up behind her. "Hi, folks. Didn't realize these tables were set so close together. Hope you don't mind us intruding on your privacy. The kids need their running time as soon as we pull up each night, but we insist they eat first."

"And they love picnics," the young woman added.

"I see," Gray returned, amused by how fast the children were dragging out paper plates and plastic silverware. "Good little helpers."

"We get to play as soon as we eat."

The mother busied herself setting out the food, what appeared to be mainly bread, lunchmeat, and a few pieces of overripe fruit. Jenna raised a brow toward Gray.

Jenna was the first to act. "We have more of this chicken casserole than we could possibly eat. Would you mind helping us out by taking some of it off our hands?"

The woman shot a quick glance at the man, who gave a slight nod. "It looks delicious. Are you sure you wouldn't rather save it for another meal yourselves?" Gray began scooping large spoonsful into a container. "We're sure. Hope it's something the kids will like."

The man accepted the container. "We'll see right now. Look, kids. These nice folks are sharing some of their meal with us. This is a treat, so you both have to show your thanks by eating everything we give you. Understood?" He turned to Jenna and Gray. "We're the Jensens. My wife, Janie, our kids, Molly and Bobby, and I'm Don."

Since the couple was eyeing them expectantly, obviously waiting for their introduction to be reciprocated, Gray cut in before Jenna had a chance to either give too much away or get embarrassed. "Jenna and Graham." He didn't add last names, nor did the other couple push.

Both children, eyes wide at the new *delicacy*, simply bobbed their heads. As soon as they were served and got the okay from their parents, they dug in. They didn't stop shoveling the casserole into their mouths until it disappeared from both plates. "Yum-my!" the girl said.

Her brother seconded her appraisal. "Is there more?"

Their mother silently moved a portion of her share off her plate onto theirs before Jenna or Gray could offer more. The father followed suit.

Gray and Jenna's eyes met as both noted the parental sacrifice. Clearly, the family was struggling. Just as apparent, though, were the family bonds they witnessed. What else could he and Jenna do for them without insulting their pride?

The children downed their food quickly, the lure of playtime fast overtaking their appetites, now apparently satiated.

"Stay where we can see you," the father called.

Other than the fact they ran and jumped and otherwise frolicked, their delight in being "free" reminded him of Jenna's earlier actions.

"They're so much fun to watch at that age," Jenna said.

The other woman eyed Jenna. "Do you two have children?"

Jenna blinked, shot a glance at Gray, but kept her cool. "A daughter. Fourteen. She's staying with other family at the moment."

"How nice. Don and I haven't had a moment to ourselves since our oldest, Molly, was born."

"Where are you headed?" Gray asked, attempting to deflect the topic of Jenna and him as a couple.

"Eau Claire, Wisconsin. I, uh, lost my job a few months back. When we had to give up the house, we went out to stay with the wife's parents in Barstow. But I'm allergic to cat dander. Stood it as long as I could by sleeping in our RV, but that meant I either slept alone each night or the kids were alone in the house with their grand-parents." He lifted his hands, palms up. "What're you gonna do?'"

"Move on, I guess," Gray replied. "What did you do? Your old job, I mean."

"Worked on tractors. Assembly, repair, what-have-you."

"Yeah? Isn't agriculture booming these days?"

"Exactly," the other man said. "Booming so much, foreign investors wanted in. Dutch company absorbed us. Brought in their own technical people. Didn't need me any longer."

"Rough."

"Got a lesser-paying job doing about the same thing in Barstow, but when my allergy kicked up— being around the kids so much and the kids being around the cats—decided I'd try my luck in Wisconsin with my parents. Janie babysits. That way, she can stay home with the kids 'til they're in school. Still a year off for Molly. Two for Bobby."

"Ever worked on a motor coach?"

"Huh? Nothing that fancy. But it's been up to me to keep our RV goin'. Couldn't afford to keep it otherwise."

"Would you mind taking a look at my rig? This is the maiden voyage. We're still working out the kinks. On our way here today, something sounded suspicious." Nothing was wrong with the coach. Mitch had done a great job prepping it. But Gray was getting good vibes about this guy, the whole family, actually. While Don had been describing their situation, an idea had occurred to Gray. Something he wanted to test out first.

AFTER GRAY and Don went off to have a look under the coach's hood, Jenna moved over to Janie's table.

"You folks headed east or west?" Janie asked.

"West. California." Alone with a stranger for the first time since arriving in Burlington, it was so tempting to clue Janie in about her real circumstances. But she held her tongue.

"We just came from there. Hope you fare better than we did." She explained about her husband losing his job and their last few months at her parents', confirming Jenna's earlier suspicion something was amiss with their financial situation.

She'd update Gray later. See if he could give them some money. She'd been ready to open her own wallet when she once again remembered her circumstances. She had less money than this family at the moment. The realization gave her a start. She understood why Gray wasn't ready to trust her with money … still, being penniless made her feel vulnerable and overly dependent. But nowhere near as reliant on the man as she'd been with Jerry. She just had to win over Gray's trust to regain her independence. "Your kids seem no worse for wear."

Janie kept her eyes on her children across the way, although there was absolutely nowhere they could get lost or any signs of strangers around. "I don't know how I would've gotten through this past year without them to keep my mind occupied. They're so hopeful."

"And full of energy." Had Paige run in circles that much when she was four? Funny how the tiniest memories could return to you unbidden, and yet, when you tried to summon them, they remained in the past, cloudy and unreachable.

Janie released a long sigh. "True. But they need this time so they'll calm down later. In a few minutes, they should be ready for me to read as many stories as I'll permit. I don't mind, although I'm getting tired of reading the same old same old. Maybe this place has some different children's books I can borrow."

"I have one for them. Brand new. As of this afternoon."

Janie cocked her head. "Really?"

"I wrote a short story. I used to make up things to get my daughter to sleep at night, but this is the first I've written down. Would you mind if I tried it out on your kids?"

"Please, do."

They gave the youngsters a few more minutes to wind down their play while Jenna retrieved her pad of paper, then Janie called them over to the picnic tables. "Besides the wonderful food she shared with us, this nice lady has another surprise for you, but you have to promise you'll go to bed quickly and quietly as soon as it's over. Okay?"

Molly jumped up and down at the prospect of a surprise. Bobby clapped his hands repeatedly. "Yes, Mama, yes," they both cried.

Janie explained how this was a very special story, because they were the first to hear it. There were no pictures yet, so they'd have to listen very carefully.

They both nodded with all the seriousness two young children could convey.

Jenna sat on the picnic table bench facing out and the two children planted themselves on each side. "This is the story of a young girl who wanted to be happy."

Molly immediately wanted to know the girl's name. Huh? Hadn't named her yet. "Jennalee," she improvised. As good a name as any for now. She'd have plenty of time on the road the next day to come up with something better.

She went on to describe why the girl, uh, Jennalee, went searching for happiness in the different lands of colors, starting with red. Each land required the listener to supply their own list of red things that made them happy.

Bobby answered first. "A red ball, just like the one Daddy got me."

"Red flowers," Molly added. "What's red that makes you happy, Mama?"

"Let's see. I know. My red sneakers," Janie replied, somewhat surprised to be included.

"Good one, Mama," Bobby said.

The search for happiness continued through The Land of Green, Blue Country, Orange-opia, Pink Land, Purpleville, and finally arrived at Yellow Land, also known as Amarillo, at which point, Janie glanced at Jenna and winked, having apparently caught on to the inspiration for the story.

When the story concluded, both children clapped. "Again, read it again, lady."

"No, only one time through for this one, kids," their mother told them. "It's special that way."

Molly and Bobby puffed their lips into pouts, but a stern look from their mom sent them scampering off toward their RV. "I loved your story," Janie said. "For a first time, you did great."

"I second the opinion," Don added. When had he and Gray returned? Had they taken in her story, too?

"Thanks. That was so much fun sharing my ideas with your kids. They were so responsive and appreciative."

Janie released a sigh. "We'd better follow them. No telling what mischief they can get themselves into even in a few minutes on their own." She took Jenna's hand. "You and your man are very kind. Plus, you've got a real talent. You should think about publishing your stories."

"I might just do that."

"I'll be in touch, Don. One way or the other," Gray called to the departing couple.

"Hey, thanks," the other man said over his shoulder.

"In touch?" Jenna asked.

"Guy's a natural-born mechanic who needs a new start. Why not in Burlington?"

"Isn't that your job?"

"I only told Mitch I'd take over for him so he'd get on with his dream of being an attorney. If the guys think we can swing this financially, this might solve all our problems."

Once the couple reached their RV, Jenna turned back to him. "Apparently my sister isn't the only problem solver in that firehouse."

"My efforts don't hold a candle to Aubrey's. I just saw a possible way I could help that family and help myself at the same time."

"Now, if you could just turn your attention to helping me with my problems."

"Sounded like you were taking care of that on your own. That story you read to those kids was great. Maybe you could augment your concert tour by writing children's books. Or drop the concert tour altogether ..."

"I still want to do the tour, once I find a smarter way to do it. But I'm also intrigued with the idea of writing children's books. If this first try isn't just a fluke, that is."

They packed up the rest of their dinner things and headed back to the motor coach. "Plus, there's this coach. What would I do with it?" she asked as they entered.

"Good point. Although you might be able to resell it for a profit. It's a great coach. Aubrey outdid herself decorating the interior."

"She did, didn't she? I'm glad I told her so before all this stress-related trouble started. I've only seen a few of the rehabs she'd done in L.A., but I have to admit, my sister found her niche. Hopefully, I will find mine."

"Now that I've heard you play, I'm a believer. If that's what you still want."

"Has to be."

"Okay, fine. Just sayin'. There might be other alternatives, if you decide to scrap the tour."

The next several minutes passed in silence. Gray busied himself putting away what was left of their dinner things. Jenna pulled out her tablet and appeared to reread the story she told the children, adding passages or scratching out every so often.

"I wasn't kidding when I said your story was pretty good," Gray said at length.

She glanced up. "Even if I did decide to go the childrens' book route, it would be years before I'd earn enough to support Paige and me. I have to find something to bring in money in the meantime. Let's give all this don't-do-the-tour talk a rest. I need some me time. Think I'll take my cue from Molly and Bobby and head to bed."

She wasn't ready to tell him she was considering giving up the tour. If she shared that tidbit now, he wouldn't let it drop for the rest of the trip, and she needed time to digest the idea on her own time, in her own way. Earning her living through concerts had been her go-to decision once Jerry left them. Did she have the courage to head in a different direction now that she had thought more about it?

Twelve

Jenna closeted herself in her bedroom while she considered her options. For now, she had only herself for counsel. Not much different than what she'd been dealing with for months. Even though her mother and Aubrey checked in with her from time to time, they had no idea the hell she'd been inhabiting. Though precocious, Paige was still a child, who should be spared any of her mother's difficulties. Jenna had done her best to keep her joyfully unaware.

"Damn you, Graham McKenna," she said to the room in general. "You made me think friendship was possible. I could really use a friend right now. But the price of your company is too high." He'd made her doubt her decision. She couldn't afford to second-guess her concert tour at this point, although to be honest, she'd already arrived at that point. "Thank you very much, Gray."

A gentle rapping on her door brought her out of her thoughts. "Jenna?"

She didn't want any further communication with the man tonight.

"Jenna, open the door."

She'd learned the hard way not to give in to a man's pleas, no matter how apologetic they sounded. Early in her marriage, she'd locked herself in the bedroom thinking she'd make Jerry pay for some crazy remark he'd made about one her friends. After he'd begged for several minutes, she'd finally let him in, prepared to hear his apology. Apologies were the last thing on his mind. Though he wasn't into his battering mode then—that came a few years later, when he'd been doing poorly in his job—he attempted to make her forget his transgression with a little more *aggressive* lovemaking than usual. Her pelvic region ached for days following.

But she wasn't afraid of Gray. She'd come to trust him that much. How many times had she thrown herself at him? At least twice. Three times, if you counted the kiss in her exuberance after her mini-concert. But she was done discussing her tour, her stress or any of her other problems tonight. She wanted to preserve what little remained of her high spirits after finally getting to play a piano and her success with the children's story.

"No more talk about your tour. I promise."

Shouldn't listen to him. Shouldn't give in. Jenna just wanted him to leave her alone.

With hesitant steps, she made her way back to the door. One minute. That's all she'd give him. Unless it took him longer to apologize. She slid it open a bit.

"Here ..." He handed her the book she'd been reading plus her writing materials. "If you're gonna hang out in there, you may want these."

"Thanks."

"Good night." He closed the door.

Didn't that beat all? He'd used her things as an excuse to get in the last word. *I see right through you, Gray. Trying to make me feel like a petulant child. Well, it didn't work.* She was not a petulant child. She was a woman with her own mind who could make good decisions and stick with them. Okay, she'd forgotten about audience testing until today. An oversight anyone who was under the gun to get her act together in record time might make. As for needing a piano coach, how many times had she considered finding someone? But for some reason, she kept putting off that action. Had she been afraid if she did, they'd discourage her from proceeding as well, because she no longer had the talent?

She changed into her nightgown and lay in bed attempting to read at least one page of her mystery. The story wasn't registering. Jenna kept replaying Gray's words in her head.

Now that I've heard you play, I'm a believer. If that's what you still want?

I wasn't kidding when I said your story was pretty good.

Maybe you could augment your concert tour by writing children's books. Or drop the concert tour altogether?

There might be other alternatives.

He hadn't actually come right out and *told* her to forget the tour. But his intent had been clear enough. She often adopted a similar approach when attempting to convince Paige to do something she didn't want to do.

Even if she wanted to, she couldn't just abandon the tour at this point. Could she? She attempted a mental list of all the commitments she'd made: costumes, this motor coach, and the tour promoter, who even now was probably busy arranging for concert dates. The costumes had been purchased outright, although it might be possible to unload them, at a loss, of course, at some consignment place. After all, she lived in L.A., where resale shops abounded.

As for this coach, Gray suggested she sell it. There were always rock and country musicians looking for rigs. Maybe Mitch or Geoff could work their contacts.

But then there was the promoter. Could the contract be broken? She'd left for the Midwest in such a hurry to claim her runaway daughter, she hadn't brought the document with her. Maybe she could convince Gray to let her call the guy, just to check.

Why was she even considering these actions? She couldn't drop the tour. Although with all her rehearsal issues and now having to take time off due to this forced rest, maybe she could move the tour back a few weeks. Or a month or so. By then, Paige would be in school again.

Her head throbbed. Too many questions for tonight.

TONIGHT, Gray adopted a different tactic to assure Jenna stayed inside the coach by climbing into the bottom bunk bed just outside the door to her bedroom. Good thing the coach included a small bathroom for guests besides the master bath, so he'd been spared having to use Jenna's space. Given how he'd practically had to beg her to open her door just so he could hand her things over, he doubted she would've been in much of a mood to let him dress in there. Unlike the night before, this evening he wore a tee along with his briefs rather than sleeping in the buff. Although, considering her current mood, she probably wouldn't be wandering around in the middle of the night and falling on top of him anyhow.

What was with her mood tonight? The result of coming off her meds too soon or was he seeing the real Jenna? She'd asked for his advice, so he'd given it, only to be met with her rejecting every idea he proposed.

As she claimed, the woman really was a talented pianist. He'd enjoyed her impromptu concert as much as, more than, the rest of her audience earlier in the evening. Standing at the back of the room, he hadn't seen much of her face as she played, except when she'd turn her head to the right as her fingers flew over the higher-pitched keys. But those brief glimpses had shown an intensity and concentration screaming contentment.

But she wasn't managing her tour very well, nor had she hired someone to do that for her. She mentioned some sort of promoter, who apparently was setting up the concert dates, but even Gray, a total outsider to the concert business, knew there was more to the business end of a tour.

She wasn't using the services of a piano coach either. Despite her ego, she was too smart to think she could enhance her technique by herself, especially after so many years off the concert circuit. Apparently most of her budget had gone to what he considered "fluff" items, the promoter, costumes and the motor coach. Even though he was grateful for her business, considered in light of her other tour needs, it was a luxury. She probably should've rented a less fancy rig.

He didn't doubt her need to make a living for herself and the kid. The dirt bag she'd been married to apparently hadn't left any choice. But this tour seemed to be messing with her head. There had to be better options.

Whatever. Once he got her to California, he no longer had to worry about either her state of mind or career. If he was lucky and she'd meant what she said about staying in her room, he wouldn't have to worry about her the rest of the night.

Two full days of driving and babysitting Jenna caught up with him and he slept soundly. Had she walked right past him and slammed the door on her way out, he probably wouldn't have known.

He rose around seven, fixed a quick breakfast then headed to the lodge to pay the bill.

The desk clerk from the previous day was on duty again. "Your lady comin' back to play some more? She shore gave folks a great concert last night."

"We need to hit the road, but I'll tell her how much folks liked her music."

"Too bad." The clerk shook his head. "We rarely get a group together around here. Most folks tend to stay in their own rigs. Don't like to mix with strangers. But last night, they hung around talking, even after she left."

"She'll be pleased to know." Gray collected his receipts and hurried back to the coach, just in case his fellow traveler was up for the day. No need for the rush. All was quiet in the back bedroom. For good measure, though, he checked her door. Locked. She was still there.

He'd been on the road over two hours before he heard her stirring, but it was another half hour before she made an appearance. "There's coffee made," he called.

"Thanks."

"We can stop for rolls or doughnuts, if you want?"

"Cereal's okay."

Silence again. She'd returned to her bedroom. No big surprise. The only question, how long before those quarters, comfy as they were, got to her? He checked his watch. Nine forty-five. He'd give her about two hours, max. She'd probably use lunch as an excuse to return then just stay on in the front of the coach without making a production of her return.

Two minutes later, she plunked down in the seat next to him. "I made a list."

Good thing he had a strong grip on the steering wheel or they might have swerved off the road. So much for trying to predict the woman's actions. Did he dare pursue her statement? She obviously expected as much. He kept his response neutral. "Sounds productive."

"Certainly was. After the grilling you gave me last night, I couldn't shake all the questions you asked, so I wrote them down to help make sense of things."

Grilling? She'd asked for his suggestions. *Hold your tongue. Give her a chance to explain.* "Did it help?"

"Up to a point. You helped me realize I need a tour manager to handle the logistics as well as a piano coach. But to be able to afford them, I have to get creative about financing."

Well, well. Progress. "How's that working?"

She glanced away briefly, as if not sure she wanted to answer. "Thought I'd ask for your ideas," she said. "You weren't the least bit shy about making suggestions last night."

"Yeah, about that. Guess I overstepped. Didn't mean to put down all you've done so far to prepare for your tour."

She clamped her mouth shut. "You, uh, right. It took a while for me to realize you were only helping, not criticizing."

His radar told him she'd come around to his way of thinking mighty fast. Especially for Jenna. What was she up to? Better play it straight until he figured out her game. "My brothers and I inherited the garage and a pile of debts from our dad, who'd gone a little crazy after our mother's death and started an RV dealership. As we structured our new customization business, we played on our strong points —Geoff's sales experience, Mitch's work as a mechanic in high school and my architectural engineering background."

"So, focus on my strong points. Like my musical talent."

"For starters. Never forget how good you are. You made a believer of me yesterday."

She no longer studied her list. "Thanks. But that's pretty much where I started. I need to go beyond my talent."

"Agreed. But whenever you're in doubt from now on, go back to that." He paused, hoping she'd take his words to heart. "What are your other strong points?" he asked.

"Could, uh, you help me there?" The request emerged in a small voice.

"I could, but for you to succeed, you have to know yourself."

"Yes, okay." She seemed to consider his question. "I'm a good mother. Does that count?"

"Sure, as long as you can leverage those qualities. What makes you so?"

"Let me think." Pause. "I'm responsible."

Right. Except when you disappear from rehearsals with some stud. That small slice of her recent history still dug at his craw.

"What else?"

"I, uh, show affection."

"Better play that one down for now."

"Okay, well, how about I set a good example for my daughter?"

He took his eyes off the road long enough to raise a brow in her direction. "Want to try that one again?"

"I do set a good example. What I told you about my bar hook-ups was an aberration. I eat well, exercise, get enough rest, I don't belittle others—"

"Back up there. What do you call the hell you put Aubrey through when she was trying to finish the interior of this thing?"

Could you hear an eye roll? Probably not, but he was sure he'd elicited one.

"I admit, I did come down a little hard on her at times, but that's part of the relationship we've developed with each other over the years. I've always been the Big Sister who tended to know better whether I did or not, who mediated her quarrels with our mother and who got her out of more than one scrape. We'd sort of grown out of that and become closer friends, but lately, I've been under so much pressure that I reverted to that old frame of reference.

"Your sister was on top of things with this coach from the first day she walked into the firehouse."

"I'm sure she was, but it was difficult gauging long distance how things were really going, thus my constant calls and questions."

He'd suspected as much, but she'd never put it in so many words. Explained a lot of things. Explained but didn't condone. "Why didn't you cancel the order? There was still time in the early days after you'd signed the contract."

"With the exception of Paige, everything in my life seemed to be in shambles, my future one huge unknown. The coach was something positive and specific I could look forward to. Like buying a new pair of shoes or getting a new hairdo used to pump me up. That's sounds so weak, now that I say it out loud, but that's what happened."

Yeah, it did sound weak, but he'd done a few stupid things himself to compensate for what at the time seemed like insurmountable problems. Like getting a co-worker pregnant. Not that he'd meant to. They'd used protection, but he never should have had sex with her in the first place. But his job had been going to hell at the time, and he'd needed some way to forget.

"Gray?"

"Huh? Oh, sorry. Your strong points. What else?"

"I have a great sense of humor."

She had to be joking. "Uh-huh. Tell me more."

"You think I'm kidding, but you've never dealt with me in any other state than frazzled coach owner, worried mother or woman on the lam."

"I'll take your word for it."

"I'm also a good listener."

He scratched his head. "A good quality, to be sure, but it's your audience you want to be good listeners."

Another audible eye roll. "What I meant was, this discussion seems all one-sided. Let's talk about you for a while, and I'll show you how well I listen."

Damn. Hadn't seen that coming. "Me? I'm an open book. You know everything there is to know about me already."

"Oh, really? "How old are you? Forty?"

"Thirty-eight!" Came out a tad too fast.

"Married?"

"If you recall, I share the upstairs apartment with Mitch at the firehouse." He lifted his left hand. "See? No ring."

"Means nothing. I'm living proof. Jerry stopped wearing his ring about two years before our break-up. Said it was cutting into his finger and I stupidly believed him. Ever been married?"

"No."

She let it go for a few minutes while they drove in silence. "Ever come close?"

"To marriage?" God, he hated this topic. "Once, a long time ago," he said, surprising himself.

"What happened?"

"Fell through."

"She backed out?"

The office dalliance that changed his life was off limits to Ms. Nosey Pants. "Mutual thing. Subject closed." He had no intention of discussing Ellen and what might've been. There was a reason he kept that part of his life buried. "If you must probe my private life, ask me about something else."

"What did you do before you teamed up with your brothers?"

"I was an architect. Got hired right out of college by a large firm in Minneapolis."

"What did you do there?"

"Not much to speak of, which was the problem."

"How come?"

Hadn't shared this story with anyone either, not even Geoff and

Mitch, but for some reason, the words just kept coming. "Shortly after I came on board, the guy who hired me left. His replacement resented me from the start. I later learned I took the job he wanted for a friend. Spent his time making me miserable so I'd leave."

"That's so unfair."

"Tried not to let him get to me. Accepted his crummy assignments and smiled at others' successes, even though I could've done a better job. As time went by, though, he wore me down. I did what I was given to do but didn't try beyond that."

"Didn't you want to fight back or find another job?"

"Tried once or twice. But he was better connected with the higher ups than I was. Instead of finding other employment, I got involved with someone else at the firm. That broken engagement I don't want to discuss? Once that fell apart, I went into a deep funk, my spirit elsewhere, sorta how you described your mental state since the business with your husband. Let things slide. I was close to getting canned when I learned of Dad's bills. Used that as my excuse to quit and come home."

"Would you go back, if you could? To architecture, that is."

"With Mitch now working in Orville Drummond's law office, I can't leave Geoff to run the company on his own."

"But if you could do something else, would you go back to architecture?"

"Yeah, sure, but I'd choose what I'd do more carefully. Like design theaters and auditoriums and solve those acoustical dilemmas. In high school I talked the principal, then the school board into applying an orange peel surface to the walls so you could hear from every seat. But there's not much call for those high-ticket items, especially for a guy with no experience in that specialty."

"Why not gain some experience on the side while you help Geoff? Do something gratis. Is there a community theater in town?"

Her comment caught him up short. He'd dismissed that part of his life as being over. Never considered reinventing himself on a small-scale basis. "Interesting suggestion, although I haven't been near a stage since high school. Wonder how it would feel."

"Welcome to my world. It's been years since I've performed for a paying audience."

"Yet, unlike me, you're not afraid to see what happens."

"I don't have much choice. You do."

She was right. Crazy, obstinate woman could see his future better than he.

Thirteen

They stopped for fuel shortly after Jenna's interrogation ended. While there, they snagged fast food for lunch: a fish sandwich for Jenna, which she promptly divested of the bun, and a chicken sandwich for him, her healthier eating habits growing on him. When they got back on the road, Jenna remained in the front of the coach and jotted notes from time to time.

"What are you writing?" Gray asked after they'd driven about fifteen minutes without any conversation.

Now he was ready to talk, as long as she was the one answering questions. "Notes for a second story. Yesterday, the color yellow took over my imagination. Today, it's more brown and gray as we head farther west. Some find those colors boring. They relax me."

"They aren't bad. But I'll be happy when we see more trees and green on the horizon."

"I wonder how many animals are brown or gray or a combination. I'll bet they make up a higher percent than any other color," she said.

"Disagree. Think about the number of fish, birds and insects there are. A lot of them are either brightly colored or their coloration matches their surroundings, like water."

"Maybe my story should consider that question. Though it will require further research, which I can't do here."

"You could start another list."

The most frequent animal coloring. How stupid could she sound? Was she just making conversation to break the inexorable silence between them? Time for a topic change. "I'm also putting together a business plan for the tour. A little belated but better than nothing." She had decided to continue with the tour, only do it much smarter.

"What've you got so far?"

"Mostly what we talked about earlier—manager, coach, audience testing."

"Got an itinerary yet? Specific places to play?"

"Left that to the tour promoter, although I told him to stay within state, so I wouldn't be away from Paige more than a day or two at a time. That way, I could go and come in the same day."

His head twisted her direction. "You're kidding?"

Was he back to shooting down her plans? "No. Why?"

"Why did you buy the coach if you only planned to be out on the road a few days at a time? The money you'd spend on hotel charges couldn't possibly add up to as much as you've invested in this thing."

The coach again. Hadn't she just explained? "Promise not to laugh. Or think I'm crazy?"

"I won't laugh, but I'll suspend judgment on your mental state until I know more."

Some promise. "When my mother dragged me to California on her quest to break into show business, we stayed in one hotel after another. Motels, once her funds ran low. Second and third-rate motels after that. She frequently left me to my own devices in our room while she was out supposedly auditioning for parts."

"Didn't she, uh, ever get in trouble with the authorities for leaving you alone?"

"Child abandonment didn't receive quite the attention then as it does these days. She left me with a little money, in case of emergencies, and plenty of food, though not the healthiest variety. Each place started looking like the last, progressively more rundown. Whenever

Housekeeping showed up, I was to tell them my mommy had gone out for breakfast, or lunch, or whatever, depending on the time of day, and she'd be right back."

No point mentioning her mother had spent more of her away time looking for her next husband than a job, her way of supporting them. "When Herb Carpenter came along, my mother believed our future was set. My new stepdad was in the entertainment business, all right, but he was a musician, not a movie star. A second-rate musician at that."

"Carpenter? Aubrey's dad?"

"Right, Aubrey was born a few years later. At first, our new life was once again spent moving from hotel room to hotel room. My mother was caught up in the glamour of the lifestyle for a while, so she didn't complain. Her daily disappearances went from jobseeking to soaking up the musician's life with her new husband."

"Was Aubrey raised on the road as well?"

"No. With two children in tow, my mother demanded a more stable life. Herb traveled on his own and took on more gigs so we could live in a small rented house in Glendale. Those days were golden. No more hotels, no more Housekeeping, although my mother didn't exactly take up the slack."

Her mother fought Jenna's having much to do with her father, but Herb had been a great stand-in, when he was home. Her stepfather introduced her to music and took time to go over her piano lessons with her week after week.

"So you don't have fond memories of hotels?" Gray asked, piercing her reflections.

"Exactly." One of those memories pricked her conscious. "Funny, my telling you this. I never did tell Jerry, because our honeymoon suite was actually pretty nice. Certainly better than the type of accommodations I'd been subjected to as a child. Of course, I didn't know at the time he'd borrowed the money from my new stepfather, Buddy Appleby, Husband #3 for my mother."

"I dislike your former spouse more and more each time you mention him."

"Get in line. I'm way ahead of you." She rose and made her way back to the kitchenette. "All this talk has made me thirsty. Want a bottle of water?"

He didn't answer. Then she remembered her antics the day before. Guess he'd sworn off the liquid for a while. But he didn't prohibit her from partaking.

She rejoined him, took several swigs. "I swear I'm past yesterday's water play."

They drove in silence while she continued to take occasional swigs from her bottle. "Why not rent a coach?" he asked just when it appeared his brain had moved on to other places.

So much for moving on to another topic. How could she derail him? "Excuse me?"

"I get the part about hotels and why you see a motor coach being a reasonable alternative for overnight lodging. But why use your inheritance and buy a rig, a deluxe version, no less, and then customize it rather than simply rent coaches as they were needed? Now you've got to worry about maintenance, storage and drivers."

If he didn't get it out of her now, he'd probably pull it out before California. "Believe it or not, I started out with the intention of renting. In the course of my web search, McKenna Custom Coaches popped up. Of course, that didn't mean anything. But your address did."

"Burlington?"

"I started thinking about the town where I was born. Where my parents grew up. Where my father had lived and died. My life was a mess. I desperately wanted to make myself whole again.

"We were a connection to your past?"

"Crazy, huh?"

"Actually, that's one of the first things you've said that makes sense. Not the buying the coach part but the rationale behind contacting us."

She took a few more sips of water. He adjusted the GPS.

"It started out a mere call. I assumed the sales pitch would include a little chitchat, something about the town. Had Geoff been in that day, I probably wouldn't have been disappointed. Instead, I got—"

"Me."

"You. All formality, facts and numbers. You really need to check into sales lessons if you plan to back up Geoff."

"Our chat was civil enough. You called again the next day."

"Hoped to talk to someone else. But Geoff was still gone, so once again, you answered. This time, when I asked about the coach, you suddenly went eloquent on me. I now know, after these past weeks negotiating with you over the phone and this trip, you hit your stride when you can describe the machine you help modify."

"I do tend to go on a bit when I talk about our product." He seemed to consider his words. "Are you saying I'm the one who convinced you to buy this thing?"

"Heavens, no! You talked a good line, actually got me wondering what it would be like to own a motor coach, but you did nothing to fill me in about the town."

"You never once asked about the town or I would have said something."

"It's all pretty clear now, isn't it? But then I didn't know what I was seeking, just that I wasn't getting it from you. But talking to you filled in a tiny part of the void inside me. From the Christmas cards she sent Mother every year I remembered my mother's cousin, Peggy Summers, still lived in town."

"Peggy claims she's the one who steered you to us."

"I let her think so. I pretended I needed references about your business. She spent about two minutes telling me about you guys and the next thirty telling me about the town."

"That's Peggy. Nice woman, but talkative."

"Geoff benefited from my call. Didn't he and Eileen get together about the same time Aubrey arrived?"

"Interesting how that happened. Peggy had her sights set on Mitch for her daughter, but once Aubrey was in the picture, both women encouraged the Geoff- Eileen match-up."

Interesting indeed. "Why not you?"

He gave a chuckle. "Couple reasons. The day it happened, I was on the playing field getting clobbered by Mitch on my way to home base. That's when I broke my collarbone. Geoff and Eileen wound up taking me to the ER. While I was out cold sleeping off meds, the two of them got together."

With all that had happened the last two days, she'd forgotten about Gray's injury. "How's it doing? Is it bothering you to sit so long driving?"

"Sleeping in the door well the other night wasn't my wisest move, but I've been okay since."

"Once again, I'm sorry I tripped over you." He'd been a pretty good sport about her landing on him. "What was the other reason Peggy didn't play matchmaker with you and Eileen?"

He slid what she might have considered a lascivious grin her direction. "I have a bit of a rep as a ladies' man. Love 'em and leave 'em, you know?"

"Tell me more." The guy seemed too serious about everything he did to fall into that category.

"I haven't been serious about a woman since my engagement fell apart. These days, I go out with a woman to be sociable and, to put it bluntly, get laid. In a small city like Burlington, word gets around, and before you know it, you've been dubbed some kind of no-strings-attached kinda guy."

"So the no-sex clause in our escape agreement put a crimp in your style? Would you have, uh, come on to me, had you not agreed?"

He kept his gaze planted on the road ahead. "Ever been to Albuquerque? Plan to stay just east of there tonight."

Diversionary tactics. Interesting. Why had he brought up the subject of his love life in the first place? "No. Until we get to California, everything on this route is new to me." She could skip topics too.

The usual suspects appeared as they made their way through New Mexico—fast food chains, gas stations, and souvenir stops, although Jenna didn't notice much. She was still back on the "no sex on the road" comment. He had deliberately avoided answering her question. Would he have come on to her if she hadn't made him agree to hands off? More to the point, why was she so interested in learning the answer? The whole no-sex thing had been her idea.

Her idea. Her dumb idea. Of course, she didn't plan to go to bed with him, but her stupid requirement had ended any possibility of even having to decide whether to do so, just in case things got ... friendly.

Why had he agreed so fast? He hadn't bargained or tried to talk her out of it. Unless he'd been feeding her a line, which she doubted, he wasn't averse to casual relationships. In fact, the latter seemed to be his *modus operandi*.

"Daydreaming?" he asked, breaking into her bubble of concentration.

"Huh? Oh, yes, I suppose I was. The scenery is becoming rather untamed with nothing to see for miles. You can get lost staring off in the distance."

"Yeah. Although every so often we pass through evidence of civilization, like a dilapidated building or rundown cars." He went back to staring at the road ahead.

She returned to the speculation she couldn't seem to shake. He said something about dating whenever he needed female companionship. Okay, a female body. Maybe he'd been with someone just prior to agreeing to take her to California. Not in need of a, what, *refresher* yet? No, it wasn't in men's make-up to pass up a good deal just because they were satiated. So, why wasn't he interested?

"Tired?" he asked.

"Pensive."

"Planning another story?"

"Something like that."

"From your short answers, you're not ready to share."

"You got it. Still needs time to gel." Hmmm. Perhaps a story about a girl who got a boy to promise not to kiss her and then changed her mind. Great idea. She could ponder her situation all she wanted to by sublimating it to a harmless story.

When they pulled into the next RV park, he had her remain in the coach while he went to register. Another mystery to add to his lack of interest in her. Though he'd readily watched the strip tease she did at his parents' house and come alive when she stumbled over his sleeping body the other night, both times he'd stopped before they got too carried away. Before he did, anyhow. She'd thoroughly enjoyed herself. He'd sparked something inside her. Something that had been missing for … ever.

Why was she thinking about him like this? Sure, he was great looking and had a body that didn't stop. Not a bad start for any affair. But there was more to him than that. Much more. He was solid. Reliable. The kind of man she should have married instead of Jerry.

"All set." He bounded back into the coach. "No piano. And I asked, so give me points for at least thinking of it. But this place does have a small café. Want to eat something that's not fast food?"

Don't get excited. He probably wants to be around others besides you. "Sounds good."

The evening rush, if such a thing existed in this place, hadn't materialized yet. An older couple was seated at one table, a middle-aged man at another, and a scruffy looking guy about thirty-five sat alone at a table across the room nursing a beer. As soon as they ordered, Gray excused himself to use the facilities. He couldn't sit here with her for even five minutes before taking off.

After speculating for the last hour about why she didn't interest him, that old feeling of inadequacy nibbled its way under her skin, tunneled into her stomach, made her feel not quite whole. She could attract the attention of any man she wanted, couldn't she? Even that dirt bag across the room who'd been eyeing her since she arrived.

Forget it, forget him. Not worth even a few seconds' conjecture.

"Z'up, babe?"

While she'd been engulfed in her thoughts, the guy across the room had become the guy leaning over her, bad breath and all.

"I beg your pardon?"

"Playin' hard to get now, huh? Didn't stop you from givin' me the look a minute ago."

"I-I don't know what you're talking about." This couldn't be happening. Not again.

"How's about you and me go somewhere more classy for a bite to eat? This place is a dump."

"Actually, the gentleman who came in with me and I have already ordered."

He didn't leave. Instead, he pulled out the chair facing her, planted a foot on it, and leaned in further, the bulge in his pants becoming increasingly more obvious. "You missed my drift. I didn't have eatin' in mind." Dramatic pause. "Eatin' food, anyhow."

"Please leave. I'm not interested."

He grabbed her arm, his grip clammy but powerful. "Coulda fooled me, starin' at me like that. Your message was loud and clear. You want what I got."

She tried to shake off his hand, but he tightened his hold. "I have no intention of going off with you. Now leave, before I call someone."

"Like someone's gonna come to your aid in this joint?"

"Someone already has," Gray said from behind her. "Take your hand off the lady and get outta my sight."

"Hey!" The guy went into macho reactive mode, stood up to his full height—about three inches shorter than Gray but at least thirty pounds heavier—hands on hips, jaw jutted forward. "What she to you?"

"You've got five seconds to remove that hand from my wife's arm before she bruises and fifteen seconds to get out of here." A steely, determined tone, one she hadn't heard before, underlined his words.

"Your wife? Better let her know, then, that givin' a stranger the look can get her into trouble, serious trouble." He backed away from the table, then slammed out the door.

Jenna released the breath she'd held while the two men's testosterone levels dueled. "Th-thanks," was about all she could get out.

"What was that about?"

"I-I have no idea. One minute he was seated across the room guzzling a beer, the next he was accosting me."

"He seemed to think he'd received an invite." His statement sounded like a question.

"Are you saying I'm responsible for his misunderstanding?"

He took the seat the guy had hovered from a minute before. Folded his arms on the table. Leaned in, blue-gray eyes stormy. "I'm asking."

She shifted her gaze to her hands. She couldn't face him directly. "No. Why would you even suggest such a thing?"

"Guys looking for a hook-up don't usually hang out in cafés. Bars are more their style."

"He was drinking beer."

Neither spoke for a bit. The silence continued after their food arrived.

Jenna couldn't shake her self-doubt. Did she cause the incident? She remembered glancing at the guy, but just for a second. She'd been thinking about … oh, God!

"We need to talk about what happened," Gray said finally.

"I don't know what happened. Not for sure."

"What was going through your mind after I left you at the table?"

She didn't want to get into this.

"This is important. You can't play this one out on your own."

She finally gazed at him. "It wasn't like my bar scenes. I wasn't trolling. You've got to believe me."

"Then what were you doing?"

He wouldn't give up until she gave him an answer. Might as well go for the jugular. Hers. "Why don't you find me attractive?'

He jerked back in his seat. "Where did that come from?"

"You've rejected the offer of my body twice. When a man who admits to casual relationships turns one down, he apparently isn't interested because the woman doesn't excite him." There. Cards on the table. She waited for his reaction.

But she wasn't expecting him to throw several bills on the table, eject her from her seat, drag her out of the café and back to the coach, locking the door behind them.

Once inside, he pushed her onto the couch. "Wait there." He stormed through the front part of the coach, closing the curtains, then went to the cabinet where he stored his duffel and returned shortly holding a telltale packet, which he set on the floor. A condom? Well, good. Did he always travel prepared?

He bent over her and placed one of his knees beside her. "You want to test me? Here's where the rubber hits the road, lady, because my agreement and patience with you have run out." In one movement, he tore off his shirt and flung it away.

Stunned by his response, all she could do was stare at the erratic dance of his pecs and the landscape of his molded abs. Gray was one mighty fine-looking man. "I assume your offer still holds? I only get it on with willing partners."

He was actually going through with this? Did she really want it? She nodded. Her ability to speak seemed to have disappeared.

He didn't need further invitation. He shoved her knit shirt over her head and threw it across the coach where it landed on top of his. She lifted her hips while he pulled down her shorts and disposed of them as well. She lay there in a lacy ice blue bra and bikini briefs, more of the goodies Aubrey bought her.

He sat back on his haunches. "Should I stop? One last chance to say no."

This was so not a good idea. They still had a few days left on the road. If they had sex, what would happen the rest of the trip? Would she even get back to California or simply hole up somewhere in Arizona in this coach with him screwing her brains out?

A fire long dead since the early days of her marriage ignited in her stomach. No, lower. Passion overtook her senses. No going back.

"Go for it," she challenged in a voice barely fueled with breath. She reached behind her back and unhooked the bra. He took it from there, flinging it over his shoulders while he gazed at her bare breasts. She thrust her chest forward, her need for his approving stare fighting with her anticipation of his touch.

He returned the look she'd been craving. His voracious gaze said he was ready to feast, and feast he did, his mouth going immediately to one breast and taking it in. One hand covered the other breast, molded it like she would the clay they purchased the previous day.

Underneath him, her buttocks tightened, the mound still covered by her briefs strained against the rock-hard bulge in his pants. Though part of her brain screamed for her to give up this insane idea while she could, the other part, the part that had nodded assent to Gray, grew increasingly stronger and more insistent. She wanted this, all right. So much, she was ready to throw caution to the wind.

How could a man be so forceful, so driven, and still turn her own body into a writhing tangle of nerve endings? Jerry had never done this to her. Nor her queue of one-night stands.

"Oh. Ah," she murmured, unable to form words but needing desperately to express her state of arousal.

Gray didn't respond. He didn't even glance at her as his hand moved from her breast to skim over her abdomen to her sweet spot, now moist with her pooling passion. Discovering her reaction, he relieved her of her briefs in short order, then his hand returned to explore the wetness further.

Finally, he raised his head, stared at her, eyes smoky, lids heavy. He paused, as if waiting for cognition to kick in. When he finally blinked, he smashed his lips to hers, his free hand dipped underneath her to hold her tighter. His lips pressed hers, his tongue commanded her to let it take over.

She kissed him back as if she'd never kiss a man again, savoring every sensation on her mouth, the unrelenting pressure of his body over hers, and most of all, the incredible sensation of being buck naked beneath him.

As brusquely as he'd captured her mouth, he popped up, his eyes focusing on her for the first time in what seemed like forever. "Hold on."

Before she could ask what he meant, he rolled them both onto the floor, her once again on the bottom, him on one knee leaning over her. "Let me look at you." An order, not a request. He leaned back enough to scan her body from her head to her most private region. He didn't ogle her nor smile, but his lips shifted slightly to the side and his breathing increased.

"Well?" she asked, attempting to sound brazen. Like females for centuries, she had the upper hand, despite her acquiescent position.

"Not bad. Not bad at all, for a woman your age. Even after one kid."

"Not bad?" she returned before taking the time to determine if he was baiting her.

He offered half a grin. "Just seeing if I could rile you. You're gorgeous, woman, like you don't know it."

"I-I don't." Damn, some femme fatale she was. She'd caved at his first show of approval. She needed to get her edge back. She lowered her eyes, and when she lifted them again, attempted to put a challenge in her voice. "Now, how about you? Great upper body, but since you took care of shedding all my clothing, it's only fair—"

Before she could finish, he'd slipped out of his jeans, followed by his briefs. "Better?" he asked, his eyes locked on hers.

She fought to keep her response level as she made a show of craning her neck to check out his lower front. He was definitely still in the game, his erection jutting out, ready for business. Her mouth had gone dry. "You're well endowed. No question," she still managed to say.

"But?"

"But what?"

"What aren't you saying?" he asked. His question telling her she had the upper hand.

This was too easy. And too much fun. She'd pay for playing him, but she didn't care. This male-female dance was just too delicious. "Why'd you stop? You've obviously got the goods, but do you have the *drive?*"

God help her, she was skating on very thin ice, ice she wanted to shatter and fall through. Only if it broke, it wouldn't be icy water she'd be treading, but instead, she'd be consumed in the fiery flames of his desire.

If possible, even more steel slipped into the dark haze of his eyes as they bored into hers for a millisecond. "It's action you want? Then hold on for the ride of your life." He grabbed the condom packet, ripped it open and sheathed himself within seconds.

He settled over her, his lips nuzzling behind one ear. His warm, soft breath drilled through her neck column, attacked every nerve ending. Energy she presumed long dead awoke, swirled and curled its way through her lower region, caused her to writhe beneath him. *Nice prelude, fella, but get on with the main event.*

She was ready. She'd been ready since his hands, fingers, sought the area between her legs. She moved her hands over his buttocks— God, they were firm— urged him to move along. But Gray apparently took a woman on his own schedule. His lips trailed downward, over one breast, leisurely tongued the taut nipple, then farther south over her stomach, burning a path of fire as he went.

Though his every move registered and her own body was one boiling pool of explosions, her mind went elsewhere, soared to heights she'd never known, floated, swooped through clouds of steam and smoke and shot back again into the bright sun.

Then he entered her and reality and the surreal combined just as their bodies became one, a man and a woman engaged in the age-old mating dance. Only this wasn't to procreate. This was sex, pure and simple. No … scratch that. Whatever activity they were engaged in was not simple. Definitely not pure.

But it was great sex. The best she'd ever experienced. She could go on like this forever. She didn't want him to stop, and for a while, it seemed she'd get her wish. Endurance didn't seem to be a problem for Gray.

But all good things must come to an end, even mind-bending sex with a masterful lover like him. He rolled over her side, clutched his chest to catch his breath. He didn't speak, didn't even glance over at her.

She waited for him to say something like. "Wow, that was great!" would've been nice. But he didn't.

She listened to her own breathing, willed it to slow.

Finally, he sat, grabbed for his pants, and rose. "Happy now? I've broken the no-sex clause. I wasn't disinterested, just trying to abide by your stupid rule, which your lack of self-confidence forced me to break." He stomped off to the bathroom. Within seconds, she heard the shower running. Couldn't wait to remove her essence from his body. How flattering.

Fourteen

Despite the close quarters of the small shower, Gray thrashed about, fought to keep himself from punching a hole in the wall. He'd given in to her and hated himself for doing so.

From the first day she'd shown up in their garage all haughty and know-it-all, he'd wanted her, though he didn't admit it, even to himself, at the time. Every instinct had told him she was trouble. She may have been trying to prove her desirability to herself by offering her body to him, but she was the kind of woman whose body came with conditions. Commitment. Marriage. Family. She had a nearly grown kid.

How could he have been so stupid? He'd sworn off all those long ago.

She'd gotten under his skin, and he'd let down his guard. Broken his promise to her, which really bugged him. He didn't break promises.

He'd also been pretty rough with her. Sure, she seemed to like it—how many guys rationalized their treatment of women with that argument?—still, he should've found some other way to help reassure her of her sex appeal. But her run-in with the sleaze back at the café had elevated his machismo beyond common sense.

Face it, guy, you saw red. The bastard was harassing your woman. His woman? No. His ward, maybe. His assignment. But his woman? Definitely not.

Jenna wasn't in the front part of the coach when he finished dressing. Just as well. He wasn't ready to talk about their tumble on the floor. Didn't even want to think about it, though he doubted he'd be successful there.

He'd take off for a while, give her some space. Give himself a chance to clear his head. Yeah, like that would happen. How would he erase the sight, the feel of her body from his brain?

Probably shouldn't leave her alone, just in case that low life from the café was lurking nearby. Jenna was a big girl—the last half hour attested to that fact—and could defend herself, but just in case, he didn't want to borrow trouble. He'd just go outside and catch some fresh air but hang around the coach.

JENNA'S SHOWER took a little more time than Gray's, as she languorously drew her soapy sponge over her body, stopping every so often to let streams of lather trail down an arm, a leg, between her breasts. At times, she'd lean against the wall and rerun the scene where she wound up under Gray's body.

"You want action? Then hold on for the ride of your life," he'd said. He hadn't been kidding. Her body still tingled and throbbed from his attentive hands.

He'd sounded angry with her, and his thrusts had been forceful, determined. Afterwards, he'd shifted his body away from hers and stormed from the room. What was with that?

She ran a hand up her abdomen and cupped a breast. Full and high despite approaching her forties. "You've still got it, girl. Jerry didn't appreciate what he had." But had Gray? Or did his thunderous exit signal disappointment?

Stop going there. He was turned on. He wanted you. She could see it in his eyes, eyes that at times had grown so hazy with hunger for her, she'd doubted he'd even seen her.

She'd gotten what she wanted, for Gray to cave and make love to her. Make love. Probably not the most accurate description of their rolling around on the floor. They'd had sex. Intercourse. Love had nothing to do with it. Therein lay the rub. As world-shaking as what they'd experienced had been, it lacked the emotion she'd always equated as part of the sex act. Even though she'd proven to herself she could interest a handsome hunk like Gray, something had been missing. Love?

Love had gotten her married at a young age to a man who was never fully committed to her. Love had kept her blindly accepting his indiscretions for years.

True. But love had also brought her the most beautiful, intelligent daughter she could have ever imagined.

Then love had died, replaced by responsibility and the desire not to hurt the child. Finally, even those faded, leaving her an empty shell of her former self.

Why was she even thinking about these things? She didn't have the time or energy to consider love in her life. She had a daughter to support with a concert tour she had to get off the ground. Did Gray think she was after something more than sex? It would explain his mood.

They needed to talk.

She took her time toweling off, blow-drying her hair, changing to different clothes. Finally, ablutions completed, she dragged herself out to the front of the coach, only to discover she was alone. Where was he?

For one split second, she wondered if he'd just walked off and left her there to get herself to California. He could have easily caught a flight back to Iowa. But he wouldn't do such a thing. Would he?

No, he wouldn't. Gray might be angry with her, but he had principles. He'd finish this, even if he didn't speak to her until he'd dropped her at the steps of her house.

She wandered about the front of the coach, seeking something to occupy her mind while she waited for him to return. Mistake. Waiting meant she'd placed everything on hold to coincide with his schedule. He'd return when he wanted to. Meanwhile, she should address her own needs. Mental and spiritual. She'd already indulged her physical needs, and look where that had gotten her.

She could work on her writing. Right, her story about the little girl who regretted making the boy promise not to kiss her would be just the ticket to take her mind off things between Gray and her. Not! Even if she were foolish enough to pursue it, how would she finish the tale, especially if the boy broke down and did kiss the girl? Send him running away also? No, the story would have to wait until she had a better idea where it was going.

Another half hour or so passed with no Gray. She started to read one of her new books but didn't get beyond the second page. Meditating got her nowhere as well; she couldn't empty her mind. She could only finish a fourth of the sandwich she made, even though he'd hauled her out of the cafe before they'd eaten.

Okay, no more trying to fool herself. She was worried. Worried about Gray and his whereabouts and his reaction to their little "session." What if he'd run into the guy who'd hassled her earlier and followed through on his threats? Worse, what if the guy had surprised Gray, wanting revenge? Oh, God! Gray could be lying unconscious somewhere on the grounds right now.

Was that why he was staying away so long? She had to find out.

She didn't stop to consider all the reasons why her speculation was completely off-kilter but instead dashed from the coach to his rescue.

The park was about three-fourths full, RVs and other vehicles rested like a herd of cattle about fifteen feet from each other. Though dusk was still an hour away, there didn't seem to be much activity. The wind had increased, swirls of dust coiled up like puffs of smoke. An odd smell, like the remains of a bonfire hit her nostrils. She picked up her pace, strode up one lane and down another. No sign of Gray. If he lay bleeding somewhere on the property, he was nowhere near their coach.

She'd almost reached the outer perimeter when the first drop of moisture hit. Then another, and within seconds, raindrops streamed down her face. Rain? In New Mexico? Wasn't it like a semi-desert? Stupid to debate herself. Best return to the coach and get out of this downpour.

But retracing her steps wasn't easy. Every vehicle looked identical to its neighbors. Had she turned here or was it the next row of RVs? Meanwhile, the rain increased. What was dust minutes before grew slick and muddy, impeded her steps.

By the time she reached the coach, she was soaked through, her hair stringy. Warmth and dry clothes never sounded so good. But as she yanked on the door, it wouldn't open. She struggled to recall how the latch worked. She'd rarely used it on the trip, because Gray had always been there to do the honors. Locked! Oh, God, no. She'd taken off so fast in search of Gray, the door must have locked behind her. What was the code? Her mind was so preoccupied, she couldn't think straight. Couldn't remember. And, of course, she had no phone, so she couldn't call Gray or anyone else for help.

She knocked, in case Gray was back. Then she banged relentlessly on the door, thinking he might be in the bathroom. No answer.

What to do? Seek respite in a nearby RV? Couldn't risk it. Might run into that guy or another version of him. Wait here for Gray? No idea how long he'd be gone or how long this monsoon would last. Return to the lodge? Right, she was so waterlogged, her clothes left little to the imagination, but at the moment, that seemed her best option.

She pivoted and collided with him.

"What are you doing out here?" he shouted over the deluge.

"I-I came to find you. I was worried you might be in trouble, if you met up with that guy again."

"Me in trouble? What about you?"

Her eyes shot to her sodden clothes. *Trouble* was a pretty good word to describe her current state. "Couldn't remember the code."

He leaned forward, keyed in the numbers, and ushered her up the steps. "Stay here and drip on this mat while I get us some towels." He returned in seconds, flinging two Turkish beauties her way. "Here." She draped one around her shoulders and used the other to wrap her hair in a turban.

He dried off with less caution, hung one towel over his head, his face and hair disappearing beneath, and mopped his clothes with the other. "Damn," he muttered, when his efforts produced little success. He ripped off his shirt to dry his bare chest.

Though still intent on getting dry herself, she couldn't help but ogle that award-winning set of pecs. She struggled to find something to say. "When you didn't come back, I was concerned you'd gone to have it out with that slime from dinner."

"That the *trouble* you mentioned outside?"

She lowered her lids. "I know you can take care of yourself. But I got to thinking maybe he'd snuck up on you and—"

"Knocked me out?" The corner of his mouth curled up slightly.

"Okay, it sounds ridiculous now when I say it, but you stayed away so long, my imagination took over."

He cocked his head, narrowed his eyes. "What would you have done if you'd found me dumped behind one of these rigs?"

He was mocking her. But then, her rescue efforts did sound pretty absurd. "I have no idea, Gray. All I could think of was helping you." She continued to dab at her shirt and shorts to no avail.

"Take off your clothes."

She jerked up her head. "What?"

"You'll never get dry like that. Strip down to your bra and panties and I'll towel you off." He added, "It's not like I haven't seen them already today."

True, but the last time she was in her skivvies, they hadn't remained for long. Did she really want to tempt fate?

He waited for her to realize she didn't have much choice. Once she shed her outer layer, his ministrations were swift and efficient. Not exactly foreplay.

Finished, he had her sit on the couch and covered her shoulders with one towel and her legs with the other. He settled next to her, a good foot away, one of his own towels slung over a shoulder.

They remained there in silence, each wrapped in his or her own thoughts.

"I'm sorry," They both said at the same time. She blinked.

He jerked.

He was sorry?

"What are you sorry for?" he asked.

Now she'd done it. But they had to deal with their having had sex sooner or later. Might as well go for it. "I, uh, may not have seduced you, exactly, but I pushed you, just because I was curious."

"I knew what I was doing, Jenna, and that it was a bad idea, but I gave in to my, uh, hormones."

"Having sex with me was a bad idea?"

He drew a hand over his mouth, as if trying to wipe away the phrase. "Bad for you. You're still vulnerable from what your creep of a husband did to you. I took advantage." He hung his head, shook it, as if he couldn't believe what he'd done. "I made a promise to you when we started this bizarre journey and I broke it. I don't break promises, but this time I did."

"I goaded you into it."

"Yeah, you did, but I let myself be goaded. That's worse."

"You're angry with yourself, not me?"

"There's a little left over for you too. You should've gotten help for your feelings of sexual inadequacy a long time ago, admitted you had a problem. Instead, you've been walking around with an open wound."

"Open wound? You make it, me, sound like an emotional wreck."

He didn't reply, but he kept his gaze steady, as if waiting for her to concede his point.

"Maybe I am. Sort of. Like I said, I'm sorry."

He put a hand on her towel-covered thigh. "Apologies offered and accepted on both sides. Where does that leave us?"

Where did it leave them? More to the immediate point, why was heat shooting up her thigh?

He seemed to read her mind and removed his hand.

"That *promise* thing? Forget about it," she said. "It was my lame way of protecting myself from myself, and I failed miserably."

"By *forgetting about the promise*, was that forget about reneging on it or forget about following through?"

Was he kidding? Trying to lighten the mood? Though she started to answer, her eyes once again lighted on his torso. His biceps were giving his abs and pecs a run for their money in the catch-your-breath hunkiness department. She wasn't done enjoying that body. She was having difficulty responding to his question, because her mouth had gone dry once again. "I'm not suggesting we, uh, do anything further about it, although—"

"Although?"

With effort, she shifted her eyes away from his chest to inspect her fingernails. "You're making me say it?"

"Safer that way."

"I, uh, seem to have misjudged you when we first met. We didn't get off to a very good start."

"I'll say."

"In large part because almost immediately you accused me of being a bad mother."

"A mother who'd gone at least three days without realizing her kid was missing. Of course, I didn't know then how much pressure you'd been under and what an independent dynamo your kid is."

He reached across and curled a strand of her still wet hair around his index finger. "Has your opinion of me changed?"

"You're still a bit stiff, but you have a kinder heart than I imagined."

Rather than smile at her compliment, he seemed to flinch. "Uh, thanks."

"You've put up with a lot from me the last few days."

A slight twinkle showed in his eyes. "True. But you were worried about me earlier. Enough to come looking for me in what turned into a cloudburst."

"You came to my rescue before, so it was my turn to help you."

First, they'd exchanged apologies, now thank yous. Their conversation ended, still begging the question of where this left their relationship.

Sitting there so close to him, clad in no more than her underwear, she was at a loss what to say next. Why was she having so much trouble explaining herself? Couldn't be the line of chest hair that descended below his jeans. Or the way his nipples seemed to wink at her.

"Jenna?"

"Huh?"

"You're staring at me."

So she was. "What do you expect? You're half naked. Earlier may have been a mistake, but that doesn't mean I'm now immune to your appeal."

"You wanted to keep things between us uncomplicated."

"I did."

"Did?" He leaned in closer. "What about now?"

Fork in the road time. What she said now would affect the rest of the trip, maybe the rest of her life. Despite her better judgment suggesting she not go there, she wanted what she wanted. Her mind was clearer than it had ever been. "Time to complicate things." She pulled his face toward hers and planted a world-class lip-lock on his mouth.

No trying to prove her feminine allure this time. The verdict was already in on that one. This time was purely because she wanted him. Forget they'd be going their separate ways when she returned to California, forget his being the brother of her sister's boyfriend and forget her concert tour. They were here for the night, tucked comfortably away in her deluxe motor coach. What better way to spend their time?

It took Gray a split second to respond. When he did, she had no doubt he wanted the same thing.

The next minute, two minutes—who kept track of time during moments like this?—were a blur. Towels flew, arms and legs entwined, body crushed body and hands wandered everywhere. Once again, they rolled onto the floor, but not until all their remaining clothing joined the towels.

GRAY COULD BARELY BREATHE. His blood pressure had shot up from normal to beyond aroused in seconds. Jenna's kiss, if you could call a frontal attack like that a kiss, shocked and surprised him when she actually took the initiative and admitted she wanted him. He'd known since he'd spied her eyes trained on his chest they weren't done with each other.

This time was just as frenetic as before, only this time he wasn't trying to prove something to her and hating himself, and her, for having to do so. This time he couldn't help himself. He was giving in to his need for her. In the back of his head, in what little brain that remained after his cock took over, he was aware he should slow down. Take this slower, help her enjoy the ride. But he couldn't. His body was primed for action, his fella ready to claim its target.

Her lips held on to his as if taking in the breath of life as her hands gripped the back of his neck. Her thumb slowly rubbed the scruff, awakening nerve endings long dormant, while her body wriggled beneath him. The lady definitely had made up her mind.

Couldn't let her do all the work. Instinct took over as his brain went on vacation. He cupped her behind, pulled her into him even closer to really enjoy her hip action up tight against his hard-on. Could life get any sweeter? Well, yeah, it could once he was inside her, but this was pretty damned good at the moment.

He let himself go, got caught up in the shifting of arms and legs, the groping and fondling, and the intensity of one body claiming the other and vice versa. "God, you're killing me, Jenna," he told her at one point. "But don't stop."

"I can't stop," she breathed back in a hoarse whisper, "not yet. Not until …"

God, he enjoyed having sex with her. No strings, no commitments, but a hell of a good time.

Her hands slid down his back to his butt, clutched him tighter, if that was possible. "Now, Gray, please," she moaned, as she squirmed under him.

What could he do but comply? He paused long enough to slip on the condom he'd removed from his pants before shedding them. He nudged her legs apart and entered. Sweet mother! Like coming home, a rough and tumble arrival, but pleasure like nothing he'd ever experienced. He almost lost consciousness while his body took over. Later, moments, minutes later, he came to, found he'd collapsed over her, his nose buried in her neck.

"Oh, lady, what you do to me."

"No, Gray. What you did *for* me."

He mustered the strength to roll away. Every ounce of blood had been drained from his body, or so it seemed. Despite his fatigue, though, God, he felt good! No more regret over breaking their pact. Jenna was a big girl. If she could dismiss it as easily as she had, then he could too.

As soon he let the boys rest, he'd be ready to go again.

"Gray? Are you okay?"

"You wore me out. Give me a few minutes." Or thirty.

"Hungry?"

"You're kidding."

"No, silly, for food," she said. "I'm ready for a sandwich. I ate before, but I'm still hungry."

The woman still had an appetite? Impressive. "You fixing? I can't move yet."

She chuckled, probably like every woman through the ages had reacted to her mate's post coital exhaustion. "Stay there and rest, strong man." She rose and slipped back to the kitchenette, not bothering to replace her clothing. She'd come a long way, sashaying her nakedness in front of him like it was the most natural thing in the world.

Nor did she seem inclined to get dressed when she returned with sandwiches, chips and apples slices. He wolfed down his snack, all the while admiring the beautiful woman before him. Her body was still in good shape. Her breasts pert and firm. Couldn't wait to get his hands and mouth on them again. Her flat stomach belied her giving birth fourteen years before, yet a certain roundness in her hips augmented her maturity.

She caught him ogling her. "What are you thinking? Should I put on my clothes?"

"No. Don't. This is too good a view. I was just calculating how soon we can go at it again. If you're still willing?"

Mona Lisa couldn't have returned a more suggestive smile. "I could probably be persuaded to repeat our, uh, earlier performance."

"Persuaded? How?" He leaned closer, liking this game.

She tilted her head, twirled a strand of hair between her fingers. "I don't know. Perhaps you could tell me more about your fiancée? Now that we're, uh, somewhat more familiar with each other."

He groaned. Why couldn't she drop that topic? "You wondering how you compare in the sack?" Yeah, a bit brutal, but maybe it would get her off the subject.

Though she appeared to flinch, she continued. "Now that you brought it up, how do we compare?" Tit for tat, huh?

"What if it was better with her? You really want to hear?"

She considered. "Probably not, but if it gets you talking about something you obviously want to avoid, fine. Lay it on me."

Her self-esteem had returned. Good. "Apples and oranges. Her name was Ellen. I was with her several years back. Who knows how it was? My hormones were on 24-7 duty then. Now, with you, I'm old enough to slow down and enjoy myself."

"Thanks. I wasn't really fishing for compliments. I just wanted you to talk about her. Ellen, huh? I want to help you deal with what's obviously your open wound."

Way to go, Gray. Give her a new phrase to use for ammunition. "Wound healed years ago."

She studied him a little too long. "Okay. But if you ever want to talk about it ..."

"Don't hold your breath, but thanks."

"I was lucky, you know, though I didn't realize it at the time."

Now where was she going? "How so?"

"That you were the one I picked to help me escape."

Speaking of *wounds.* Her words sliced through his chest, though she had no idea she'd fileted him. He glanced away. Couldn't let her see the guilt that must be in his eyes. How much longer could he go before telling her the real reason he'd become her driver?

Fifteen

Gray woke the next morning to find Jenna already dressed and at work in the kitchen. She held up a mug of coffee, which he gratefully accepted. "Ready to get this show on the road?"

Within minutes, he'd checked out and fired up the coach. They rode in silence the first several miles. The day was overcast, but the rain had passed.

"Not writing today?"

"Fictional, I presume?" He shot a smile at her.

She smiled too. "Completely."

"What does she do?" He took a sip of coffee.

"After much deliberation, she stays, realizing she'd imprisoned herself. When she no longer considers herself locked away, she makes it her home."

What was she telling him? He got the *stay* part but not the why. "Figured out how she realizes she made herself a prisoner?"

Her smile this time was more enigmatic. "Hard to explain, which is why I haven't finished. Once she discovers locks don't exist, the thrill of escape is no longer there. What remains is an appreciation of what she's got."

"Hmmm. 'No place like home.' That kind of theme?"

"Sort of but more like breaking out of the prisons we build for ourselves."

Jenna had been doing some deep thinking. She'd made progress understanding why she'd been under so much stress. "Think you can finish in the next two days?"

"I guess. Why?"

"Should make it to Palms Springs in a day. Could probably keep on going all the way back to L.A., but we wouldn't arrive 'til the early hours of the morning. By stopping, you'll be rested when you get there."

"We'll be there that soon?"

"You should be turning cartwheels to hear you're almost home."

"Uh, I am. Figuratively. It's just … I don't have a place to store the coach yet."

He almost spilled his coffee at her announcement. "You're just getting around to telling me this? Surely you've got some sort of plan?"

"Of course. There's a garage not too far from my home where business and professional vehicles are stored. But I wasn't expecting to need them until next week or later. If you'll loan me your phone, I'll contact them."

He debated. She could still put in a 9-1-1, but he doubted her words minutes before were a sham. She seemed to have turned a corner. Unless his brain had gone to mush after all the times they'd had sex the night before. At length, he handed over his cell.

He listened in on her end of the call. Not good news.

"Time for Plan B," she said when she hung up. "They weren't expecting me until next week and don't have space right now."

"What's Plan B?"

She released a long sigh. "I have to come up with one."

She spent the next few hours checking other garages or potential places to park her rig to no avail. Finally, she handed back the phone. "No one has room. Now what?"

"Couldn't you park it temporarily at your place?"

"My two-car garage isn't high enough for the coach, nor is my driveway long enough. And parking isn't allowed on the street."

"Were you planning to pay rent in some commercial garage whenever you weren't using the coach?"

"Yes. Why do you ask?"

"Seems like a huge expense. Guess you'd just chalk it up to the cost of doing business." An unnecessary expense, if anyone asked him, but this was her tour, not his. "Why don't you check in with your sister and daughter?" he said to get her mind off the issue.

"Good idea. I've gotten out of the habit. She input the number. "Hi, Aubrey. Guess who?"

"Uh, hi yourself, Sis. Where are you?"

"On our way to Flagstaff. Gray says we'll be back in L.A. day after tomorrow."

"Gray?" Aubrey said. "He doesn't let anyone but Geoff and Mitch call him that. And Paige." That statement came in lieu of following up on Jenna's comment.

"Well, now I do too." She glanced at her traveling companion. "We've gotten to know each other pretty well during the last few days." She wouldn't tell her how well.

Gray raised a brow, grinned.

"How, uh, do you feel?"

"You mean have I been able to relax? Yes, thanks to Gray." Aubrey could just wonder about that comment too.

Short hesitation. "Great. Good to hear. Then all is set for your tour."

"Uh, no. Wouldn't go that far." She related the problem finding a place to house the coach.

"Why don't you leave it at Mom and Buddy's place? They've got that huge drive."

Mom and Buddy's. "Not sure I want Mom too near this coach, but I'll think about it."

Aubrey put Paige on next. "I'm having the best time, Mom. Aunt Aubrey and Mitch took me to a jalopy race. A demolition derby. Ever seen one of those cars bump into others on purpose? The winner finished with the front half of his car gone."

"Sounds intriguing. Was anyone hurt?"

"No, pretty tame that way, even with all the smashups."

"How's Tommy? Baseball season still going?"

"Who? You mean Eileen's little brother? That loser?"

"They argued the other night," Aubrey said, when she came back on the line. "She suggested a change to his pitching style and he wasn't amused."

Jenna had to laugh. "Probably the first of many misunderstandings with the male gender for her."

"Exactly what I told her."

"Put her back on the line. Let her ole Mom soothe those sensitive teenage feelings."

"Can't. She just rushed off to find her phone. Something about a text she owed him."

"Ah. Next chapter."

The conversation ended shortly after. Jenna clicked off and smiled.

"All is well?"

She told him first about her daughter's latest discovery regarding boys.

"Figures."

"Huh? Oh, wait. You're insinuating 'like mother, like daughter,' aren't you?"

"Something along those lines. Tommy is in for quite a ride."

She slid her eyes his direction. "Like we've had?"

"God, I hope not!"

"I meant the male-female dance, not the uh, well, the *other* dance."

He redirected his gaze to the road again. "Have to admit, traveling with you hasn't been bad, once we got past the initial misunderstandings. It's almost been like a vacation from the business."

"Was that a compliment?"

He stretched in his seat, rolled his shoulders. "Fishing?"

"Maybe. Or maybe I want to talk about last night. I enjoyed the sex." Let that sink in a moment. "I've never said that to a man, even to my former husband. You've made it possible for me to talk about sex without feeling guilty."

"What about actually having sex? Feel guilty there?"

"I feel terrific. That's what I wanted to tell you. Thanks to you, I was able to let go and thoroughly enjoy myself."

"But?"

She liked how he discerned her nuances. "You don't have to worry about my making more of it than two people taking advantage of their mutual attraction."

"No strings?"

"Maybe a few, since Aubrey and Mitch seem headed to a permanent connection. But no expectations."

He nodded but didn't say anything. Couldn't he at least thank her, or was he trying to refrain from showing too much relief? "No comment?" Why was she pushing? She should just let the topic drop?

He seemed to be considering how to reply. "What do you want me to say? Hurray?"

"I don't know. How about 'I enjoyed being with you too. We had great sex. Memorable sex.'"

"I enjoyed being with you, too, Jenna. We had great sex. Memorable sex."

"You're mocking me."

"No. Just don't know what else to say. If I ever stay the night with a woman, I'm gone before breakfast. I've never remained with her for hours, days, afterwards. This is new territory. What you suggested sounded as good as anything."

"Oh."

They were approaching a small town. Signs announced a few fast food places. Gray suddenly took the exit and pulled into one of them. "How soon do you want to get to L.A.?" he asked as soon as he applied the parking brake and turned off the engine.

"As soon as we can, whenever that will be. Why do you ask?"

He folded his arms in front of him. "Because all this talk of having sex last night has made me hard again. Since you started this line of talk, the least you can do is help relieve me of my, uh, condition."

"Here? In daylight?"

He returned a lewd expression. "You one of those people who can only do it in the dark?"

"Well, no. I, uh …" An interesting idea occurred to her. "Let's try out my bed. I have blackout shades."

He rose, pulled her up, kissed her knuckles. "Thought you'd never ask."

GRAY LED Jenna to her bedroom, laid her across the mattress. Despite the demanding bulge in his pants, he removed each garment from her body at a leisurely pace, admiring the curves and valleys revealed as he went. Though she wore a basic white cotton bra, those delectable breasts underneath were anything but basic.

He ran a finger across the skin just above the top of the garment, mesmerized by the rounded softness, the gentle rise and fall of her chest. "You're really beautiful, Jenna."

She eyed him, her eyes cloudy, languid. "Thanks."

He lifted one of her hands and raised her arm, running his lips down the inside, breathing in the intoxicating fragrance of her shower soap, a subtle blend of floral and spice. How like her, a mix of opposites, if there ever was one.

Her shorts removed, his mouth trailed down her taut abdomen to the top of her bikini briefs, eliciting moans and undulating movement from Jenna. His penis ached for release, but something held him back to appreciate this luscious creature while he still could. Once they reached L.A., this phase of their relationship would be over and his best sex partner ever would be off to her new career. The idea made him pause, catch his breath.

"Don't you have some immediate business to attend to?" she asked.

"I'm taking that ride you mentioned earlier. Enjoying the scenery."

"Then shed that shirt and let me appreciate the landscape as well."

He readily obliged, and the next half hour was filled with a gradual strip tease-touch-and-taste session. The intense kissing from earlier was now less hurried, less frantic, more profound. Gray fought himself to delay release, attempted to make what could be his last time with Jenna as pleasurable as possible for her before he stuck on protection. "That was good. Better than before," he breathed, when at last he lay spent next to her.

She took a few seconds to calm her breathing. "Practice makes perfect."

"About that practice?"

"Yes?"

"Keep smacking your lips. That's a real turn-on."

"I told you before. I don't smack my lips."

"Right. Whatever you want to call it. I like it. A lot."

ONCE BACK ON THE ROAD, Jenna remained either in her room or out on the couch, leaving Gray to concentrate on the road. Didn't stop her from replaying their latest tryst in her head, though. At times like these she wished she had a close girl friend to provide counsel. Someone she could take into her confidence and reveal some, not all, of the details of having sex with Gray.

Back in L.A. and before Mitch, Aubrey sometimes talked about the revolving door of men in her life, although those times were more for entertainment rather than counsel, since Aubrey picked some real losers. Jenna had withheld telling Aubrey much about her failing marriage until it was obvious. Probably should've been more forthcoming with her sister, but hindsight would no longer help.

She could hide out in the bedroom and call Aubrey now, if Gray loaned her the phone again. And tell her wheat? That she was enjoying the best sex in her life with Mitch's brother? The brother who'd be only so happy to drop off when they reached L.A. and catch the next flight back to the Midwest and never see her again. Well, no, if Aubrey and Mitch got married, she'd probably see Gray then. Oh, God! She and Gray would be matron of honor and best man (were divorced women called matrons of honor?). Would he still be tempted to take her to bed, or were all those stories about best men hooking up with the maid of honor just urban legends?

Whoa! Slow down. Their unscheduled sex stop was supposed to be a swan song, cherry on top of the sundae, not incentive for repeat performances. She should be sealing the memories away to take out and relive later when he was gone, not contemplating the next time. But she couldn't rid her mind of the possibility of the next time and the time beyond.

Her notebook lay next to her on the couch, awaiting the launch of a new story, but her children's tales didn't lend themselves to the ideas flitting through her brain today.

She couldn't get over how this last time differed from all their prior bouts. She'd been raring to go, to tear his shirt from that magnificent chest, nibble his shoulder, and answer him thrust for thrust. Instead, Gray slowed things, focused on gentle touching, caressing. Tasting replaced tonguing. She hadn't objected. Far from it. For now, she was completely satiated.

But she couldn't dismiss the notion Gray had been trying to tell her something in his lovemaking. Something he'd chosen not to tell her in person or couldn't tell her. Back up. When had the word "lovemaking" entered the picture? Lovemaking, not sex. But that was it, wasn't it? They'd been making love, communicating with their bodies. Telling each other good-bye. Or something else?

Stop it, Jenna. Yes, they'd grown closer in the last several days, but certainly not that close. Even if, by some ridiculous joke of the fates, he was starting to feel something for her, she couldn't reciprocate. Other considerations, like keeping food on the table, took priority.

They continued on this way for another hour, Gray alone up front, Jenna seated on the couch attempting to capture the essence of another story to no avail. She didn't even realize they'd stopped until Gray called her. "Need to fuel up. Want to get out and stretch your legs?"

Anything was better than staring at a blank page.

They stopped at one of those super truck stops priding itself on clean facilities and good food. It was late afternoon and they still had a way to go before stopping for the night. As anxious as she was to get home and start her tour, these last few days had been unreal. Pleasant, actually, once she got past the jitters of the first day. She and Gray had developed a good rapport, a much better partnership than she'd ever known with Jerry.

While Gray attended to the fill-up, she wandered inside the combination restaurant/convenience store seeking nothing in particular except diversion. Snacks didn't appeal, nor did they need maps, sunglasses or newspapers. A few more circuits through the aisles and she was ready to return to the coach.

Gray was engaged in conversation with a guy who looked to be around thirty when she approached. The man was dressed in casual clothes and clean looking in appearance. Then she noted another motor coach parked next to them.

"Here's the owner now," Gray said as she neared. "Jenna, this is Shane Tunney. He's the driver of that rig over there."

She offered her hand. "Nice to meet you, Shane. Are you headed back to L.A.?"

"Nah, we're just getting started on a twenty-city tour."

"Oh. Whose? Or aren't you allowed to say?" Some performers and groups slapped a huge banner on their vehicles, others preferred anonymity.

"Sure, I'll share, since McKenna here says you're about to go on the road, too. It's Kirsten Parker."

"Kirsten Parker?" She started to scream, immediately toning down her response, since he was telling her this on the QT. "She's really big," she said in a much softer voice. "Nice job. Do you enjoy it?"

Tunney scratched his head, apparently not sure how to answer. "Sometimes. She's kinda gettin' bored with this tour scene, although she knows it's her bread and butter and what keeps her name in front of her fans."

Interesting observation. "Bored? How?"

"Don't want to reveal too much. I signed a confidentiality clause. Let's just say the pastimes that used to keep her mind occupied on the road—knitting, songwriting—no longer do the trick."

Would that be her in a few years? Tired of the road routine but trapped by the lifestyle. Jenna resolved to keep things fresh, even if she had to keep changing hobbies.

"McKenna here gave me a quick tour of your rig. Hope you don't mind? You didn't spare anything making yourself comfortable."

"Apparently Ms. Parker's digs aren't anywhere near as nice as yours, Jenna," Gray said.

"All thanks to McKenna Custom Coaches and my sister's interior decorating."

"You mind if I ask why you decided to purchase rather than lease? Did your business manager see it as a great write-off?"

She shot a glance at Gray, hoping he'd fill in the blanks on this one, but he eyed her back, as if waiting to hear how she replied. "It was a personal decision. I don't like hotels."

He seemed to accept her answer, at first. "Most touring companies don't own their vehicles. They rent. That way, any problems are the responsibility of the rental agency."

Hadn't Gray said something similar? "Good to know. I'll keep that in mind."

He reached in his shirt pocket and withdrew a couple cards. "This is the company that contracts my services and this is the company that rents the rigs. You ever need a driver, call them first and ask for me. I'd love to get my hands on this coach. And if you ever decide to sell, this other card lists the company that might be interested in obtaining it for high end customers."

He turned to Gray. "Don't know much about the tour bus business in the Midwest, but you might want to consider adding a rental arm to your outfit."

Gray rubbed his jaw, apparently considering the guy's suggestion. He and Tunney shook hands, Tunney saluted Jenna and then took off.

"Was that just talk?" she asked as soon as they were alone.

"Probably, but he brought up an interesting point. Selling it to another concern and then renting it from them could save you money and a lot of frustration in the future."

"Maybe." She glanced at the cards Tunney had given her. "I'll keep these, in case I decide to follow through on his suggestion. For now, though, I'm sticking with my original plan."

Gray headed for the door. "Suit yourself. But keep in mind how much trouble you've had finding a place to leave this thing. If you rented, that'd be someone else's worry."

He had her there. What she wouldn't give to lose just one of the worries weighing her down.

Sixteen

They climbed aboard and resumed their journey. Jenna left her notebook unattended on the couch and joined Gray up front. "As pleasant as our time in bed has been, we need to get back to finding a place to store this rig," she said.

"Didn't your sister suggest your parents' place?"

"I told her I'd think about it."

"What's to think about? You're gonna pay a minor fortune at any commercial parking garage. Besides, we'll be in L.A. soon. I need to know what route to take. I'd planned to turn south when we get to Flagstaff, so we can avoid the Mohave Desert. But if your mom and stepdad live farther north, maybe we should stay on this road."

"It's just … you don't know my mother."

"I know she came to Aubrey's defense and got her out of that lawsuit."

"After she set her up with that flaky client in the first place. Unwittingly, but she still brought on Aubrey's trouble."

Gray didn't pursue the subject. He had no idea how overbearing and difficult Iris Appleby could be to her daughters. If Jenna showed up with her coach in tow, her mother was sure to question why she hadn't made the proper arrangements. Then Jenna would have to explain why she'd found it necessary to return to California in her own coach. Anticipation of the first degree her mother would give her gave her a headache.

"Here." He handed her cell phone to her. "Time to give this back to you."

"Thanks. You finally trust me?"

"Wouldn't go that far. Yet. Although as I get to know you better, I understand your motivation a lot more."

She glanced at her phone. "It's charged. How did you manage that after all this time?"

He raised his eyebrows. "I have my ways."

She returned the lascivious gaze. "That you do." She continued to stare at her phone, considering his timing. "You returned it now because I didn't have much choice."

His lips curved upward. "Best to let you reach that conclusion on your own."

"I don't like being handled, Gray."

"Sure seemed to like it earlier, back in bed."

"You're exasperating."

"Want me to hold your hand while you call?"

"No. Just don't laugh."

"S'pose it wouldn't be prudent to remind you you're a grown woman with a teenage daughter who shouldn't be afraid of her own mother."

"You sound so wise, but just you wait. You can't park the coach and run. I expect you to stick around long enough to help me get settled."

He angled his head, gave her a you've-got-to-be-kidding look.

"I shouldn't have said expect. I meant, I hope you won't return to Iowa as soon as we get there. I really could use your counsel as I decide what to do about my tour."

He still didn't comment.

"I know, I know, you've already taken more time away from the business than anyone has a right to ask. I've just come to depend on your input." She hadn't known she would admit as much until her words were out. But she meant them just the same.

His mouth relaxed, his eyes seemed to take on a certain sparkle. "Huge admission from you, lady. You could barely tolerate my presence when I hauled you to the emergency room against your will."

"Funny how that happened," she said in her best impression of a coquette, trailing a finger up his arm.

"You think the promise of more mattress time will keep me around?"

She fluttered her eyelids.

"Don't do that, woman, or we'll never make the next stop. We'll be too busy parked on the side of the road indulging ourselves."

"We're not … done? Wasn't this morning like a sweet goodbye?"

"Maybe. That what you want?"

"What do you want?" she asked.

"I asked first."

"Don't do this to me, Gray. I can't think about my tour if I'm holding my breath until our next time together."

"Right." His eyes went back to the road ahead. "If all was well with your tour, I'd be back in the picture?"

"Hypothetically, since all isn't well with the tour."

"Okay. I'll stick around. A day or so."

Did that mean Gray didn't want to end things just yet either? Better sense told her to let it go for now, not to push him into a corner defining his intent, or he might just change his mind. "That's wonderful! Thank you," she said.

"Let's get started on your tour plan. Since I'm an architect and data man, planning a tour should be a great change of pace." His first suggestion was that she check in with her tour promoter, since he'd been party to keeping them separated.

The news from the guy putting her tour together wasn't good. "Where've you been?" His first question. She played up her illness, making it sound like she'd been quarantined. She had been, sort of. He showed little sympathy. "Had a couple possibilities pop up in the last week, but when I couldn't get hold of you, which you insisted I do before I signed you up for anything, had to let them pass. I'll get back with them now, if you want, but no guarantees." When he told her what they were, she liked one and rejected the other.

"So what have you lined up?" she asked, a knot growing in her stomach.

"The same two you approved three weeks ago."

"That's it? Two plus one more potential?"

"Told you when we started, this was a tough time of year to book, end of the summer, especially for an unknown to this generation."

"This time of year works best for my schedule."

"Your decision. I'll seek more venues, but if I were you, I'd step back and give myself more time to get my act together. I can still get you out of these commitments, but not for much longer."

She hung up more dejected than ever. The knot in her stomach had reproduced during the call, giving birth to several more knots. "Besides needing more rehearsal time and having to locate a place to store the coach, I now may be facing a very short schedule. Things keep getting worse rather than better."

Gray asked, "Ready to change your mind?"

"It's all I've got to fall back on." Could she sound any more defeated?

"I'm partially at fault for preventing you from learning this news sooner, so I'll put up with a couple more minutes of self-pity, then I suggest you get over it and start figuring out your next move."

Not exactly the reaction she was expecting, hoping for. She wasn't pitying herself, was she? She was merely laying it all out there, all the negative, sad reality of her life. "That's not fair. I just learned all this bad news. I need time to adjust."

"Time you don't have. So go ahead, immerse yourself in gloom a bit. Then get over it."

"I know I asked for your help, but do you have to sound so logical and blunt?"

"You don't have time for my sympathy, lady."

"Why do you do that? Call me 'lady' all the time? It makes me sound like a, a self-centered bitch. Do you really think of me that way?"

Once again, he turned his attention to the road ahead, which for seeming to be in the middle of nowhere boasted continual traffic, both oncoming and passing. A lot of trucks. A lot. Off in the distance, a freight train hauling a long queue of shipping containers disappeared behind a butte. "I've changed my opinion about the 'self-centered bitch' part since I've gotten to know you. I say 'lady' out of respect, because I admire what you're attempting to do. You're a real trouper, someone who's been knocked down and refuses to stay there."

Surprise. First time he'd revealed this take on her. Maybe he had started to like her.

"Guess I also say 'lady' so I don't blurt out something we'll both regret."

Was he suggesting there was more between them than either had yet admitted? Probably best to leave his comment alone. Though, why had he even mentioned it?

"Before you invest too much time analyzing my last statement, let it go for now. Your brain is needed elsewhere."

He'd read her mind, and unfortunately, he was absolutely right. "Okay, where do we start?"

"Let's go back to my earlier question. Your motor coach has and will continue to drain all your funds, you don't have much of a concert schedule, and you yourself say you need more rehearsal time. Given all that, you sure there isn't a better livelihood? You could teach piano, play locally for a club, write children's stories or work at any of a dozen other occupations."

He didn't appear to have much confidence in her concert career. "Look, I know you're trying to help me realize I have more options, but this is what I know. All I know."

"Then sell the coach and rent it from the buyer like Tunney suggested. From what that guy said earlier, it was a good investment. You could get top dollar for it and plow that money back into the tour."

She rubbed her forehead. "So many ideas. I'm not rejecting them, but I need to think them through."

"Ever been to Flagstaff," he asked, changing the subject.

"Huh? No. Why?"

"We'll be there soon. At least on the outskirts, where we're stopping for the night. Let's table any talk about your tour, eat, and enjoy the scenery a bit."

Too tempting an idea to resist. "Okay. A break would be good."

THOUGH THE IDEA had been to take her mind off her tour for an hour or so, Gray couldn't get his own mind to relax. What in the hell had he gotten himself into? He didn't know anything about running a concert tour, yet he'd been bombarding her with ideas. Ideas counter to what she wanted, which was to get her ill-fated concert tour up and running. Was he able to think that much clearer than her or was he concerned about her tour bombing?

She had the talent. But was that enough? She had to somehow get on top of the details hounding her now.

Why did he even care? He'd almost completed his part of the deal, getting the coach back to L.A. Once they arrived, all he had to do was walk away and leave her with this mess, even though she'd asked him to stay on longer.

But Jenna's problems weren't the only thing bothering him. Though he'd attempted to sublimate his thoughts about mountain travel, tomorrow he'd have to face his fears. Probably should've warned Jenna by now, except she had enough on her mind. Tomorrow would be soon enough.

"More fries?" Jenna's voice broke through his thoughts. "I let you talk me into them, but I've had enough. You went through yours like you hadn't eaten in days."

"Huh?" She was right. There was nothing left of his meal. "Uh, sure, if you don't want them."

"Want them, yes. Need them, no. I have concert gowns to fit into.

If they even arrived. Oh, my god, if the delivery people left them on my doorstep, someone could've made off with them in my absence."

He placed what he hoped was a comforting hand over hers. "Don't worry about them now. You've got enough on your plate."

"It's just that," she shook her head as if this newest problem was the one that could break her, "my dressmaker mixed up the colors with some country singer's touring costumes, so mine had to be redone. Should've tipped me off that my life was about to go downhill."

He pushed the fries back toward her. "Here, you eat these. Costumes or not, chow down and get over yourself. You've come too far to let the small stuff defeat you. Once we're done eating, we'll spend the rest of the evening getting your life back on the road."

Half an hour later, fed and relaxed, as much she could relax, Jenna leaned into the couch, steepled her fingers, and pressed them into her chin. Beside her, freed up from his driving duties, Gray stretched out his lanky frame, his own hands behind his neck. "Okay, where do we start?" she asked.

"What do you need to do right now?"

"Find more venues."

"That's your promoter's job. Try again."

So much for taking a break. All the unsolved issues that had clouded her brain earlier were back, stronger now because there was less time to deal with them. Finally, she blew out a breath. "Find a home for this thing. And since I can't seem to come up with anything better, I guess it's time to call my mother."

She picked up her cell. "Hi, Mom." She listened. "Yes, I'm feeling much better." More listening, some head nodding. "Oh, she told you. Right. We're on the road right now."

Apparently Aubrey had been keeping their mother informed about her cross-country trek.

"Yes. Uh-huh. No. Actually, that's why I'm calling." She backed farther into her seat, appeared to stiffen. "I need a place to park the motor coach. The place I lined up wasn't expecting it until next week and can't take it yet."

How would this next part go down?

"You guessed correctly," she told her mother. "Could I park it at your place?" She winced, shot him a not so nice look. "You're right. I should have called sooner." More listening. "Okay, let me talk to him."

She leaned over and whispered to Gray. "I've made it through the muck of Mother's censure and now I have to get my stepfather Buddy's approval. Like she lets him have any say. Hello, Buddy." Her tone turned more friendly.

She listened more. "I don't have an exact ETA yet, but we can let you know when we're an hour or so away." She nodded again, scrunched up her face. "It's a fine piece of machinery, Buddy. In great shape. But if something gets on your drive, sure, I'll take care of it."

Damn, he should've had her put this on speaker. She was a different person as she interacted with these people.

"Okay. Thank you so much, Buddy. Tell Mother the same." She ended the call, her body appearing to deflate. She didn't speak immediately. Instead, she turned her head toward the side window.

Give her time to come down.

"We're heading to Glendale," she said after a few beats.

"Your mom's place?"

"Hers and Buddy's. Aubrey told her I had remained in Burlington to spend time with Paige. We were supposedly off exploring her hometown every time Aubrey called. To save money, I decided to bring the coach back myself, so they weren't completely surprised by the request."

Good old Aubrey. He hadn't known about the calls to their mother, apparently to keep her from racing back to the Midwest to bring home her daughter à la Jenna's style. "What's this about saving money?"

She returned a guilty expression. "Uh, that would be you. Don't worry. It was a ruse. I'll pay you for your time and the expenses along the way."

"Fuel and lodging, fine. But don't worry about paying me. Consider it my contribution to your career. Besides, I needed this break."

She quirked a brow. "I'm a *break*?"

"Yeah. You don't think so? You've certainly taken my mind off work."

"Is that a good thing?"

She was fishing, but hell, he might as well come clean. "This trip has given me a chance to evaluate where I'm going with my life."

"With all my problems, you've had time to think about your own life?"

"I've put in a lot of hours in this driver's seat the last few days. While you were busy writing and whatever, I thought about my own career direction."

"Care to share?"

"Been thinking about your suggestion I get involved with the local theater on props or sound. They may not need my design skills, but it might help reacquaint me with the special needs of the theater."

"That's terrific. Something good might come out of this trip west besides getting my coach back to California."

"I've tucked this dream away for years. You're the first person I've told."

"I-I'm flattered."

"You may not be able to see clearly where your own career is headed, but you're a pretty good career counselor otherwise. Both you and your sister. Whether intentional or not, together you've managed to realign two-thirds of our company. You don't have another sister in the wings waiting to rearrange Geoff's life, do you?"

She laughed. "Actually, we do have a stepsister. Buddy's daughter. But don't worry. I hardly know her, she doesn't want to associate with us. I doubt she'd consider leaving her cushy life in California, obtained after her mother took Buddy to the cleaners when she divorced him."

He shook his head. "How about we just concentrate on our own lives for now. Geoff will have to punt if your sister, uh, stepsister, ever shows up. Besides, he's pretty tied up with Eileen Summers these days."

"You know, talking about Buddy got me thinking. He was a secondary character on a major sitcom a few years back until a vicious rumor purportedly circulated by his ex-wife got him fired. He may not have found his comeback vehicle on television yet, but he still has a number of ties to the entertainment industry. Maybe one of those is a retired pianist who'd considering coaching me in exchange for meals or something."

"Great idea."

"It's like my brain relaxed enough to start dealing with the other details of the tour once we found a place to house the coach temporarily. In fact, I think I'll call the people on the card Shane Tunney gave me right now and get an estimate for renting a coach."

Ten minutes later, she had her answer. "Wow. Renting may be cheaper than owning, but these people certainly aren't giving away their coaches." She shared the amount she was quoted with Gray, both for a basic package and a more luxurious vehicle like her own.

"Does that include the driver?"

"No, that's a separate service."

"Maybe you could sell them this rig for a reduced price, which would include your rental costs?"

She ran a hand through her hair. "Maybe. What if you and your brothers bought it back and acted as the rental agent?"

"You're kidding, right?" He glanced at her. "No, you were serious. Sorry, babe, our cash flow couldn't handle it right now. Not a bad idea, though. We have the space for storage, if you consider the back lot, but the bank won't float us a loan to purchase even one coach, if we don't recoup the purchase price through an immediate sale."

She let a few beats go by. "Okay, for now I table the idea of either renting or renting out. I stick with my original plan."

"Then attack the problem from a different direction."

"Different direction? Like what?"

"Move the tour back?"

"Then it would take even longer to see a return on my investment."

"Not if you fired your promoter. You'd have to set up your own schedule, but you couldn't do much worse than he's been able to do. That would give you time to get in the rehearsing you think you need as well as find someone to promote you."

She started to refute his suggestion but stopped.

"Hey, I'm not trying to pressure you into doing one thing or another. I just want you to see there might be other ways to skin this cat." He chuckled. "Listen to me. Maybe I should spout a few more clichés while I'm at it. Look for the silver lining. It's always darkest before the storm. Hang in—"

"I get the idea," she said, cutting him off. "But every deviation from my plan means more decisions, more work, more chances to screw up. I can't risk doing that to Paige."

He rose, pulled her up, too. "Enough for tonight. Go back to your bed. Read. Listen to music."

She didn't resist. Time was running out for him to help her get her act together, but from the sag of her shoulders and bags under her eyes, she'd had enough for one day. He stayed behind. "You're not joining me?"

Although he really wanted to sleep with her again, he shook his head. "You won't be able to relax with me there."

Though tired, her eyes assumed that come-hither look every man worth his

erection recognized. "Probably not, but I bet I won't think a bit about my tour."

"Well, then, that's one challenge I can't refuse."

Seventeen

Gray was up long before Jenna the next morning, too preoccupied with today's leg of the trip to sleep. Yet again, they'd had sex before dropping off. Only a few more days to enjoy her inviting body, but he wouldn't let himself think about that.

Another concern nibbled at his brain today. He'd put it off during their first days on the road, because the road, if not the landscape around them, had been relatively flat or sloping. Even the Continental Divide had been anticlimactic. But he could no longer defer his fear.

He'd dressed but not been able to eat. Instead, he'd retrieved a map of Arizona from the console next to the driver's seat and spread it out on the counter in the kitchen area. Though the answer was inevitable, he continued to study the various roads going south, southwest and west. With desert, rough terrain or mountains the main features of the landscapes in those directions, there weren't many choices. It didn't hurt to double-check his options, but his decision didn't change. I-17 would take them south to Phoenix, where they could pick up I-10, which would take them into California and the home stretch.

All he had to do was get through the next few hours. By then, the baby tornado swirling in his gut would have subsided. Maybe.

Once the sounds of Jenna moving around in the back of the coach reached him, he made himself productive by preparing her usual breakfast, coffee and cold cereal. How the woman could live on that stuff mystified him, but it kept that great body in shape.

Jenna was a morning person. He usually was also. Not today. He nodded to her bright, "Good morning." She thanked him for making her breakfast. "No problem," he murmured. Did his best to smile when she mentioned their go-to-sleep sex. All this upbeat cheerfulness exhausted him.

He went back to studying the map. Not that the answer would change, but he did so as a gentle hint to his traveling companion that he needed his space. Didn't want to talk.

"You swear by your GPS," she said.

He blinked, came out of his fog. "Grew up reading paper maps. They're my go-to when I need to get my bearings." Damn, wrong phrase. Sure to prompt her interest.

"Bearings? We're can't be lost. Even I know we're right outside Flagstaff."

He chose not to reply. Maybe she'd get the hint he didn't want to talk if he refolded the map.

"Gray? What's up?"

The woman could be so dense when it suited her. If he wanted to make it to Phoenix safely, he had to tell her. Just hated the idea of sharing one of his innermost fears. He retrieved a bottle of water from the fridge and headed toward the front of the coach. He tucked the bottle into its holder. "We need to put off further talk about your tour until we've been on the road a few hours."

She studied him a beat before replying, "Okay. Why?"

"Something I haven't told you."

She lifted a brow, cocked her head. "You mean I don't know everything there is to know about Graham McKenna?"

"Seriously."

She set her cereal bowl on the counter. Straightened. "Oh."

Just say it. Spit it out. "Mountain driving, especially in a rig like this, isn't my thing. I-17 has some serious downhill slopes."

She stared at him as if his words hadn't resonated. "What do you mean? You're quitting as my driver?"

"No, of course not, unless now that you're aware of this information, you want me to quit?"

"I don't want you to quit, but why are you just getting around to telling me?"

Because she wouldn't have let him help her escape if she'd known. Instead, she would've found another way to take off, more than likely something self-destructive. "No need to mention it until now. These are the first real mountains we've hit."

"Back up. You said mountain driving isn't your thing. Explain. You freak out? You can't drive? What?"

"Fair questions. I've only driven through mountains a few times. Had no idea until the first time that I'd freeze up. Got through only by keeping my eyes on the road and tremendous mental focus. I can do it again today, but I need your help."

"Me? How can I help?"

"Once we get underway, don't talk. No radio. No noise, period."

"Sure. Do you even want me up here?"

"As long as the views don't get to you."

She flicked off his remark with her hand. "You forget, I grew up in the mountainous terrain around L.A."

"Too bad you can't drive this thing."

She took her seat beside him. "What if I'd considered driving back to California on my own? Not the smartest idea I've ever had, but given my mental state before we got underway, I might have tried. Who knows what kind of trouble I would have brought on myself if I had?"

Self-discovery. She was getting there. Might not be quite there yet when it came to her tour, but other parts of her life were coming into focus. Now it was his turn to face his devils. He fastened his seatbelt, pushed up both sleeves, and adjusted his wristwatch. He released a long breath. "Ready?"

"Are you sure you're okay doing this? Isn't there any other road we could take?"

He still hadn't started the engine. "This is the best route. I'll manage. Now, done talking?" She nodded instead of speaking.

They set off, passed through a fairly flat area of resorts and ranches for several miles. A few horses, some cattle occupied the fields. Shortly, though, most signs of population disappeared, replaced with occasional signs warning of deer and elk crossing. Still, the terrain was merely rolling. He used this time to relax as best he could, prepare himself mentally for the imminent challenge.

Within minutes, things changed. At first the number of pine trees flanking both sides of the road increased, came nearer. Then they fell back as outcroppings of rock appeared.

Gray kept a tight grip on the steering wheel. The steady drone of the tires on the road, the whooshing of other cars passing them and his breathing were the only sounds he heard. He'd already zoned out Jenna, although at times he sensed her sneaking a peek at him.

Though he stayed in the right lane, he didn't let himself view the dramatic drop-offs on the passenger side, tempting as the urge might be. Occasionally, a butte would split southward traffic from vehicles heading north. Then there was only their coach and the occasional vehicle in front, behind or to the side.

It was coming, the downward drop in the road. Knowing didn't help. If possible, his grasp on the wheel tightened, the blood drained from his knuckles. He tried to keep his breathing steady, but every so often he'd skip a beat. *Take it one mile at a time. Stare straight ahead. Don't worry about the rest of the way.* It would come soon enough.

Just as he began to hear his heart beating in his ears, the sound of an old-time car horn pierced the silence. He jumped in his seat, causing the coach to swerve dangerously close to the right side of the road. Instinct kicked in and allowed him to correct his steering. Only then did he realize the sound had been that of Jenna's phone. It blared again. He didn't need this distraction. He shot a glance at the offending instrument. Jenna let it go off a third time, probably afraid to answer.

"Pick up!" he shouted after the fourth blast. "Anything's better than that obnoxious ring tone." Damn call had broken his concentration just as he'd passed the first sign announcing an upcoming six-percent descent.

JENNA CRINGED, furious with herself for forgetting to put it on mute. She'd been without her phone so long, she'd forgotten that step. Had to be Aubrey or Paige. She'd tell them she'd call back later. Her hand shot out to stifle the honking. "Hello?"

"What'dya think you're doing, leaving our daughter to fend for herself while you go off on some cross-country trek with your new boyfriend?" Jerry Waller, her former husband, said in his slimiest voice.

Her brain went on overload. With one question, he'd pressed several buttons that ripped through her core—appearing to be the concerned parent, accusing her of being the flaky one, assuming Gray was her boyfriend, okay, he wasn't too far off base there, ambushing her over the phone. Though it had been months since she'd last tangled with the jerk, memories of the last few years of their troubled marriage came flooding back like they'd merely been off stage, waiting for their cue.

She struggled to frame a dispassionate response, avoid all the old rejoinders that had brought her nothing but shame, heartache and unquenchable anger.

"You okay? Who is it?" Gray asked over his shoulder. His voice was strained.

"That him?" Jerry charged. "How comforting. Wait'll he discovers what a fraud

you are. Pretending to be so sweet, so devoted, when the real you is such a bitch."

Name-calling and putdowns had been Jerry's stock in trade in the latter days of their marriage. But not this time. If she'd learned anything since being single again and especially after being with Gray, she didn't have to take this. His tirade was simply vitriol. "I won't discuss anything with you as long as you have that attitude." She hung up.

Gray raised a brow. "Husband?"

"Former."

"Right. You okay?"

"Me? What about you? I'm so sorry about that ring tone. I'll change it right now and put it on mute."

"Good idea." His eyes didn't stray from the road, but he did manage a slight grin.

She considered his question. Yes, she was okay. Her heart rate was slowing, the lump in her throat had disappeared and she could feel her fingers again. "To answer your question, yes, I feel damn good. I've never talked back to him like that."

"What did he say?"

"Sure you want to keep chatting like this?" She wondered how long he could lock his knuckles without his fingers going numb.

"Talk fast. For now, road's better than I anticipated. Real drop-off's coming up."

"Somehow, he discovered I'm on the road. With you. He accused me of abandoning Paige." A jagged sliver of ice sliced through her stomach, dissipating her pride seconds before. "Oh, my God! Do you think he's considering regaining custody?"

"He say as much?"

"Jerry? Not his way. He's more into innuendo. And intimidation."

"Hardly on the line long enough to threaten you."

"Long enough for Mr. Raid the Bank Account and Run Away to accuse me of enjoying myself on a junket with you while leaving my daughter alone in Iowa." The irony had her insides churning.

Gray turned his head her way briefly. "He's blowing smoke."

"Yes, I know."

"Your tone suggests otherwise." He seemed to think through his comment. "Wait a minute. He struck a nerve, didn't he? You feel guilty leaving the kid behind."

"We could have brought her."

"Really? Think about it. How long did it take before you got bored? So how long would it have taken her enthusiasm to dry up? Plus, she seems to be having a great time."

"True," though she didn't sound convinced, even to herself.

Gray put up a hand. "Road's changing. Gotta table this for now."

"Okay." A sign appeared on the passenger side of the road announcing a six-percent descent. This was it. She took a deep breath and prayed for Gray to keep his cool. He was strong in so many other respects, she guessed she could abide one drawback. Although at the moment, she sure wished it wasn't fear of driving through mountains. *The man is putting himself through this for you. Give him a break!*

Like Gray, she directed her eyes forward. The road itself didn't appear to be dropping off the side of the world. If it weren't for the slight pressure on her chest as the coach accelerated and the top of the rock piles on the driver's side steadily growing higher, she wouldn't have known they were descending the mountain.

"Gum," Gray said tersely.

"Where?"

"Console."

She fished around until she found the pack, quickly removed a stick, peeled off the wrapper and handed it to him.

He accepted it like a man who'd been without water for days and started chewing immediately. Within seconds, an audible sigh escaped him. His grip on the wheel relaxed ever so slightly.

Even as they made their way down the mountain and she helped Gray calm his nerves, she couldn't get Jerry's call out of her head, especially the potential threat of taking Paige from her. This couldn't be real. Stressful as it had been to get through the horrible last days of her marriage, then the strain of the divorce, those periods were nothing compared to her current terror. The last several months of rehearsals and planning her tour were nowhere near as frightening as the prospect of Paige with her father.

She kept staring at the phone, wondering if it would ring again. Sure, she'd come on tough with Jerry and told him not to call unless his attitude changed, but her bluff wouldn't stop him. The best she could hope was he'd hold off long enough for them to reach more level road.

After a series of turns, the highway remained fairly straight, especially on the slopes. Finally, mercifully, the surface leveled off. Gray's hand reached for his bottle of water, but his eyes stayed plastered ahead.

"How are you doing?" she finally dared ask.

He twisted his head enough for her to see the glimmer of a smile. "Better. Thanks. Appreciate how you got me through that. I was a real wuss."

"No, you weren't. You were a true example of how to gut it out and face your fears."

"Which brings us back to you and your ex. Let's talk before the next section of rough road."

She shook her head, still dumbfounded at Jerry's continuing ability to bring her to her knees. "I hoped I'd never have to deal with him again. He had the bulk of our money, he'd found himself a girlfriend out east and he had no parental responsibilities. Hearing from him today took me back to those awful days of our marriage."

"He'd call you a name and you'd convince yourself you'd done something to deserve it?"

Gray had a pretty good take on her relationship with Jerry. "I told you, I didn't have much self-confidence."

"But you were married for over a decade. Was it like that from the start?"

"Maybe. But I doubt I would have recognized it then. I was so used to my mother ordering my life for me, I guess I assumed his doing similar was to be expected. He really did try to support me for a while. Even after Paige came along. He did—does—love her. But after he lost his job when the company was bought out, he went a long time before finding another job. He was forced to take something that paid less. That's when he changed. Started looking for the easy out. Gambling. Making bad investments."

She was about to expound further when Gray's phone rang. Aubrey. He handed the phone to her.

"We've got a problem," Aubrey told her. "Jerry called Paige a little while ago and blew up when she told him you were on your way back to California."

"He called me too. What happened? He hasn't been in touch with her in a long time."

"Paige wants to tell you herself."

"Dad called you already? Sorry, Mom. His call came out of the blue. I haven't heard from him in months."

"Did he say why he was calling?"

"Not to find out how I was doing. He was pumping me for information about you."

Paige was on to him? "You must have told him I'm on the road right now."

"I told him about your tour. Then he wanted to know where you were and where I was."

Jerry could make it sound like he was so interested in you when all he wanted was a way to extract something to use against you. "Did you happen to tell him that Gray is driving the coach?"

"Yeah, wasn't I supposed to?"

"I'm afraid your father got the wrong impression about Gray. That he's my boyfriend."

"Oh, Mom, I'm sorry. No wonder Dad kept asking about Gray."

Then it hit her. Oh, God, no! "You, uh, didn't tell him about my uh, needing to relax, did you?" She held her breath, waiting for the response.

"Gosh, Mom, no way!"

Jenna collapsed in her seat. It was bad enough Jerry had accused her of abandoning Paige, but if he knew about her breakdown ... "Good. Because I'm fine now. This trip is helping me relax. Look, if he calls again, be pleasant but try to keep your conversation short and your comments general. Okay?"

"Gotcha, Mom. But he probably won't call. He said something about having lost his charger and he was running down his battery."

"But if he does, let me know. Okay?"

"Sure. Aunt Aubrey wants to talk to you before you hang up."

In a few seconds, her sister was on the line. "Jenna? Paige took off. I think she sensed I wanted to talk to you in private. Tell me, are you okay after talking to that jerk?"

"I'm okay. I didn't let his shouting get to me, at least during the twenty seconds I stayed on the line. He accused me of going off on a lark with my new *boyfriend* and had abandoned *our* daughter."

"Apparently he was all caring parent, encouraged her to go on and on about what she'd been doing. When she figured out he was baiting her, she ended the call. Right after, she told me he'd called."

"You both did the right thing. I want her relationship with her father to remain positive, unless he threatens to hurt her. It's bad enough he rarely calls. I asked her to keep her conversation brief, if he calls again, and she seemed to go along with me. I was surprised she saw through him."

"She's growing up before our eyes, Jenna. She knows more about the problems you've experienced with her father than you realize."

"Has she said as much?"

"Not exactly, but when she and I discussed your need to relax, she seemed pretty aware of the pressures you've been under. She's heard you crying more than once. And she doesn't understand how your finances have changed so much. Look, if he calls again, hand him off to Graham, if necessary."

"Gray doesn't deserve to deal with the jerk."

"He's a big boy. Plus, like his brothers, he's got this white hat thing going. If he's listening to this call, that's okay."

Jenna glanced at her driver. *White hat thing*. Even though he could be a pretty bad boy in bed, he truly was the hero type. So different from Jerry. "He's not listening, but I'll be sure to tell him. And ... I agree."

"I hear Paige coming back from telling Mitch about her call. Gotta go."

"Be on the lookout. I doubt Jerry would make the trip to Iowa, but alert everyone else and plan how you'll handle him if he does."

"Got it. Take care. Let me know his next move." She hung up.

"What's up?" Gray asked.

"For reasons unknown, Jerry called Paige and got her to tell him where I was and what I was doing. After that, he called me. You know the rest."

"Want to talk?"

"No. Yes. I need to move around first, shake this off."

"I'd almost give in to a water fight, if it would help get you past that call. But let's not go there."

"Fortunately for you, I'm beyond water fights. Although I do want to throw things."

"Think I've got just the ticket."

Eighteen

Within ten minutes, they were pulling into a truck stop. Gray steered the motor coach off to the side. Once stopped, he went to one of the cupboards and retrieved a box that read "rubber horseshoes."

"Where did you get those?" she asked, this being the first time these had made an appearance.

"Picked them up as we went through the sporting goods section of the discount store the other day. This is a lawn game. The shoes aren't real."

"I didn't mean horseshoes when I said I wanted to throw things."

He led her toward the door. "I didn't think to pack a couple catcher's mitts and a softball, so these will have to do."

Once outside, they made their way a certain distance from the coach, after which, Gray broke open the box and lifted out the contents. "Ever pitched a horseshoe?"

"Haven't had the pleasure."

He removed two round rubber mats and laid them several feet away with maybe ten feet between them. Then he stuck a ten-inch peg in the middle of each. Returning, he held out two blue shoes in one hand and two red ones in the other. "Take your pick."

Jenna chose the red. "You go first. Show me how it's done."

"Step back, away from me. Even though these are rubber, you don't want to get hit with one." He demonstrated. "Hold it in the middle with the ends, the caulks, pointing down. Bring your arm under and back, step forward and release." He let go of the shoe and it went sailing, landing between the two mats.

"Was that good?" She had no idea how points were earned, although she remembered the saying about "close only counting in horseshoes." Was his throw considered close?

"Uh, no, other than I lined up pretty well. Rusty. Probably should've taken a few practice swings."

"Do the other."

"We're supposed to take turns, but okay, I need to remind my arm what to do." He threw the next one, which, though it touched the first peg, landed several inches behind it. Rather than leave the shoes there to see how her pitches compared, he scuttled over to retrieve them and sent them sailing again. One landed just in front of the farther peg and the other sailed past.

"Uh, remember me?"

"Right. But you get the idea?"

"More than." She stepped up to the position he'd occupied. Unlike his technique, she held her shoe by one end and shot it toward its dual targets. It flew several feet behind the farther peg. "Oops. Guess I've got a lot of pent-up energy to expend."

"Glad I didn't suggest boxing."

On her next lob, despite the remaining need to blow up, she dialed down her pitch. The shoe ringed the second peg but flipped away. She jumped up and down, clapping. "I did it! Do I win?"

"We're not really playing a game here, just channeling your anger."

"You say that now that I've done better than you. With only two tries."

He grimaced. "Let's focus on you." He recovered the shoes and handed them back to her. "Try again. Show me up even more."

She flung the shoes again with even better results. Still no ringers, but with each heave, her wrath diminished.

"Horseshoes! I haven't played in years." A trucker had approached them, unnoticed. "Don't suppose you'd let another player join your game?"

Dressed in a pair of worn blue jeans, dirty sneakers and a rust-colored t-shirt with a four-inch stain of unknown origin on his chest, the guy still seemed friendly enough. Nonetheless, Gray stepped in front of her, the white hat apparently back on his head. "We're just taking a short break. Don't really have time for a full-out game."

"Hey, no sweat. Hoped I could throw out a couple pitches. That's all."

"The lady just took a call from someone she'd rather not tangle with, so we're out here trying to ring the shoes rather than this guy's neck."

The guy shot a glance at Jenna. "Oh. Sorry. I shouldn'ta interrupted."

He twisted to walk away. "No. Stay. I'm feeling much better. Now that I've been introduced to this game, I'm curious to observe others' styles."

A smile broke across his face. "Hey, thanks. Appreciate it." He grabbed the shoes and took his position. His stance immediately morphed him into someone else. A sportsman. Competitor. He released a shoe and barely missed the first peg. But the second landed exactly right.

The game took on new meaning. Gray had been good, but this guy was better.

Gray passed over his two shoes, and both tosses landed squarely around the far peg.

"Wow! That was something." Jenna went over to shake the trucker's hand.

Gray, too, was impressed. "Man, you're great. If we had more time, you should be the one teaching her."

"How 'bout taking five more minutes while I watch the lady throw?"

Jenna checked out Gray, who nodded, then went to gather the four shoes for her.

"Let's see your release," the guy told her. She followed through. "Not bad," he said as the shoe flew past the second peg. "Too much power. But from the way you're dressed and the way you stand, ma'am, I can tell you're no stranger to restraint. Even though you're here to burn off that anger, direct it inward into your release. Now, try again."

Feeling herself sucked into his vortex of expertise, Jenna sent his message from her brain to her arm and let go. Ringer! "Oh. My. God. I did it!" First she hugged Gray and without thinking then grabbed the other guy and hugged him.

Surprised, even a little embarrassed, the trucker took a step back, hung his head for just a second, then hunched his shoulders. "You're quite the student, ma'am."

"And you're quite the instructor." He turned to Gray. "Where'd you get these? I'd like to stick something like this in my cab for times when the driving gets to me."

Gray mentioned the super discount store and the guy nodded. "No kidding. Didn't know something like this existed. Figured I had to dig a sand pit for the pegs whenever I wanted to play. This is much better and easier."

They said good-bye to their new friend, picked up the shoes, mats and pegs and headed back to the coach.

Jenna flopped into her seat. "That was actually fun."

"Good. Didn't go exactly as I planned but close enough. And in horseshoes …"

"Close counts," she finished for him. "I take it you weren't planning on our friend showing up."

"How about showing me up?"

"C'mon, Gray, surely your ego can take it."

"I was fine with his pitches outdoing mine. But I wanted to be the one who helped you make your own ringer."

"It was all your idea, Gray. Besides, the point wasn't to help me score so much as help me get rid of the bad taste in my mouth following Jerry's call."

"That guy didn't need to hang all over you."

"He didn't *hang all over me*. He stood a couple feet away from me when I threw."

"Didn't stop you from hugging him."

"I hugged you first. Hold up. You were jealous?"

"Of course not. I don't have any claim on you."

Although she agreed, he didn't need to offer up his lack of claim quite so fast. "Okay, forget about him. What I really appreciate is you helping me clear my head."

"Hate to break the spell, but your ex is still out there. How you gonna handle his next call?"

Damn. He was right. "Would've been nice to have five more minutes of peace, but he could call back at any time. I need to be ready." Only then did she remember she hadn't taken her phone with her. Checking it, she discovered she'd already missed two calls from Jerry, though he hadn't left any messages. "Now he's probably frothing at the mouth because he couldn't reach me."

Before she had a chance to figure out how she'd handle him the next time, the phone rang again. "Avoid my calls and I'll just keep calling." If possible, her ex's tone had grown even more menacing.

Enough of her recent serenity remained that for once, she didn't plunge right into answering him. Instead, she put the call on speaker, so Gray could get a better feel for the pest, took a long breath and considered his words. "Where did you find the time to call, Jerry? Did you lose another job?" Okay, putting him on the defensive might not be the best idea, especially when she noted Gray's raised eyebrow, but for once Jerry's shouting and snide tone of voice hadn't prompted her to respond directly to his comment.

"My work status is none of your business."

"Not very civil, Jerry. I told you not to call if your attitude didn't improve." Once again, she was pushing back rather than supplying non-answers, but now that the floodgates of her ire had been released after years of taking his tirades, it wasn't easy to curb her tongue.

"My *attitude* was fine the first time I called back."

"Not that I care, but why did you call, Jerry?"

"Told you before. You left our daughter on her own to play house on the road with a guy you just met. I want it to stop."

"You know this only because after weeks without contacting her you called your daughter and used her to get information about me."

"Doesn't matter how I found out. Besides, I've been busy."

She was tempted to pursue his last statement, but her main goal was to end the call. "Did Paige complain about her situation?" She wouldn't have asked if she didn't already know the answer. Her teenage daughter might thrive on drama at times, but she was one happy kid these days.

"Said she was being tossed around from one caregiver to another."

"Really? And how were these *caregivers* treating her?"

"How do I know? No one's really responsible for her. She seems to have landed in some kind of hippie commune."

Don't take the bait. "She's fine. She would've told me if she wasn't happy."

"Really? That's why she ran away from you and took herself to Iowa?"

Oh, God. Paige hadn't mentioned that. Jenna started to reply, but Gray held up a hand, silently counseling her to think twice before responding. "I suppose you read her the riot act on her actions?"

"You're a better candidate for the riot act. Have you not established rules, warned her about the hazards of a kid traveling alone?"

"Let's not get into parental responsibilities. You don't have a leg to stand on. If you have any more *concerns*, contact my attorney. I'm sure she'd be happy to go over the terms of the custody decision." She hung up, stifled the urge to throw the phone and dropped it instead onto the console between them.

Gray spoke first. "He's a real winner."

"Not exactly the term I'd use for my former spouse, but I get what you mean. How'd I do? Did I stand up to him?"

Gray's mouth assumed several shapes before he spoke. "Yeah, I'd say as far as standing up to him, you did fine. The guy's the kind who someone either fears or dislikes. You seem to have gotten past the fear, which is a big deal, but now you've moved into anger. You're challenging him."

"That's wrong?"

"Depends. If he's the type who'll back down when challenged, then go for it. But he didn't strike me as such. Push him into a corner, he'll come out slugging. That what you want?"

"No, of course not."

"He called for a reason. When you cut him off the first time, he came back again, three more times until he finally reached you. He's draping his goal in concern for the kid's welfare and safety, but there's something else he's hiding. From what you've told me about the guy, I'd say he's after more money."

"Money? He took it all."

Gray shrugged. "Maybe it's gone."

"Gone? All that money he stole from Paige and me? The judge allowed him to keep it, because by then Jerry resided in another state where the court had no authority, and once Jerry's attorney found my trust fund, which was unbreakable, they convinced the judge it would be my share of the property settlement, along with our mortgaged home."

"Bummer. You still have the same attorney?"

"No, I got rid of him as soon as the divorce became final. I found a woman who specializes in family law, especially where one partner has cheated or shortchanged the other."

"You might want to check in with her. Just to see what kind of damage that rat can do."

"Damage? Not just harassment?" Her palms had begun to perspire.

"You said the trust fund was unbreakable. But now that you've withdrawn funds from it to buy this coach, is the coach safe from Jerry?"

"How could Jerry possibly justify taking my coach?" Then she remembered. Her one-night stands. Could Jerry find out about those? She couldn't mention this fear to Gray, because he'd then bring up her blackmailer. Her *fake* blackmailer. Unfortunately, her bar pick-ups weren't.

Nineteen

Jenna called her attorney, Linda Harris, and went over the two calls she'd received from her ex-husband. "What do you think? Should I be worried or was he just harassing me like always?"

"It's hard to tell from just two short calls. He apparently didn't make any demands, nor did he threaten either you or your daughter."

"Not directly, but that's the way he operates. Through suggestion rather than direct threat, so if you accuse him of anything, he not only readily denies it but suggests you're paranoid."

"Even though he accused you of leaving your daughter alone with your sister, you think he's only using her as an excuse to get more money?"

"Money I don't have, but yes. If he was so concerned about our daughter's welfare, he would have stayed in contact with her."

"Let me make some calls and get back to you."

"Okay, but call me back as soon as you learn something. He sounded really anxious."

Jenna and Gray continued on their way. After a bit, she caught him shooting a glance at her every so often. "What?"

"How are you doing?"

"Not falling apart, if that's what you mean. I learned today I could stand up to him. I also found out that Paige isn't completely oblivious to his tactics. We're both recovering, in our own ways."

"So I've observed. You've come a long way in a short time."

Short time. Mostly these past few days on the road. "Don't tell Aubrey, but I guess I did need to stop and catch my breath. I'd gotten so accustomed to fighting Jerry, I wasn't ready to listen to her and my doctor."

"Big admission."

It was. Strange. Though her tour had been constantly on her mind the last seventy-two hours, she hadn't made much progress with the planning, other than finding a temporary home for the coach. Now, on top of that wealth of issues, she had the threat of Jerry to worry about. Yet, despite the growing load of stress on her plate, she felt more optimistic than she had in months.

She turned to him and offered a smile. "You've played a big part in getting me to this point."

"Me?"

She reached over and patted his forearm, since she couldn't grab his hand from the steering wheel. "Yes. You've listened to me go on and on about my woes, then you've patiently talked me through one option for ridding myself of them after another."

"Ready to consider some more of those options? The road is fairly flat and straight for now."

"Not just yet. The idea of delaying the tour start is rolling around in my head. I'm getting used to it, but I'm not ready to make any decisions yet."

"What else, then? Or do you want to read or write?"

"Let's talk about you a bit?"

He rolled his head. "Ah, no. Not me again."

"Suit yourself. I just thought I could return the favor." She pulled her tablet and pen from the side pocket on the seat. "What about me?" he asked after a minute.

"I'm curious about something. You don't have to answer, if you don't want."

He cocked his head in her direction. "Like you could make me. Okay, shoot."

"You're the oldest brother, right?"

"Yeah, a dubious distinction at best."

"That's what I was getting at. I'm the older sister. I've already described how that has affected my relationship with Aubrey. But from what little interaction I observed between you and your brothers, you don't come across as the oldest sibling, the leader. In fact, Mitch, the youngest, seems to assume that role."

Gray returned his attention to the road. Didn't say anything for several beats. Were their sibling interactions that easy to detect? When it came to reading people, Jenna outdid Aubrey. "I should be insulted, but you're right. Mitch does tend to take the leadership role in the family. Don't know if it's because he's an attorney or he gravitated toward the law because of this tendency. He's a lot younger than Geoff or I, so he sorta grew up on his own."

"Are you okay with that?"

HOW MUCH DID he want to reveal? What the hell, she was already on to him. "Hasn't always been the case. While he was in college and law school, Geoff and I became his surrogate parents, paid his tuition, counseled him about girls and grades. But when our dad's debts started to haunt us, Mitch took over with the creditors. When we decided to customize coaches, he put aside his legal aspirations to join us. Thanks to Aubrey, we only recently learned he put law on hold because he felt he owed us."

"You didn't answer my question. Are you okay with Mitch always taking the lead?"

Persistent. But then, he'd come to like that about her. "I was okay with him handling Dad's debts and filing the papers to set up the new business. It's other things, like always wanting to be the one in charge, that don't sit well." Why was he telling her all this?

She seemed to mull his statement a bit. "What have you done about it?"

Signed on to be your driver and guardian. Withheld information, like swearing to a no-sex clause that fizzled within two days. No, couldn't go there. "Did my own thing, I guess."

"How'd that make you feel?"

"Jenna! You sound like a psychologist."

"Hit a nerve? Sorry. Let's drop it." She retrieved the pad of paper.

"His actions anger me." There, he'd said it out loud. "I love my brother, but sometimes I want to sock him when he gets all authoritative."

"You've never told him how you feel?"

"No. I've either ignored him and done my own thing or just gone along." As soon as his words emerged, he prepared for her inevitable response.

But it didn't come. A pregnant silence developed. He waited. Finally, he could curtail his curiosity no long. "Go ahead. Say it."

"I don't need to. You already know what it would be."

Damn the woman. Get him talking and then drop it before he was finished. Damn her also for being right. Yeah, if Mitch's behavior bothered him, he should tell him. Work it out. Mitch had told him and Geoff how much he disliked working on the coaches and how much he wanted to practice law. Finally. He and Geoff had been oblivious to their brother's frustrations. Maybe the same was the case for Mitch. Damn Jenna also for doing to him exactly what he'd been doing to her —helped her arrive at her own decision without telling her what it should be.

THEY CONTINUED to ride in silence, although as the minutes passed, both became more comfortable. At length, Jenna's phone rang again. It was her attorney reporting back.

"What did you find out?" Jenna asked.

"He hasn't been seen by his employer for over six weeks, and he's no longer living at his last known address," Linda Harris, her attorney, said.

Jenna's heart jumped into her throat. "No one knows where he is?"

"His employer didn't want to divulge the details of his disappearance until I suggested he might be a threat to his daughter. Seems your ex was dipping into several of his employer's accounts."

"Embezzling?"

"Exactly. He was about to be brought up on charges when he stopped showing up for work. When the police went to his apartment to arrest him, he'd already gone. A few days later, some shady character appeared at his office looking for him. His boss suspected the guy was connected to local gambling."

This was worse than she suspected. Jerry was a low-life, but now he was also wanted on criminal charges and hiding both from the law and the people to whom he must owe money. What had happened to the man she married? Had he been like this all along and she'd just been too blind and too naïve? The only positive part of this news was that there was no way Jerry could possibly get custody of Paige with all this against him. "Do they have any leads on his whereabouts?"

"No. He must be using cash wherever he is, because there haven't been any charges on his credit card for a while. Apparently your daughter is the only one who's spoken to him lately."

"Can't they track his calls by GPS?"

"Not if his phone is off. He must only be turning it on long enough to call you and your daughter."

"This doesn't sound good, Linda. He could be anywhere, including on his way to see her."

"Would he hurt her?"

Jenna tried to speak, but nothing came out. Her ears pounded so hard she was compelled to hand the phone to Gray.

"Ms. Harris? This is Graham McKenna, Ms. DiFranco's friend and her driver. What did you tell her? She doesn't seem able to talk. I'll put you on speaker."

"I told her no one knows where her former husband is at the

moment. Her daughter and Ms. DiFranco are the last persons to have spoken to him."

"You think he's headed to Iowa?" he asked.

"He'd be more likely to be hiding out somewhere. The daughter would only slow him down."

"But it's a possibility," Jenna said, finding her voice.

"Yes," though her voice sounded tentative. "Or he could let you think so, to get you to part with more money."

"My funds are stretched to the limit right now. All that's left in my trust fund is the money I saved for Paige's education and a tiny operating fund to keep our heads above water for a few more months." Then it dawned on her. Jerry was desperate to save himself. His daughter's education didn't count. "My God! Paige is in danger."

"Ms. DiFranco … Jenna," the attorney said, "to protect your interests, I suggest you give your sister temporary guardianship of your daughter, so if your ex-husband shows up, your sister will have the legal right to keep him away from her. I'll also alert the authorities in Burlington. If he does show up, they can arrest him and send him back east."

The woman's calm tone kept Jenna from freaking out. "Yes, do that. I'll call my sister and figure out how we'll protect Paige."

"If he's after money, he'll probably call again. You need to be prepared. Mr. McKenna, do you also have a phone?"

"Yes."

She gave him a number to call the next time Jerry contacted Jenna. "This will alert the authorities. Hopefully, he'll stay on the line long enough for them to triangulate the call to get his location. Get him to spell out in plain language exactly what he's after. The authorities can subpoena the phone conversation from your carrier, if he says enough to convict him."

"I'll help her," Gray said.

"I know this is difficult, since you're on the road, but you're not alone. You've got family and friends plus the authorities ready to go to bat for you. I'll get back to you if I hear anything more, and feel free to call me, if you need anything else."

"What do you want to do next?" Gray asked after the call ended.

"Get in touch with Aubrey. I've got to warn them." Fortunately, she got right through to her sister. "Has Paige spoken to her father again?"

"Not that I'm aware, but she's been with Geoff and Eileen all afternoon. Why don't you call her yourself?"

"I will, but I'm sending her back to you immediately. I need your help, sis." She brought Aubrey up to speed about her ex's latest activities.

"I can be on a flight to L.A. with her in a few hours, if that's what you want."

"No. If he can't find her in Burlington, that's the first place he'll go, presuming he has the means to get there."

"Where should I take her?"

Jenna glanced at Gray. This would be news to him too. "Can you and Mitch meet us in Palm Springs? We should be there tomorrow. All five of us can finish the trip to L.A. together."

"Won't that be a little, uh, close? Five of us in that coach?"

Gray nodded.

"It'll just be overnight. But that way we can all keep an eye on her as we head back home."

Aubrey rang off after promising to get in touch as soon as they finalized their travel plans.

"We're meeting up with them?"

"I should've talked it over with you first, but it just occurred to me."

"There's an exit coming up with at least one fast food place and a gas station. One of them should have Wi-Fi."

"Why do we care about Wi-Fi?"

Within minutes, she had her answer as Gray retrieved a notebook computer she didn't know he'd brought. He had her contact Linda Harris to request she email her the necessary temporary guardianship along with the means of providing an electronic signature.

"Do you think that's still necessary, since Aubrey and Mitch will be meeting up with us tomorrow?" she asked.

"Probably not. But why not err on the side of caution, just in case the guy were to show up in Burlington yet today?"

The document was waiting for her once they were set up. Five minutes later, Aubrey had become Paige's temporary guardian.

That task checked off her list, Jenna allowed herself a few minutes to sit back with a latte before they hit the road again. "At what point did you plan to tell me you had a notebook along with you? I could've used it to write my stories."

"Deprive you of writing them longhand? What kind of friend would I be, if I kept you from the divine experience of composition?"

"Please, Gray. Spare me the high road attitude. You didn't want me checking on things back in L.A. without you listening."

He raised his palms in surrender. "You got me. I made no secret of my conditions before we left."

"Which you've enforced until yesterday. My one condition fell apart before we'd barely gotten on the road."

He reached for her hand from across the booth. "I'm glad it did."

She almost said, "Really?" but caught herself in time. She'd already appeared needy enough.

"Why don't you call the kid while we're here?" he asked as if to change the subject.

"Right. Thank God you're helping me stay on top of this."

He rubbed a thumb across her knuckle. "You've got a lot on your mind. Least I can do."

She placed her hand over his. "More than I deserve for the way I treated you at first. You're becoming … more than a friend."

He raised a brow, his hand tightened around hers. "Agreed."

Her mouth became cotton. Of all the inappropriate times for this relationship to intensify. All she could manage was a nod.

"We need to talk after we get you to L.A. Too much other stuff going on right now."

She attempted to clamp down on her increasing heartbeat. "Okay."

"Hi, hon," she said once Paige came on. "I hear you're out with Geoff and Eileen."

"Hi, Mom. Yeah, we're playing miniature golf. Can I call you back later?"

"I hate to break up your game, but I have good news. You, Aubrey and Mitch are leaving town later today to join me."

"What?"

"I miss you, sweetheart. I want you to spend a day on the road with me."

"Well, yeah, sure. But I'm having a great time here, Mom."

"I'm sure you are. Since it appears Aubrey will be staying there from now on, you and I can go back sometime and have a real visit."

"But—"

"Please, Paige. I don't want to debate this."

"When can we come back?"

The child in Paige was negotiating for a better deal. Gray had claimed her daughter was such a grown-up. But to get the child on the move, she'd promise her whatever. "After my tour ends. Maybe Christmas."

"That's five months away." A whine undercut Paige's tone.

"You'll be in school until then. But think of it. There'll probably be snow on the ground. Not mass-produced snow like on a ski slope but real snow."

"Oh, all right."

"Can't wait to see you, sweetheart. Now, let me talk to Geoff so we can make arrangements." When Geoff came on the line, she gave him a headline version of what was happening and what she needed Eileen and him to do before Paige got curious.

"Okay, Jenna. We're leaving now."

She hung up and heaved a huge sigh of relief. "I wasn't sure I could get her to agree without threatening her."

"You did great."

"Great. Right. Now all we have to do is wait to hear they've made their flight without Jerry showing up."

An hour later, Aubrey called to say they were packed and ready to catch an early morning flight to Chicago, where they'd then pick up another flight to Palm Springs. "We're staying the night in a motel near the airport, just in case."

"Call when you're about to board. I'll breathe easier once you're in the air, but I won't feel secure until I can hold her in my arms."

THE CHIRPING of the phone sounded ominous. As if a ring tone could suggest a mood. Jenna shot a quick glance at Gray, who removed his hands from the steering wheel long enough to put two thumbs up.

She cleared her throat. *Stay strong. Don't let him goad you into saying anything.* "Hello?"

"Took you long enough."

"I told you if you still had that attitude, I wouldn't discuss anything more with you."

Gray immediately placed his call to the authorities.

"Let's *discuss* this, then. I'm very concerned about our daughter's welfare. You've left her with relatives or on her own too much. She'd be better off with her old dad."

"You want to share custody? How would that work, Jerry, with me in California and you on the East Coast?" To obtain her evidence against him, he had to spell out his intentions.

"I don't plan to share custody. You've had your chance and you've botched it."

"Get real. You couldn't possibly obtain shared, let alone full custody. Not after cheating on me repeatedly and then running off with all our savings."

"That was all hashed out in the divorce settlement. But I'm a changed man, ready and willing to reclaim my parental responsibilities. Certainly could do a better job than you."

"It's been less than a year since the decree. How can you expect a judge to believe you've changed that much in so short a time?" Her insides split apart as she kept him on the line. They were almost there, almost at his real reason for calling.

"But you've changed, haven't you? Claimed yourself nearly penniless so the judge would let you keep the money your dad left you. No sooner was the decree final than you were dipping into the trust fund that should have been part mine. Buying that expensive bus you don't need."

She took a deep breath. One more parry, distasteful as this whole discussion was. All she had to do now was get him to admit what he was really after. "Y-you can't do this, Jerry." She had to sound scared, pleading. Not difficult at all. "Paige is all I've got."

"Should've thought of that when you left her so often."

"I had to rehearse. She understood. My concert tour is the only way I can support the two of us since you're not contributing anything to your child's welfare."

"You won't have to worry about that when I get custody."

"Please don't do this." Sounded like a pretty authentic plea to her. "Isn't there anything I can do to convince you to drop your suit?" Here it was. But he had to be the one to say it.

"Hey, I miss her. Can't wait to see her again."

"Please, Jerry. Reconsider."

Silence for a few beats, like he was actually rethinking his suit. "You'd have to promise to be around more for her, change your lifestyle."

"And in return?"

"Get rid of that damned coach, downsize to something less grand. In return, we split the proceeds, seventy-five percent to me."

"You'd give up custody of Paige in return for three-fourths of the money from the sale of my coach?"

"Sounds so crass put that way. Let's just say, we could all benefit from such a decision. What'd'ya say?"

She prayed this exchange would be enough to keep him away from Paige forever, because she couldn't continue. "I'd say, go to Hell." With great pleasure, she hung up.

She immediately got in touch with Linda Harris and went through, word by word, her exchange with her ex.

"You did great, Jenna. If the authorities can access the recording of that conversation, it would appear we have him."

"I just hope we were on the line long enough for them to track him. I won't feel my daughter's safe until I hear he's under arrest."

"THE FLIGHT GOT in fifteen minutes ago. They should be coming through that gate any minute," Gray told Jenna. He'd spent the last couple hours attempting to distract her by discussing the tour. Hadn't expected her to be so antsy about seeing her daughter again. Per Aubrey earlier in the morning, they'd made it to Chicago, where they caught their flight west without any sign of Jerry. But until Aubrey had the kid with her, she wouldn't relax.

"There they are!" Jenna shouted as the trio emerged from the secured area. She took off running, leaving Gray in her wake. The kid ran too.

The pair embraced, even jumped up and down, as each tried to outdo the other with greetings. Finally, the kid broke away. "We had such a cool flight, Mom. Aunt Aubrey let me buy a huge bag of pastries in Chicago, which we shared once we were in the air."

"Sweets?" Jenna glanced at her sister.

Aubrey shrugged. "We didn't have much time between flights. Danish and bagels were the fastest and easiest way to get a meal."

Please, Jenna, don't put down their meal choice. Aubrey and Mitch had just spent a fortune to get the kid out of town fast.

Jenna tipped up her daughter's chin. "But I'll bet after all that time in the air, you're hungry again. The motor coach is right outside. How 'bout we get you all settled and stop for something to eat?"

While the three females discussed the flight, Mitch pulled Gray aside. "Why didn't you call me when Jenna's husband threatened her?"

Gray had wondered about his brother's readiness to jump on a plane with Aubrey and the kid without questioning the plan. Too passive for Mitch. Apparently he'd come along with the idea of taking over once he arrived. "This is Jenna's issue, Mitch. She had to be the one who decided how to deal with her jerk of an ex."

Mitch leaned closer, so the women wouldn't overhear them. "But Jenna was in no condition to handle any more stress. I could've contacted people who handle this kind of criminal case and spared her having to deal with this on her own."

His brother had become so accustomed to taking charge in their family, he didn't get that other people could lead their own lives without his "help." Even after Ms. Fixit, Aubrey, had entered his life, Mitch still saw himself as the one who called the shots. In an instant of perception, Gray realized his issue with Mitch wasn't so much his own inability to step up as it was Mitch's inability to step aside. That shed a totally different light on things. Jenna had suggested he tell Mitch how much it bothered him that Mitch had this need to always be in charge of family matters, but at the moment, he didn't need to fight Mitch for control; his task was to help Mitch relinquish some of it.

Gray laid a hand on Mitch's shoulder. "I'm sure you could've cut right through this problem with Jenna's ex-husband, but rather than cave from the additional weight placed on her shoulders, by dealing with it herself and standing up to the guy, Jenna's come a long way toward getting her life back. Surely you can understand how important that was to her."

Mitch narrowed his eyes, as if processing Gray's words. "She's really doing better? Aubrey and Paige have been worried about her."

"We all may have overreacted to Jenna's situation," Gray said. "We pushed her into a corner where the only thing she could do was fight back."

"She's sure won you over now." Mitch raised a brow, gave him a look he probably reserved for cross-examining witnesses.

But Gray wasn't ready to share any more information about the last several days on the road with Jenna. Their time together was precious and something to be shared by only the two of them. "I've gotten to know her better and come to understand some of the reasons why she was close to a breakdown."

Their talk was cut off when the others joined them and they all made their way to the coach.

The women and Paige went on to the bedroom, where they would stash their luggage. "Bet you could use a break from driving. How 'bout I take the wheel for a bit?" Mitch asked.

Mitch was trying to take over again, but in this case, Gray didn't mind. It'd be great to sit in the passenger seat for once. "Don't mind if you do."

"First thing, though, I'll check the AC," Mitch said. "It's an inferno out there."

"Shouldn't be a surprise. We're in the desert in the middle of summer."

Mitch familiarized himself with the dashboard, then went to check the temp. "That guy you recommended as our new mechanic is due to check in with Geoff today," Mitch said when he returned. "If he works out, I'll be able to increase my hours with Orville, so we can pay this guy. Good find, especially for being on the road when you met him."

"Yeah, this trip is accomplishing more than just returning the coach to the coast."

"You mean like befriending our client? You've certainly become sympathetic to her plight. Before you left on this excursion, you gave us the impression you couldn't stand her."

Gray checked the women's whereabouts before replying. "She's got her good points, though worry about her tour and now the kid has kept her on edge most of the trip. Leaving her meds behind didn't help, either, at first."

Now Mitch looked over his shoulder as well. "Does she suspect anything?"

"Hasn't said anything to make me think she's on to us. But I don't like keeping things from her, especially now that you're all here."

"I hear you, but from what you've told me about her tour concerns and her ex, do you really want to shake things up further by 'fessing up to our role in her escape?"

Gray ran a hand through his hair. "No, I suppose not. She was so jumpy this morning until you all arrived, I don't want to add to her mood."

They didn't go far before Gray spotted the burger place Jenna had mentioned. "Where are we going once we hit the City of Angels?" Mitch asked as soon as they pulled in.

Gray related the issue of where to store the coach. "Whether we're ready for it or not, looks like we're about to cross paths again with the infamous Iris Appleby."

Twenty

"Sure you can eat all those fries on your own?" Gray asked Paige after the waiter delivered her lunch.

"Why didn't you order your own, if you want some?" she threw back.

"Just wanted one. Or ten. All this road food has gone directly to my hips."

Jenna smiled to herself. Gray was attempting to bond with her daughter, lame as his efforts might be, since Paige didn't seem to be taking to it. Or was that her daughter's own lame attempt at kidding him back?

Mitch pulled his carton of fries closer. "Gray knows better than to take mine."

"How should we spend our time in Palm Springs?" Gray asked, moving the conversation along. "There's an aerial tramway that takes you up the mountain where we could check out the scenery. Would you like to go there, Paige?"

Paige finished downing a fry then shoved the container toward Gray. "I'd rather talk about why the big rush to get me out here."

Aubrey, Mitch and Gray became very interested in their food. Paige kept her eyes on Jenna. "I told you why, sweetheart. I missed you. I shouldn't have taken off like I did. I wanted you to experience some of the *thrill of the road* too."

"C'mon, Mom. You've barely seen me the last few months while you've been so busy with rehearsals." Paige wasn't letting this drop. The child still resented her recent absences.

"You're right. I didn't realize how much my time away—though for good cause—bothered you, until you took off on your own for Iowa. Ever since we started this trip without you, I've regretted not bringing you along."

"How come you decided you missed me the same day Dad called?"

Aubrey stacked her dishes and gathered the others. "Are you finished eating yet, Paige? We should be going."

They all rose before Paige. "Bring your burger with you," Mitch told her.

Though Paige obliged, her pace was much slower than her usual sprint. In fact, at one point, she actually pulled up, and tilted her head.

"Paige? Are you coming?" Jenna asked.

"Yeah, sure, Mom."

Back in the coach, Aubrey unfolded a couple of brochures she'd taken from the restaurant lobby. "I found some info about that tramway. Here, Paige, you check out this one. It's about shopping areas."

Though she accepted the document, Paige didn't open it. Instead, she turned to Jenna. "Okay, I get it. You don't want to talk about Dad in front of everyone else. But can just the two of us go off and talk somewhere?"

Although Paige had asked countless questions when Jerry first moved out of the house and then during the divorce, Jenna had sugar-coated her answers, believing the girl wasn't ready to hear about the realities of love and marriage. Paige loved her dad, and Jenna hadn't wanted to burst that bubble. But now the man had offered to sell his custody rights and all bets were off. "Yes, Paige, I think it's time you learn what's been going on. But let's wait 'til we can be alone. Okay?"

"When?"

The child wouldn't let this drop, not that Jenna had believed for one minute she would. "Let's do that aerial tram thing. When we get to the top, you and I can go off by ourselves."

"Okay."

A half hour later, along with several other summer visitors, all five of them entered the tram. Though Jenna, Aubrey and Paige had lived in California most of their lives, only Jenna had ever been to Palm Springs. That was as a child, when she was dragged along with her mother, and later as a teen, when she appeared here for one concert. She'd stayed in her motel room until just before the performance. So the view as they ascended the sheer cliffs of Chino Canyon was new for all of them.

"Oh, my," Aubrey murmured. "The brochure said this was a rotating car, but I had no idea that meant full three-hundred-sixty-degree movement."

As the car first began to turn, Mitch backed away from the windows and edged his way farther inside.

"What's the matter, bro?" Gray asked. "A little too breathtaking for you?"

Mitch stared at the floor. "I'm a Midwestern guy. Not used to heights."

"And you were so proud of Burlington's bluffs the night we ate dinner along the river," Aubrey said, coming up to him.

"Yeah, well, you don't have to rotate to admire them. Hope you're enjoying this, Paige. I'm making a huge sacrifice to come along on this trek."

Paige, who was glued to her window view, glanced over her shoulder. "You don't know what you're missing, Mitch."

Jenna slipped in beside her. "This is quite the mechanism. My brochure says we go up two and a half miles in about ten minutes." Though she tried to sound brave, she was in Mitch's camp. Every time their side of the car faced the cliff, she clamped her eyes shut. Just ten minutes to reach the top? It already seemed like hours.

The temperature seemed to have dropped twenty degrees when they emerged from the tram, one of the attraction's selling points, escape from the heat below. After agreeing to meet back at the Mountain Station in an hour, Aubrey and Mitch took off on their own. Gray stayed with her and Paige but kept a discreet distance.

"What would you like to do while we're here?" she asked Paige.

"You said we could talk."

"You don't want to try one of these trails? We wouldn't have to go far."

"Another time, Mom. Let's go over to those benches." Paige sent a meaningful "scram" glance at Gray.

"I'm, uh, gonna check out the gift shop. See if they have any stomach tablets. That ride up didn't mix well with the burger I wolfed down at lunch."

They were all deserting her. Giving her and Paige their space. Stranded on the top of a mountain. She couldn't avoid telling Paige about her father much longer.

Paige headed off for the benches. "Over here, Mom."

Something told Jenna when she rose from the indicated bench, her life would have shifted yet another direction. *If this has to be, please let me tell her with compassion. Please help her understand.* "Okay, I'm coming." Each step was like treading her way through a bog.

Paige waited until she was seated before she spoke. "Tell me what's going on. Why'd you really rush me out here? Why don't you want to talk about Dad?"

They had arrived at a crossroads. "This is very difficult for me, Paige. I'm going to tell you the full story, but once I do, it will change things forever. I don't want to hurt you or make you sad."

"Too late, Mom. I was sad months ago when Dad first left the house. As for hurting me, unlike Dad, you could never do that. Even when you wouldn't let me go on tour with you. "

"Your dad hurt you?" She couldn't stop herself. The words just tumbled out.

"He didn't abuse me. Not physically, anyhow. They warn us about that at school. But it hurt a lot when he left town and didn't call very often."

Jenna pulled Paige into her arms. Jerry had hurt her as well, but that didn't matter compared to what he'd done to his own flesh and blood. "I wish I could explain why he hasn't contacted you much, but I can't. I've tried to spare you from finding out what he did as much as I could, but things have happened in the last day that you need to know for your own protection."

Paige twisted around to stare at her mother. "Dad's dangerous? That's why I'm here?"

"Your dad accused me of being a bad mother, because I left you behind. Said he was taking custody. I-I couldn't let him do that, Paige."

"You've been a great mom. I don't want Dad to take me." She hesitated, then went on. "If he really cared about me, he'd have called more often. Maybe even flown me out east to visit. Please don't let him do this."

Jenna closed her eyes, said a silent prayer of relief at her daughter's support. "I won't let that happen."

"Was Dad coming to get me? Is that why you said I might be in danger?"

"I, uh, think he was using you as a way to get more money from me, but I couldn't be sure he wouldn't show up at the firehouse and take you away."

Paige folded her hands, seemed to process Jenna's statement. "Yeah, that's more like him. He took most of our money with him when he left town, didn't he?"

"You know about that?"

"I heard you and Gram talking about having to cut back."

"You mean you eavesdropped."

"Nuh-uh. I came home early from a bike ride and overheard you. She said she and Grandpa Buddy could help out a little, but in their retirement, they had to watch their pennies too. After that, you didn't go shopping any more, go out to movies, you even stopped buying my favorite ice cream."

A small chuckle emerged from Jenna. The wrong ice cream. Funny how people had difficulty conceiving of huge issues until some small detail brought it home to them. She made a mental note to buy Paige's favorite ice cream again. One tiny way to make her daughter's life better. "We're not poor, Paige. Nor are we homeless. But our lifestyle has had to change given our reduced finances."

Paige cuddled closer. "I still love Dad, because he's my dad. But I don't like him. I heard him hassle you sometimes. I wanted to make you feel better, because you're my best friend. But all I could do was try to be a good kid and not make your life any worse. I never should've taken off on my own for Iowa."

Sniffling to hold back her tears, Jenna held Paige tighter. Her precious daughter understood much more than Jenna had given her credit for.

That was about as far as she'd go. No point letting Paige know her dad was unemployed and had gambling debts. Jerry's cheating during their marriage and the way he'd treated her were the last things she'd tell Paige, although her daughter apparently had heard more of that than Jenna realized.

But Paige wasn't content to leave it alone. "We still need money, don't we? That's why your tour is so important."

"Yes. When we divided up our assets for the divorce, your father discovered the trust fund your grandfather left me years ago. Because it was set up before I married your father, it was something that couldn't be part of our settlement. I used some to buy the motor coach. The rest is still quite safe, waiting for your college bills. But the motor coach could now be considered an asset, providing there was cause to reconsider the divorce settlement."

Paige digested her words. "Dad wants the motor coach?"

"Not the coach itself, the money I'd get for selling it. If the court required me to do so, I would have to sell it and give him half the money."

"But if you have to do that—"

"It would directly impact my ability to tour and earn a living for you and me."

Paige rose abruptly. "That's so unfair."

Jenna didn't know what to say. Of course it was unfair. The last few years of her life had been unfair, but complaining to her daughter wouldn't change things.

She remained seated while Paige paced around the benches, shaking her head, kicking an occasional stone or twig.

At length, Paige returned and flopped next to her. By now, tears streamed down her cheeks. "Can we stop him, Mom?"

"I don't know. I think so, but now that you know, we've already won. Even if he were to win more money from me, the only way he could really hurt me would be to take you. I couldn't bear that."

Once again, Paige came into her arms and hugged her so tight she could barely breathe.

"Hey, you two. Is it safe for a guy to join this party?" Gray sidled up to them.

"Can you stand a few tears?" Paige returned.

"Depends. Are they tears of happiness?"

"Couldn't say I'm happy, but I'm glad Mom finally told me why I'm here."

Gray studied Jenna, as if seeking a sign about how much she'd shared. "I told her we think her father is trying to get more money from me by threatening to get custody of her." That should let him know she hadn't mentioned Jerry was on the lam.

"You know about my dad?" Paige asked Gray.

Gray pursed his lips, as if debating how much to say. "Some. We've had a lot of time to talk while we've been on the road."

"Good. I'm glad she's had a friend to talk to."

Friend? Since when had her daughter placed Gray in that category? He'd been her accomplice in getting out of town.

Maybe things were actually looking up.

Twenty-One

The five of them spent the night in the coach in the parking lot of a super grocery store in Palm Springs, the women in the bedroom and the two guys occupying the bunk beds. Paige got the couch. The previous night may have been Gray's last night in bed with Jenna. Just needed time and he'd get over her. Who was he kidding? Somewhere along the route west, his feelings for the woman had gone beyond sex. Even great sex.

Thus, sleep eluded him.

"How're you and Aubrey doing?"

"This a slumber party? I'm beat, man," Mitch said from above him.

"Deliberately not answering?"

"I'm crazy about her. Don't think that's gonna change any time soon. How 'bout you and Jenna?"

Whoa! Mitch was on to him? "Told ya, once she settled down, we got along okay."

"Not just okay. That's a changed woman, bro. Not the high-maintenance broad who showed up on our doorstep chomping at the bit to chastise her sister."

"She'd been under a lot of pressure. But this road trip has forced her to relax."

"I'll buy that but not your changed opinion of the woman. Unless ... something's happened between you ..."

Should've kept his mouth shut and let Mitch get his z's. Mitch, the attorney, wouldn't end his interrogation until he had an answer. "Of course, something's happened. We've been together round the clock. What do you expect?"

"Didn't expect you to be so touchy. She's gotten to you."

"Go to sleep."

Fortunately, Mitch was apparently so exhausted from their early morning flight he didn't pursue the subject further but instead dropped off to sleep within seconds.

A SIMILAR INQUISITION was taking place in the bedroom, as Aubrey pumped Jenna for information about her days on the road with Gray. "You and Graham seem to have gotten past your initial meeting."

Jenna wasn't ready to tell Aubrey that she'd gone to bed with Gray. She'd done a quick sweep of the room that morning to assure any signs of his presence had been removed. "It was either that or spend six days on the road not talking."

"Graham probably could have managed, but I doubt that would have worked for you."

"Actually, Gray talked as well."

"Gray? You sloughed off explaining that one over the phone, but I'm not buying. Mitch told me his brother only tolerates that nickname from Geoff and him. For some unknown reason, Paige has gotten away with calling him that also. But you? Why? And how?"

Jenna unhooked her bra and slipped into her nightgown. "What's the big deal? It's just quicker to call him Gray."

"So you're not planning to tell me everything that's happened. Okay, I kept my feelings for Mitch from you until you showed up in town and I couldn't avoid our little confrontation. Just know, I like Graham. Already consider him a brother. If something's happening between the two of you, I couldn't be happier. You need a decent man in your life."

Aubrey approved of her and Gray. But there was no *her and Gray*. Just two willing sex partners. If there were more, she'd be tempted to bring her little sister into the loop. "Thanks, sis. Don't think I haven't considered the irony of two sisters finding two brothers, but it's not to be, if for no other reason than I've got a concert tour to launch and he'll be returning to the Midwest tomorrow."

"Your tour's the only thing keeping you apart?"

"Don't jump to conclusions. You may have decided Mitch is the love of your life after a few weeks, but I can't afford to fall for someone so fast. I did that with Jerry and regretted it ever since."

Aubrey slipped under the covers. "Just remember, if you need an ear, I'm there for you. Even back in Iowa. I wish you'd let me know about your problems with that jerk long before you did. You shouldn't have had to face all the difficulties you've been through alone."

"Thanks. I'll remember."

THE NEXT MORNING, they entered the outskirts of Los Angeles. Mitch drove the coach while Gray navigated. Their first stop was Aubrey's apartment. She and Mitch planned to stay on a few days, long enough to pack up some of her worldly goods. Then they'd return to the Midwest in her car, so she'd have her own means of transportation.

"I'll let you know when we get back," Aubrey told Jenna. "Sorry we can't take you with us, but my car will be loaded with my stuff," she told Gray.

"No problem. As soon as I get your sister and niece settled in, I'll fly back. Too bad Mitch won't have the pleasure of seeing your mother again, like I'm about to experience."

Aubrey chuckled. "Right. He's full of regret." She pulled him into her arms and hugged him. "Thanks again, for getting Jenna home safely."

"Actually, I enjoyed seeing this part of the country."

And then they were three.

Jenna rejoined him in the passenger seat. "Ready to meet my mom?"

"You'll like Gram," Paige put in from her roost on the couch. "She's a hoot."

Jenna rolled her eyes. "That's one way of putting it. Just don't let her get to you, Gray. Once she smells compliance in someone, she doesn't stop."

"I stand—well, sit, forewarned."

Iris Appleby was nothing like Gray pictured, given Jenna's description of her mother. A two-headed crone holding a broomstick had taken shape in his mind. Instead, the woman who greeted them at the door was human, not a creature of the underground. Her blonde hair was lighter than Jenna's, but it looked natural, not derived from a bottle, and like she'd just returned from a visit to her stylist.

"Well, hello," she gushed, looking him up and down. "You're Jenna's driver?"

"This is Graham McKenna, Mother. He's one of the three brothers who customized my coach. I prevailed upon him to bring me and the coach to California so I could get back to my tour preparations." She glanced up at the older man who stood behind her mother. "Hi, Buddy. Thanks for letting me park here."

An aging, overgrown teddy bear grinned back at them. "As long as I get a personal tour, consider my driveway your coach's new home."

"Temporary home," her mother added, the smile never leaving her lips.

"Hi, Gram." Paige stuck her head around Jenna. "I'm back."

"Paige?" her grandmother replied.

Before Jenna could explain, her mother invited them in—rather, commanded they enter her bastion.

By Iowa standards, the Appleby home was a mansion, huge, imposing and impeccably furnished. And intimidating, if Gray let it get to him. But Jenna had already prepared him for what to expect, so he acted like being a guest amidst such luxury was an everyday happening.

"Are you hungry? We already had lunch because we didn't know when you'd arrive, so we don't have anything hot to offer, but Cook stocked us up on salad and sandwich makings before she left."

"Thanks," Jenna answered for them, "but we ate on the road. Don't feel you have to entertain us. If you could drive Paige and me to my house, I'll stay there and Gray will stay in the coach overnight."

"Nonsense!" Buddy exclaimed. "We have more than enough guest rooms."

"Uh—" Jenna said.

Spending the night in a real bed sounded like a good plan to Gray, but this was Jenna's call. He waited for her to respond.

Jenna's mother, smile still frozen in place, gave her spouse that look reserved for married couples. "We've offered, don't push," it appeared to say, but the man seemed unaware of her reaction. "Other than Paige, your mother and I rarely have overnight guests. Please humor us."

Jenna turned his direction and raised a brow. "It's up to you, Jenna."

Jenna appeared trapped. "We don't want to be in the way any more than we already are, but if you insist—"

"Which I do," Buddy said. "Unfortunately, I have a doctor's appointment in an hour, so your mother and I have to leave soon. After that, we have tickets for a concert in Pasadena, so I'm afraid you're on your own for several hours."

Gray caught himself just in time before a smile spread across his face. "Not to worry. Jenna and I will spend our time finding another place to park the motor coach."

Buddy nodded, as if relieved, then left them to their own devices.

"Are you okay with this arrangement?" Gray couldn't help but ask as they gathered their things in the coach.

"Spending any time under my mother's roof is not my idea of fun, but Buddy didn't leave us much choice. He means well, thinking all my mother and I need to improve our relationship is a little more time together.”

“Nice guy.”

“Yeah, we both like Buddy,” Paige chimed in.

“You notice that Mother doesn’t challenge him openly in front of others, but I’m sure she’s back there now giving him a piece of her mind.”

“She didn’t want us here?”

“I’m guessing she doesn’t want the coach here because it will draw questions from the neighbors. If I were a big celebrity about to take off on my road trip, she’d be delighted to show us off, but having to concede I’m hitting the road again to make a living for Paige and me probably embarrasses her.”

“Gram’s a snob. She can’t help herself.”

“Even though Mother’s the one who pushed me into this tour, she was against spending so much money on the coach. Probably right on that count. But then Aubrey wouldn’t have met Mitch, and I ...” she seemed to remember the kid, “would have been forced to spend my time on the road in hotels.”

“And I wouldn’t have had such a great time the last few weeks,” Paige added.

“So I’m probably in the dog house, since she associates me with the coach.”

“That’s why I held off asking to park here until I had no other choice. We’ll stay the night and hopefully find a new home for it tomorrow.”

They hurried back to the house, so they wouldn’t keep their hosts waiting. “Paige, you’ll be in your room. Jenna, take the guest room next to ours,” Jenna’s mother directed as they entered, “and you’re down in the den, Mr. McKenna.”

“Please call me Graham.”

“Uh, yes, of course, Graham. The bathroom is on the other side of your room.”

A dismissal, so Gray carried his things to his temporary quarters. So much for impressing Iris Appleby, as if he’d ever considered the notion. Though she hadn't said a word to the effect and her smile had never left her face, she clearly wasn't happy with the situation.

What was with Jenna? The independent, never-afraid-to-express-an-opinion woman disappeared the minute they pulled into the Appleby drive. He remembered how reluctant she'd been to contact her mother, even when the old biddy had come through to save Aubrey from the suit against her. The woman seemed to have a real effect on both daughters.

Best for him to get a good night's rest in a comfy bed, help Jenna find a new parking place for the coach tomorrow and get the hell back to Iowa. No, there was one other task where Jenna was concerned. Her blackmailer. Funny, they hadn't spoken much about him during the trip. In fact, she hadn't said anything about the guy, which was odd, thinking back on their earlier discussion about her options concerning the tour. And that was even before that jerk of an ex had threatened her. Hopefully, her mother would make herself scarce the rest of the day so he could find out what Jenna wanted to do about the guy.

"OKAY, GO AHEAD AND SAY IT," Jenna admonished her mother as soon as Gray made his exit and Paige ran ahead to the room she used whenever she visited.

"Whatever do you mean?" Iris Appleby returned. "The fact that your stepfather and I have suddenly become a parking lot for an RV or the idea of you traveling cross country alone with a man you hardly know. When did Paige join you, because Aubrey told me my granddaughter had stayed behind in that hick town?"

Jenna followed her mother upstairs to the room she'd be using. "Let me get settled before we talk about Paige. As for parking the coach here, I'm sorry about the late request, and it's a motor coach, not an RV. Like I said on the phone, I just learned the place I'd lined up to store it wasn't ready yet."

"Fortunately for you, your stepfather, for reasons still unclear to me, is delighted that monstrosity is on our property. I'll let him explain to the neighbors, who clearly will not share his excitement."

Explain what? How her daughter had been reduced to playing the piano to support her daughter and herself because, when she was still a young girl, she'd picked a snake of a husband to escape the concerts her mother had pushed her into? Probably not. "I'll get right to finding new housing for the coach. It shouldn't be an eyesore in your drive for long, although personally, I think it's a pretty classy addition to your spread."

Her mother swept through the room, smoothed pillows that were in perfect shape, pulled down the duvet. "We were expecting you and Paige days ago. What have you been up to all this time?"

Her *episode* and enforced rest were the last things she wanted her mother to learn about, so she turned her story around. "I ran into your cousin, Peggy Summers, and her children, Eileen and Tommy. It seemed a great opportunity for Paige to get to know her Midwestern family. Besides, I wanted to revisit my roots."

"You spent time with Peggy?"

"Both Aubrey and I have gotten to know her. She's pretty great. Even showed me some old photos of you. And my father."

Her mother brought a hand to her mouth, obviously caught off guard. "She kept all those old pictures? Whatever for?"

"Because we're her family, and she hoped someday, now, maybe Aubrey and I would like to know about your early days."

Her mother angled her head, studied her. "What did you, uh, learn?"

"Actually she told Aubrey and Aubrey filled me in. You were almost in a movie that was shot locally, then Grandpa got sick and you had to drop out. Why haven't you ever told us about that part of your life?"

Her mother continued to smooth the top of the duvet long after she'd folded over the top. "That part of my life is over and done with. Peggy overstepped."

"Maybe so, but her little history lesson helped me understand you better. You came so close to achieving your dream of becoming a movie star. It wasn't your fault, or Grandpa's, that you had to drop out when he died. You've been trying to regain that chance ever since and the stars never seemed to align at the right time."

Her mother finally faced her. "Don't go psychoanalyzing me, Jenna. I am who I am. That's all there is to it."

"Tell me about Paige, why she's back with you already." she said as if searching for some way to shift the topic.

"Paige never would have taken off to find Aubrey if she hadn't discovered the address you left out on your desk after I asked you not to tell Paige anything about Aubrey's whereabouts."

"And Paige wouldn't have been so anxious to find her aunt if you hadn't abandoned her."

"I didn't ..." She stopped. "Okay, I don't deny leaving Paige with you as I prepared for my tour. She's had a lot to deal with this past year. But back in Iowa we began to repair our relationship. It was her idea to stay longer with the new friends she's made."

"Then, all of a sudden, you hustled her home."

Give me strength. This won't be easy. "Jerry called the other day. Acted like I'd been the one to abandon our daughter, totally overlooking his own disappearing act. His subsequent calls got more threatening." She told her about Jerry's offer to drop his suit in exchange for the bulk of the proceeds from the sale of the coach.

Her mother sank into a chintz-covered chair, her hand covering her heart. "After all he put you through, he had the gall to demand more money?"

"He's apparently a very desperate man." Jenna relayed what she'd learned from her attorney. "I was afraid he might find Paige and take her as a bargaining chip. That's why I gave Aubrey temporary guardianship and asked her and Mitch to bring Paige to meet up with us in Palm Springs."

"Aubrey's here too?"

"For a day or so. She and Mitch went on to her apartment." No point informing her mother of Aubrey's plans to depart again. Aubrey could handle that part herself.

Her mother didn't reply for a bit as she appeared to absorb the news. "I told you buying that RV was a bad idea. That's the only good thing to come out of that man's actions," she said at length.

Jenna let that one slide. "Paige is on to her father," she added. "You've advised me all along to tell her about Jerry's antics, but I didn't want to disillusion her." *Like you did with my own father.* "Paige suspected something was up when she was suddenly shuttled out of town and wouldn't stop hounding me until I spilled. I told her as much as I could, except how Jerry treated me the last years of our marriage, his affairs and that he's currently on the run from the law."

"In other words, you soft-pedaled everything, like you always do?"

"She still loves him, Mom. I didn't want to destroy everything. Once the authorities track him down, he'll most likely go to prison. That will be difficult enough for her to understand."

Her mother released a huff. "It's that hasty trip to the Midwest that's responsible for all this."

Her mother could be so obtuse, choosing to see the world from her own distorted perspective. "No, Mom. My concert tour put all this in motion."

Her mother straightened, as if dismissing Jenna' words. "Whatever, at least you're back now so you can make up the time you've lost. When is your first concert?"

"I don't know. My promoter hasn't produced the schedule I wanted. I'm debating whether to move the tour back, fire him, and put my own schedule together or find another alternative."

Her mother's mouth shot open. "You have to get this tour underway as soon as possible. You need money, soon. You're hardly prepared to earn a living any other way."

Brutal words, but mostly true. Still, would she have ever said something like that to Paige? "You're right. I need money. But maybe there's a better solution than the concert tour."

"Thirty-eight years old and you're as naïve as you were two decades ago when you first went on the road. Heaven knows how you would have wound up had I not steered your career and kept you going."

Most likely, she wouldn't have married the first man who showed an interest in her just to get away from her mother's influence. But no point stirring that pot now. "Heaven knows, Mother."

Apparently sensing her comments were going nowhere, her mother stood, saying she and Buddy needed to leave.

Jenna spent several seconds staring at the door after her mother left. Naïve, huh? Of course, she'd been naïve in her late teens. Her mother had been the center of her life since they'd moved to California. Aubrey added a new dimension to the family. But with a span of nine years between them, they hadn't been close until much later. She'd gone years thinking her baby sister a rebel, undisciplined. It hadn't occurred to her until she'd been on the road a few years that Aubrey enjoyed a kind of freedom she'd never known and now wanted for herself.

When her mother figured out how to use Jenna's musical talents to augment the family coffers, Jenna had gone along with the scheme without questioning. When her mother had signed on as her "manager," taking fifty percent of the profits, Jenna had also said nothing. It never occurred to her the arrangement should be any different until Jerry came along. He was perfectly content to let her keep touring, because they needed the money, until he learned about her mother's cut. When it proved difficult to "fire" her mother, Jenna simply quit the tour, no longer the naïve, dutiful daughter. Instead, she became the naïve, unsuspecting wife.

Not naïve anymore. So, if that was the case, if she believed herself no longer naïve, why had she immediately seized upon going back on the road as the way to support Paige and herself?

She found her way to the den, tapped on the door. "Gray," she whispered. "Are you in there?"

He came to the door, stripped down to his briefs and t-shirt. "Come in. Let me slip back into my jeans. Wouldn't want your mother to think anything improper is going on in her house." He raised a brow. "Unless that's why you're here?"

"Cool your jets, McKenna. As tempting as that sounds, I need a sounding board at the moment." She didn't tell him her mother and Buddy had already left. No need raising temptation.

"Have a seat."

She related her "chat" with her mother, ending with her mother calling her naïve. "The other day, you threw out several alternatives to launching my tour immediately, most of which I poo-pooed. But now I'm wondering if I did come to this solution too quickly."

"You want me to talk you through it?"

She liked how he jumped right in, ready to help. "I've told you most of the story about Jerry's leaving Paige and me. That night in the motel parking lot, when I confronted him in the act, when he could deny his guilt no longer, he begged me not to leave him. Said he'd go to counseling. I wasn't naïve enough to believe him, but for Paige's sake, I stuck it out."

"You didn't throw him out then and there?" He sounded incredulous. Could she blame him? It had been easier to tell herself Jerry would change rather than strike out on her own.

"Sounds pretty lame now, but at the time, I wanted to make sure Paige didn't suffer. When I returned from the library the next day—I volunteered there in the children's section—I found all his clothes and belongings gone, only a short note to Paige telling her he'd gotten a job offer out East he couldn't refuse. He even had the nerve to suggest he'd send for her when he got himself established. Paige believed him for months."

"When did you start thinking about returning to the road?"

"I didn't think to check our bank accounts right away. Still the trusting little wife, I guess. But when I couldn't withdraw cash from an ATM the next day, the realization hit like a bomb, although it didn't set in completely until my bank manager confirmed our accounts had nothing in them."

To underline her point, she repeated, "Nothing, not even enough to keep his own daughter in groceries for a week. When I attempted to pawn my engagement ring, I learned it was a fake."

"That's tough."

"Miraculously, the car was paid off. I immediately traded it for a cheaper model. That netted a small amount to tide us over for a bit."

"Did you, uh, consider getting a job?"

Did he think she was completely helpless? "Of course. But because I had no college education and no prior work experience, my choices were limited."

He held her hand. "From what I've observed the last several days, that shouldn't have been a deterrent. You're quite talented."

"Thanks. But at the time I was so hurt I could hardly see straight. Finally, desperate, I contacted my mother. She and Buddy were traveling at the time, but I was able to text her. Didn't tell her much, because I wanted to avoid her inevitable, 'I told you so.'"

"And?"

"Since she was texting, which she hates, she said it in fewer words than if I'd seen her in person. I must have said something about now having to support myself and Paige, because her next text was short and to the point. She told me I'd have to go back on the road again, since that was all I could do."

"You agreed, just like that?"

She forced herself to remember. Most of the time, she blocked that day from her memory, it was so difficult to relive. But now it was important to get this clear. Had she just gone along with it and not tried to come up with something else? "I was so scared. For the first time in my life, I had to take care of myself, plus Paige. I didn't know if I could do it. I'd had firsthand knowledge of my mother struggling to keep food on the table and a roof over our heads. I didn't want that life for Paige and me. I guess I leapt at the first plausible way to make a living."

Then what happened?"

"I was so determined to beat her at her own game before she returned, I started making my own plans, which as you've observed, haven't turned out so well. In my haste to put something together, I didn't stop to consider what else I could do." A wave of regret swept through her. "It never occurred to me I could do something else. Not until you questioned me."

"IN TIMES OF GREAT STRESS, we all tend to jump to easy conclusions rather than think through our options. We need immediate reassurance we can handle whatever faces us." Like assuming Ellen would respect his wishes and lay off running during her pregnancy.

"Even you? You seem to always know what you're doing."

"Boy, have I got you fooled."

"Besides agreeing to drive me out here, when have you ever made a bad decision?"

"That wasn't enough?" He smiled to let her know he was kidding.

"Okay, I won't push. Misery loves company, that's all. I was hoping I wasn't the only fool around."

Why her wish not to be alone in her foolishness suddenly pierced through years of secrecy, he had no idea, but in a heartbeat he was ready to reveal his darkest secret. "You're not. I lost a child because I trusted my fiancée to do the right thing."

Her jaw dropped. "What?"

"Ellen and I had a casual work relationship which resulted in a pregnancy. I did what I thought was the right thing and asked her to marry me, even though I didn't love her. I told her I did, just so she wouldn't do something foolish and get rid of the baby."

"Is that what happened?" she asked in a very quiet voice.

"No. She wanted the baby. But she used poor judgment. We were both runners, her more than me. She refused to give it up even after she discovered she was pregnant. Insisted on participating in a 5K run, although her friends, doctor and I begged her not to."

"It didn't go well?"

"She claimed she knew her body better than any of us, but that didn't prevent her from slipping on wet pavement. Lost the baby immediately."

She reached for his hand, gripped it hard. "Oh, Gray."

"I've never told anyone this story, even my brothers. They have no idea I was ever engaged. I'd grown quite attached to that child, though she was barely more than seven weeks along. Didn't feel I could go through all that pain again. Which is why I haven't let myself get attached to anyone since." When he finally found the courage to gaze at her, tears filled her eyes.

"No wonder you didn't want to talk about it. I should have let it drop."

"No, as much as I've put you off, I'm glad you pushed. Over the years, I thought the memory would disappear if I didn't think about it or discuss it with anyone else. Instead, it's been tucked away inside me like a cancer, preventing me from moving on, from living a full life."

"I'm glad you felt you could confide in me."

"Tell you the truth, I'm surprised I did. It just poured out."

She seemed to consider his words. "Is that why you've kept your distance from Paige? You always refer to her as the kid, not by her name."

Besides persistent, Jenna was also perceptive. "Uh, yeah."

He took a giant breath. For the first time in years, he didn't feel the unbearable weight of loss as his lungs moved in and out.

She squeezed his hand again, softly ran the knuckles of her other hand across his cheek. "That explains your behavior. You're such a good man otherwise."

There didn't seem to be anything else to do but lean down and kiss her. "I'll miss making love to you once I return to Iowa."

"Making love?"

Had he really used that phrase? But now she'd called him on it, no point taking it back. The last few times had been pretty special.

"Hey, I was teasing," she said. "No need to wrinkle your brow."

"We'll soon be two thousand miles apart. I've, uh, kind of gotten used to you."

"That's some admission."

He stopped himself before going further. The woman had grown on him, and not just for the sex. Her stubbornness exasperated him, but he was learning more and more about the frustrations and self-doubts behind it. She'd been dealt some rough blows from her ex-husband and apparently her mother as well. But he and Jenna had issues to resolve before they could consider what might happen if those two thousand miles between them disappeared. "It's been good. I feared I'd be battling you all the way across country, but that didn't happen."

"Just the first day. I never should have left my meds behind. Yet another not-so-intelligent decision on my part."

He touched her hair, pulled a strand behind her ear. "You've got to stop putting yourself down." God, her mother had done a job on her. If he were to stay here much longer, the chances were high he'd have words with Iris Appleby.

She ran a hand down his cheek, over his accumulation of stubble. "Easy to say, harder to follow through on. But thanks for the support."

Tempting as it was, probably not the best idea to follow through on her touch either. He forced his brain to come up with another topic. "What's next on your to do list?"

"Top priority is finding a place to store the coach."

"Okay, let's get started. Your folks have Wi-Fi? I've got my laptop. We can start searching the internet."

"You'd do that?"

"Sure. You called the obvious places. Now it's time to dig a little deeper, get creative."

"We've got a couple hours at least before Mother and Buddy return, meaning we can stay here in the den. I'll let Paige know where we are."

"See if the kid, uh, Paige, would mind making a few sandwiches with the makings your mom said were in the fridge. I'm famished," he said as she reached the door.

As it turned out, Paige was delighted to have something to do, and after she fixed sandwiches for herself and Gray and a salad for Jenna, joined in their brainstorming session. "What about a parking lot?" she asked when told the gist of their problem.

Gray considered. "Not a bad idea, except we need somewhere that's locked all the time and preferably inside, so the weather won't be a factor."

Paige's shoulders collapsed. "Oh."

"But your thinking was spot on," he said.

"So let's run with both your ideas," Jenna added. "We need to find a locked parking lot with a roof. What kind of business would that be?"

"Wait!" Paige cried, jumping up. "Your business is in an old fire station. Could we find one of those here?"

Gray joined her, took both her hands in his. "That's a brilliant idea … Paige."

"Really?" Paige shot a glance at her mother. "What do you say, Mom?"

Jenna joined them, pulled both of them into a bear hug. "I say you've earned your way onto my team. Let's start searching for fire stations no longer in use. Maybe auto shops too."

An hour and a half later, their quest was successful. They located a firehouse that had been closed a few years back but was still on the market. The town's facilities manager was willing to rent it to her for at least a week, until a spot opened up in the commercial lot, or longer, if this alternative proved more cost-effective.

As they were once again high-fiving each other, Paige turned to Jenna. "Are you still going on tour, Mom?"

Twenty-Two

J enna looked to Gray for help, but he simply nodded while offering a half-smile, as if to say, "You can do this. Just give it a moment, then say what's in your heart."

"Good question, Paige. One that's been bouncing around in my head for some time, probably before I ever left California, if I'm honest with myself."

"So?" Paige persisted. "Are you still going on your tour?"

"No. At least not right now. I rushed into this way of supporting us without thinking it through. I need to give myself a chance to step back and reconsider my options."

Gray unobtrusively backed away.

Paige settled onto the edge of the sectional that took up most of the room. "You could do all kinds of things, Mom. I'd eat beans and franks every day if you made less money because you didn't go on the road."

"Good to hear, until that first pair of jeans comes along you just have to have."

"I'm fourteen, Mom. I could babysit for money to buy things like jeans, if you'd let me."

Could her daughter look more sincere with her eyes so wide and hopeful? Paige had no idea how difficult babysitting could be, although maybe it was time to let her find out. "I haven't decided to cancel the tour yet. But since my promoter hasn't been able to line up a full schedule, I'm putting it on hold. Indefinitely."

With that announcement, Paige popped up and hugged her again. "That's great!"

Gray finally spoke. "You want to help, Paige? Help your mother come up with other ways to earn a living. Tell her about the books, Jenna."

"What books?" Paige asked.

Thanks, Gray. She hadn't been ready to discuss her infant career in children's books. Now she had no choice. She told Paige about the stories she'd created the last few days.

"Terrific, Mom. You're gonna be a big shot author."

Jenna raised a hand. "Not so fast. First I have to find a publisher, maybe an agent. Even if they buy the books, we have to wait months before they're published, and then they have to sell. Even if people buy them, it takes months to get royalties."

"So, you find something else to do as well," Paige counseled. "Wait a minute. Didn't you tell me yesterday that Dad wanted you to sell the motor coach and give him some of that money?"

"Yes?"

"Then do it, just don't give any of the money to Dad."

Had Paige been talking to her grandmother? "I-I've considered selling the coach, but I'm hesitant to part with it so soon." She shifted her gaze to Gray. "Believe it or not, I've grown rather fond of it."

"Could you rent it?" Had Gray had been coaching Paige. Coaching? *Funny one, Jenna.*

"I've played with the idea. Even called an agency that rents this type of coach, but that was to get an estimate of how much it would cost me to rent from them. I hadn't considered doing the renting myself. I have no experience with celebrity tours. I wouldn't know how to go about it."

"Could you call them back, ask how they do it?" Paige asked.

"Good idea, hon, but business people don't share their secrets with potential competitors," Jenna replied.

"How about with kids doing a report for summer school?" Paige asked.

"Summer school?" Then she got it. "I don't think so. That wouldn't be honest."

"I'll use whatever I learn for school this fall."

Jenna glanced at Gray, who returned a "why not?" expression.

For once, Paige's pluck might just work to her benefit. "I suppose you could try, if you think you could do it."

Paige rolled her eyes. "I keep telling you I'm not a kid, but maybe just this once, I could pretend I still am and let them take pity on me."

Her daughter's audacity scared her. Nonetheless, why not let her interrogate someone else for a change?"

She handed Paige the card and sat back to observe her daughter undermine the rental agency's reluctance to reveal their secrets. By the time Paige thanked the person on the other end of the line, she had a list of standard rental terms and requirements, including average length of rental period, average number of miles traveled and stops and types of special requests made by the celebrities.

"Here." Paige handed her the list. "Now you have a start. I can't wait to tell my friends we rented the coach to some big rock star."

"Didn't that person at the agency stress the confidentiality part of their deals?" Gray asked.

Paige shrugged. "Sure, but that doesn't mean I can't brag *after* the tour is done."

Now Jenna rolled her eyes. Who was this child, er, young person?

Gray just shook his head.

"I need a break," Jenna said. "How about we watch a movie? Buddy should have something here that appeals to all three of us."

Several hours later, though fatigued and lying on a mattress even more comfortable than the one in her coach, Jenna still couldn't sleep. Though her brain was preoccupied rethinking her comeback plans, irresistible thoughts of Gray wormed their way in. She hadn't believed she'd ever love again, if that was what this was with Gray. He certainly excelled at giving a woman physical pleasure, but he was also turning into a pretty special friend. She hadn't enjoyed many close friendships in her life. Despite the difference in their ages and outlooks, Aubrey had been her closest confidant, and these days her baby sister's attention was focused on someone else.

Since she'd jumped into this tour idea too soon, whatever she did from here on, about the tour or with her relationship with Gray, she had to carefully consider her needs and wants and Paige's as well. She could do this. She was capable of more than just playing the piano.

This conclusion reached, her body relaxed and sleep took over.

THE FOLLOWING MORNING, she joined Paige, Gray, and Buddy for breakfast around eight. Her mother never made an appearance until later in the morning at what she referred to as "a more civilized hour."

Though Cook—her mother used the generic title rather than the individual's name—had fixed them a hot breakfast of scrambled eggs, sausage and oatmeal, Jenna prepared herself a glass of orange juice and a bowl of cereal.

"Only driven to the Midwest once," Buddy was telling Gray, "but I took the northern route through Colorado and Kansas. 'Course I was headed up to Minneapolis, not southern Iowa. Had a part at a dinner theater in the area."

Gray set down his coffee cup. "I considered going that way, but I've never driven one of these rigs through the mountains."

Jenna choked on her orange juice, wiped her mouth with a napkin. "Sorry. Go on."

"Probably a good decision," her stepfather said. "Some of those higher curves are a little tight, though you see RVers going through them all the time."

She waited for Gray to correct Buddy on terminology, but Gray was too polite. Even Paige held her peace. "When do I get my tour?" Buddy asked, his plate now clean.

Gray was about to answer when they were interrupted. "Who does that rig out front belong to? Is it yours, Dad?"

A gorgeous woman younger than Jenna had come into the room. Dad? Was this dazzling brunette Buddy's daughter, Alexandra? It couldn't be. The Alex Jenna remembered was overweight with mousey brown hair and glasses. This dynamo was fit, stacked, wore no eyewear, and most telling of all, the anemic hairstyle had been replaced with a dark brown pixie cut with a slash of bangs that covered the better part of one huge brown eye.

"Alex, what a nice surprise. You remember your stepsister, Jenna, don't you? And this is her daughter, Paige, and Jenna's friend, Graham McKenna."

The newcomer nodded to the three of them, then switched her attention to her father. "What's up, Dad? I got a call from the Petersons across the street. They're beside themselves with curiosity."

"But too snooty to come over and ask for themselves. You're here to do reconnaissance?"

She pulled a slight grimace. "You got me. But I have to admit, when they described that bus parked in your drive, I couldn't resist checking it out for myself."

"It's mine, Alex. If that's who you are? You look so different than the last time we were together," Jenna said.

Her stepsister blinked, drew a hand through her hair to shift her bangs out of her eyes. "Occupational necessity. I leveraged some of Dad's contacts in the industry to launch my own agency. Even those behind the camera have to look good out here."

"Alex manages Loretta Kinsolver," Buddy said, obviously very proud of his daughter.

"Loretta Kinsolver?" Jenna responded. "The up and coming country star?"

"None other," Alex replied. "Loretta and I started about the same time. A newbie like me was about all she could afford, and thanks to her huge talent and a few good breaks on my part, she kept me on as her career took off."

"Alex downplays her role in promoting her clients' careers." Buddy rose and placed a fatherly hand around his daughter's shoulder. "She's accomplished a lot in a short time."

Alex turned to Jenna. "That's really your coach?"

Jenna nodded. "Just got in from Iowa last night. Gray and his brothers customize the things back there."

"What's the story—you going on the road?"

"That's the plan. I'm returning to my concert career. I was once considered a rising star in the concert world. A piano virtuoso." Couldn't very well announce to Alex as well as Buddy that, after spending a significant amount of her trust fund on this vehicle and bringing it halfway across the country, she was reconsidering her decision. Fortunately, neither Paige nor Gray contradicted her.

"Oh, right. I couldn't miss all the pictures of your days on the road your mother placed around the house. Didn't you end that career when you got married?"

Even though Buddy and his former wife had nothing to do with each other, surely he would have told Alex about her divorce? "I'm now a single mother with a daughter to support." She nodded toward Paige. Unlike Alex's mother, she hadn't sued her former husband for almost all his worth. In fact, the opposite had occurred, yet she was still embarrassed to share what Jerry had done to her, despite opening up to Gray.

"Hey, maybe you need a manager to handle your concert tour, Jenna? Alex is the best," Buddy said.

Her stepsister's eyes flickered, as if someone had stuck a gun in her ribs. "Uh, Dad, I , uh, don't really deal with concert artists," Alex said.

"I already have a promoter, Buddy," Jenna added. *But probably not for much longer.* "But thanks."

"I was just about to give your dad the nickel tour of the coach," Gray said as if to break the awkward silence following their reactions to Buddy's suggestion. "Would you like to join us, Alex?"

Jenna shot him a grateful look. Alex may not have meant to put her down. Buddy's ex-wife's negative opinion of him, his new wife, and her family was probably too strong for Alex to ignore.

Buddy clapped his hands. "Great idea!"

Alex surveyed Gray from head to toe and back up again, offering what Jenna could have sworn was her stepsister's best come-into-my-lair smile. "Sure."

"I've met Alex before. Guess she didn't remember me. I'm just a kid," Paige said once the men and Alex left.

"No, Paige. Somewhere along the way these past several months, you've become a young woman. A very intelligent young woman who I intend to listen to more often."

Paige sat up straighter. "Yeah? Wow."

"Thank Gray. He told me to take another gander at how grown up you've become."

"Gray? You're calling him Gray now? Does that mean you've become friends?"

Apparently Paige had failed to notice that change yesterday. "I guess so. We spent the last several days together. Plus, he's the one who helped me escape. I'm sorry I had to leave you behind, but you seemed to be enjoying yourself, and I had to get out of there."

"Uh, Mom, about that?"

"Yes?"

"I need to tell you something, but first, I've gotta know you haven't freaked out anymore."

Since when had she and her daughter traded roles in the caregiving department? Still, it was comforting to know Paige had it in her. "I've done great. These past several days on the road seem to be just what the doctor ordered. Plenty of time to think and rest and not stress out. What do you have to tell me?"

Paige pulled in her lips, as if debating how to proceed. "You didn't actually escape. We all helped you."

Jenna blinked. "What do you mean, *helped*?"

"You were getting so restless staying at the McKennas' we didn't know how long you'd stay."

"I was being kept prisoner in that house, Paige. The walls were closing in on me."

"Yeah, well, we were all afraid you'd take off on your own before you rested enough. We, uh, let you think you were getting away."

A wave of ice shot up her fingers through her arms to her chest and squeezed her heart. Jenna attempted to speak, but her vocal cords seemed to have frozen as well.

"Mom? You're not angry, are you? You got what you wanted, to get back here."

They'd played her? Even Gray, with whom she'd shared so much? And Paige was in on it too? Or had they played her as well, convincing her this was for her mother's own good? No need to chastise her. Jenna's issue was with Aubrey and her merry band of conspirators. Jenna cleared her throat, cleared it again, before sound came out. "No, I'm not angry. I sensed something like that was going on and went along with it, since my main goal, like you said, was to get back home. Now I am."

Paige sighed in relief. "I'm so glad. I was afraid … well, never mind."

"Don't worry, kiddo. I'm feeling much better … now." Best change the subject, prevent Paige from figuring out she was about to explode. "Bring me up to date on what you did after I left."

Apparently delighted to have gotten past the subject of her mother's escape, Paige blithely rattled on while Jenna struggled to digest this information and regain control of her nerves. She was barely able to respond to Paige's comments. Her mind kept returning to what Paige had told her about them helping her escape. Helping her. It was all she could do to keep from immediately running out to the coach to confront Gray.

"I, uh, need to talk to Gray alone. Thank him again for bringing me here, especially after what you've just told me. So I need you to stay here with your grandmother and Buddy. Okay?"

"I guess." It came out as a mini-whine. "But what if Dad shows up?"

"Let your grandmother handle him. Don't open the door. Do you understand?"

"Yeah." Paige went off to shower and dress.

Jenna was pretty sure Jerry wouldn't come anywhere near her mother's house, but she was relieved Paige was on the alert.

The tour group barreled into the room as Jenna finished rinsing her cereal bowl. "That is one well-equipped buggy, Jenna." Buddy pulled out a chair.

"I'd have to agree," Alex added, although she didn't join her father at the table. "I've ridden on several tour buses, and this one takes the cake. You say you had it customized?"

Jenna swallowed, attempted to focus. "That's right. Gray did the reengineering and his brother and my sister, Aubrey, finished the interior." Though they didn't deserve her endorsement, she wouldn't give Alex one crumb of negativity to report back to her mother.

"Your company did that?" Alex asked Gray.

Gray's lips curved up on one side. "Yes, ma'am. All to Jenna's specifications."

Alex's eyes traveled from Gray to Jenna and back again. "I'm impressed, no small feat for someone who's grown up here in La-La Land. Glad I didn't bring Loretta with me, or you'd be arm-wrestling her for the keys."

She placed a kiss on her father's cheek and went for the door. "You ever change your mind about going on the road, give me a call. I can earn big points with my client if I could set her up in a rig like that."

This couldn't be happening, a solution just falling in her lap like this. Surely Alex was just blathering, making her job sound more important than it was.

Whether Alex was serious or not, Jenna couldn't deal with her suggestion right now. She had to confront Gray. She seized upon the first idea that came to mind. "If you'll excuse us, Gray and I need to leave, if we can borrow your car, Buddy. We've found a place to store the coach temporarily. I want to check it out before I sign a contract."

Buddy's face wrinkled, as if offended. "Moving it so soon? I was hoping I could spend the night there. Didn't have the nerve to ask yesterday."

"It'll probably be here another night. Mom would just prefer it not be here much longer."

Buddy hung his head. "Your mother is much too concerned with the neighbors' opinions." Nonetheless, he handed over his keys.

"There's a park coming up. Turn right when you see the entrance," she said to Gray once they were in transit.

He twisted his neck to check her out. Raised a brow. "Private time before we hit the garage?"

"Something like that." She didn't wait for him to round the front and open her door when they parked. She sprang from her side and found her way over to a bench. Gray followed and sat beside her. "What's up?"

"I've been thinking about our road trip."

"Fond memories, I hope."

"They were until I started considering how easy it was to get away from the house that day. Everyone was conveniently away doing other things. Only you were there to guard me."

"Best time to make our move."

"Despite your recent commitment to take over Mitch's mechanic work, you were still able to get away this long to bring me here."

"I told you. I needed a break. The job had been wearing on me. This trip has given me time to think about where I'm going with my life."

"How opportune you had so much frozen food on hand so we could enjoy hot meals along the way."

Gray studied her, a quizzical expression on his face. "Where are you going with this, Jenna?"

She burst from her seat and stood facing him. "How dumb do you think I am? You set me up. All those so-called conditions you made me agree to—no money, no phone, no drivers' license. I was still a prisoner. You'd just changed my jail from your parents' home to my own coach."

She paced in front of him. "I saw you as my liberator. More recently, my friend. And lover." The last came out a mere whisper. She leaned into his face. "Instead, you've been conning me. Guarding me from myself. With the help of my sister and your brother. Even my own child."

Her eyes swelled and ached from the effort of holding back tears. "All of you, traitors. Conspirators. But you especially. Something seemed to be happening between us. Was that your own special touch, seduce the lady along the way to make time go faster?" Was she that poor at judging men? She really had come to trust this one. He didn't answer her question. "How did you find out?" he asked instead.

"My daughter thought I should know."

"I was going to tell you. Not right away, because I didn't want to lay anything more on you while you were dealing with your tour."

"How considerate. But you're still as guilty as the rest of them. More so, because you made me believe you cared about me."

Gray shot up, grabbed her hands. "Okay, I'm guilty. Guilty of getting you here safe and sound. Of challenging you to consider all the options you have for getting yourself back on your feet, not just with a concert tour. Guilty of respecting your sister's plea not to tell you about their role in your escape, because she wanted you to feel like you were once again in control of your life. Aubrey, Paige and the rest of them care so much for you, they were willing to let you take off, even though they worried whether you had completely recuperated."

She attempted to pull away, but he held tight. "I'm also guilty of breaking my promise to steer clear of sex because you turned me on so."

He made his part in all this sound so rational, logical. Jerry used that tactic also. "Nice speech. How am I supposed to believe anything you say when you've been playing me all along?"

"Because I love you, you stubborn woman. I spent days trying to talk all of them out of this scheme. But when it became evident how much you hated being confined at the house and how determined you were to get away, I agreed to help you escape."

His reply stopped her momentarily. "You love me?" Had he said that to excuse his part in this scheme? Jerry had told her he loved her once too.

"That's what you heard in all that?"

"I heard the rest, but the love part got my attention."

"Yeah, well, it sort of came out when I wasn't expecting, but now that I've said it, I meant it. I've fallen in love with you, Jenna, despite how much I've steeled myself against personal involvements."

Confronting him seemed to have dragged the admission from him, like he couldn't hold back. Yet he seemed to regret revealing his feelings. The feelings of indignation and betrayal that had boiled her blood a minute before cooled. But not entirely. "If you were so opposed to fooling me, why did you go along with it?"

"Mitch was the only other one who could've driven the coach. Geoff can't be on the road for very long with his MS. Aubrey would've insisted she come along. Would you have really wanted that arrangement?"

"No, I—"

"Even though you'd been a real long-distance pest while we worked on the coach and you and I seemed to tangle as soon as you arrived in town, I also witnessed a very vulnerable, broken woman. Despite my preference not to get involved, I couldn't help myself. You got under my skin from the minute you stormed into the garage."

Had she sensed his interest even then? Was that why she'd bristled so at his comments about her parenting style and later offered herself to him? Because she was just as attracted to him. Even in the midst of her so-called breakdown, problems with Paige, and worries about her tour, something inside recognized a soul mate in this man? "You, I, uh, that part was real?"

He went on, "Then there was the matter of your blackmailer. Did you really want anyone else to know how that had come about?"

Oh, no. Not now. Not when she'd glimpsed a brighter future for herself and Paige with Gray. He was such a straight-shooter, could he forgive the lie she told to get his cooperation? Her stomach clenched. This topic had to come up at some point, but did it have to be in the middle of Gray telling her he loved her?

"About the blackmailer?"

"Yes?" *Just say it. You knew you couldn't avoid it forever.*

Thank God he hadn't brought up her blackmailer until now. He might have stranded her on I-40, if it had come up sooner. "That guy, uh the one I said was blackmailing me, won't be a problem. He, uh, doesn't exist."

Gray backed up a step. "He … what?"

"You were so close to agreeing to help me, I could feel it. I added this one little detail to seal the deal. How was I supposed to know you were setting me up as well?"

Gray clamped his mouth shut, studied her like she was some kind of mischievous child whose shenanigans had just been exposed.

"Gray? Say something."

"There was no musician who threatened to expose you to the media if you didn't give him a place on your program?"

"No. Aubrey says you and your brothers operate under this *white hat* complex. This need to play hero. I must have sensed it, used it to my advantage."

He shifted his feet, kicked away a clump of dirt. "In other words, you played me, too?"

She hung her head. "Yes."

"Yet you're upset with all of us for deceiving you because we were trying to protect you. Don't you realize how hypocritical that is?

"Yes, of course I do. But I told you, I was desperate. Doesn't condone my lying but explains it."

"What about … the other guys?"

"You mean the one-night stands?"

If only she could tell him she'd made that part up as well. She studied her shoes.

Better get on with this. She gazed up at his serious profile. "I didn't lie about those men. As much as I'd like to forget they existed, that's the hell I created for myself."

Her eyes locked with his, searched for signs of disgust or disapproval. But she couldn't discern what was going through his mind.

"I never lied to you about that period. I'm not proud of my actions. Nor do I excuse them. My ex-husband's head games ate through whatever confidence I had in myself as a woman." She lifted a hand to his face, touched a cheek with her forefinger. He took another step back. "You never took advantage of my emotional state. I pushed you into action. I love you for your restraint and then your response. You gave me back my self-confidence as a woman, something I didn't know whether I'd ever feel again."

His expression softened. "You love me, too?" His voice was hoarse, his tone uncertain.

"Stupid, huh? When neither one of us is particularly strong on our feet right now."

"Is that how broken spirits heal?" He ran his hand through her hair. "They help repair another broken spirit?"

"We are a pair of the walking wounded, aren't we?"

"The point is, we're still walking. I don't know how we'll do it, with me back in Iowa and you out here, but we'll find some way to walk together."

"You forgive me for making up the blackmailer?"

"Do you forgive me?"

They both nodded, then fell into each other's arms.

Later, as they returned to her mother and Buddy's house, her phone rang again, now playing a piano riff. It was her attorney, Linda Harris. "Good news. Your ex-husband was picked up by the police near Gary, Indiana. It all happened because you kept him on the line for them to triangulate his location. He's on his way back east to be arraigned. Since he's already demonstrated he's a flight risk, I doubt he'll be out on bail soon."

Jenna collapsed in her seat, relief surging through her. "Thank, God. Did he put up a fight?" Not that it mattered. She wanted him caught any way it took.

"No. Apparently he was so low on funds, he may have just given up, thinking he could at least get a bed and meals in jail. I'll keep you informed about further legal proceedings."

"Thank you so much for all your help, Linda. You've made my day."

One huge problem addressed. Now, to deal with the rest.

Twenty-Three

By the time they returned to her mother's house, Alex had left. Buddy stuck around long enough to retrieve his keys then suggested Gray might like to see his rose garden. Though she suspected Gray wasn't the horticultural type, Jenna didn't offer him an excuse to escape the invitation. Her mother would be up by now and most likely had prevailed upon her husband to get Gray out of the house. *Get ready. The show's about to start.*

She wandered into the vast living room. Might as well do this in the open rather than the enclosed quarters of the guest bedroom. She settled on the flowered chintz sofa and picked up a magazine from the nearby coffee table. One of those weekly entertainment news pieces that built celebrities' careers by the number of their photos displayed week after week.

She had only reached Page Five before her mother interrupted her reading. "There you are. I hope you were able to convince the garage to provide a new home for that monstrosity parked outside, because I'd rather not deal with that particular detail. Heaven knows, I've had enough other items to handle this morning, but you can now rest easy. Everything's settled."

And there it was. She would have bet money her mother couldn't resist this challenge. "What's settled, Mother?"

"Since you haven't managed to fill the gaping holes in your schedule and your tour plan in general, I took the liberty of stepping up." Iris Appleby remained on her feet.

If her mother had stuck a hand in Jenna's middle and pulled out her insides, her stomach couldn't have been more savaged. Her mother was once again taking over her life. Jenna was the reptile immobilized by the snake charmer. Her mother's announcement left her momentarily speechless. She had to put a stop to this.

"I called some of the halls you played years ago to ascertain their interest in having you back," her mother continued. "So far, I've got three definites prior to contract, four interested and two more maybes." She crossed her arms over her chest, seemingly enjoying the limelight.

How had her mother lined up more venues in one morning than her promoter had in over a month? Never mind, this was Iris Appleby. The woman was a steamroller, which was exactly what she was doing to Jenna right now. Time to get out of her path.

Her mother wasn't done. "You'll need to catch up on the rehearsal time you've missed the last few weeks. I've rented a spot for you less than a mile from your house. The rent includes a separate studio with a six-foot baby grand, tuned once a week, a key for private access, and you have it from eight in the morning until eight at night. You can start tomorrow."

"That's, uh, all very nice, Mother, but—"

"Buddy has prevailed upon one of his old musician friends, an instructor at Santa Monica College, to act as your coach. He'll sit in tomorrow and the next day and from that will present you with an analysis of your current level of proficiency and an improvement plan."

Her mother was ticking off several of the to-do items Jenna and Gray had discussed. How had the woman put this together so quickly?

Jenna finally found her voice. "You made all these decisions without me?"

Her mother looked up from the file she'd been referencing, startled. "Since Paige will be staying with me the better part of the next several months while you're on the road, she might as well get used to my being in charge." Her words emerged with a clipped finality.

It was one thing to run her life, entirely another to take control of her daughter's. She took a long, calming breath and rose to her full height, two inches above her mother. This was it. *Just do it.* "No, Mother, I don't want you in charge of my life or Paige's."

Before replying, her mother placed the file on the coffee table, then straightened to address her older daughter. "Excuse me?"

"You won't be in charge, because I'm not going on the road. At least not in the immediate future. Maybe someday but only under the conditions I choose. Not yours."

Her mother opened her mouth, closed it. Then took a seat on the couch Jenna had just abandoned. "I don't understand. You have to go on tour if you expect to support yourself and Paige without our help. Paige will be perfectly fine here."

"My place is with Mom now, Gram. She doesn't have to go on tour to support us."

Paige had apparently been doing her thing again, listening at doors. But for once, Jenna was glad her daughter had heard the exchange with her grandmother. It would save explanations later. Still, Paige's penchant for eavesdropping needed to be curbed. Soon.

"I don't expect or want any help from you, Mother. Your definition of help is control. I allowed you to take over my life once before when I didn't know any better. I won't let you run my life again."

"Where are those photos of my entries in last year's Rose Competition, sweetheart?" Buddy called from the doorway.

"I think we may have walked in on a private conversation, Buddy," Gray said, attempting to lead Jenna's stepfather back to the part of the house from which they'd come.

"Did you have something to do with my daughter's abrupt change of mind, Mr. McKenna?" her mother charged.

Gray shot a questioning look at Jenna. "Uh, I'm not sure what you're getting at, Mrs. Appleby."

"Really? When I spoke with her yesterday, she was planning a concert tour, though her schedule was barely developed. Now she tells me she's dropping the entire idea. The only person she's been with in the interim is you. I want to know what you said or did to make her change her mind."

Gray's eyes appeared to be reading Jenna's, trying to determine how she wanted him to respond. "I, uh, wasn't aware there'd been a change in plans."

"Gray didn't make me do anything," Jenna cut in. Okay, there may have been a few moves on the floor and bed back in the coach where he was somewhat the master, but she'd let him take that role. "I made this decision on my own, although I have to thank him for helping me get there. For helping me open my eyes and realize I was more than a concert pianist. I told myself I could do this again, and when it wasn't coming together, blamed myself for being such a poor manager. But the real reason I've been floundering is because I've started to recall how much I hated it when I was younger."

"I see," her mother said, her eyes having narrowed to mere slits. "So much for respect and gratitude." She turned to her husband, "I seem to have developed a nasty headache, Buddy. I'm going to my room. Would you mind seeing my daughter and granddaughter home before you take Mr. McKenna to the airport?"

"Uh, sure, dear," Buddy replied, confused.

Her mother made her way to the staircase on the other side of the room from where Jenna, Gray and Buddy stood. The woman never missed a chance for a dramatic exit.

Once she'd departed, Gray asked, "You okay?"

"Never better. But I have to get out of here."

"If it's okay with Jenna, I think I'll hold off returning to Iowa for another day," Gray said to Buddy. "If you could take the three of us to her house, we'd appreciate the ride."

"Uh, of course," Buddy answered, a look of bewilderment on his face.

Jenna sat next to Buddy on the front seat of Buddy's car. "I'm sorry you had to witness that little scene. When I was eighteen, I just assumed my mother being in charge was normal. But I've changed since then. I couldn't let Mother take over again, not when I now have my own daughter watching me as a role model."

"Your mother means well, kid. She's in awe of your talent, because she doesn't see herself as blessed. She just wanted to be part of your success."

"Help her find some other way to use her talents," Jenna said. "She did a phenomenal job putting a tour together for me in a few hours this morning. A much better job than my soon-to-be-fired tour promoter delivered. She just needs a more willing recipient."

Buddy chuckled. "Not me. The woman controls my life enough the way it is. Plus, I've had my own manager for over thirty years. But I'll see if I can't redirect her energies another way from both you and me."

JENNA'S HOUSE, a rambling bungalow, was also in Glendale but a little farther up in the foothills. Even though she'd left in a hurry for the Midwest, it appeared neat and orderly.

While Paige ran off to her room, Jenna went through the rest of the house checking things, raising window shades. "I did the dishes, took out the trash and straightened up a bit before I left, but it's been three weeks, so overlook the appearance. I can't afford a cleaning person. Never had one anyhow, although the weeks before I left I could have used one."

Gray set his things down in the living room. He liked the décor, a light blue and gray combo. Though not luxurious, it reflected Jenna's special flair.

An hour ago, he was ready to throttle the woman when he learned she'd conned him about the blackmailer, but considering the huge conspiracy he and his fellow plotters had thrust on her, he'd consider things even. He was sorry he'd missed the better part of her confrontation with her mother. What he had overheard made him feel like a proud parent discovering his child had actually listened and was following through on what she'd learned.

By the time they arrived in L.A., he'd already formed a pretty negative opinion of Iris Appleby, but whether Jenna would wake up and rebel had remained to be seen. Even if she did, would she have had the backbone to act? But she had, and he was happy for her.

Finally, Jenna returned and dropped beside him, her nervous energy apparently having run its course.

"That was some show you put on for us."

"The old me stepped back to observe, and the new me, whoever she is, took over. I couldn't believe those words were coming from my mouth, but they just kept rolling out. I meant every word of it, except—"

"Yes?"

"Now what will I do, Gray?

"Now that you've eliminated concert tours from your list of career options? What about selling the coach? Or renting it?"

"I have to do one or the other."

"You want help?"

"You're offering?"

He took her hand. "Yeah, but a lot more than just helping you decide what to do with the coach. I'm offering you whatever help you need to support yourself and Paige, at least until you're no longer questioning your abilities and your desirability. If you're going to hang out in bars, I want to be sitting right next to you.

She returned a weak smile. "I don't love the idea, but I'm willing to give counseling a try."

He squeezed her hand. "I'm glad you came to that conclusion on your own. But I'd like for us to become a team."

"I'd like that too."

"Then come back to Iowa with me."

"Live in Iowa? Leave California?"

"Think of it this way, there you'll be free of your mother's influence should you be tempted to backslide."

"What about you? Are you going back to a job that's more a familial responsibility than your passion?"

She wouldn't let him off the hook, even though so much was changing in her own life. "For now. I owe it to the guys to get the place in the black. We're almost there."

"Mitch is leaving."

She did have a point. "All the more reason for me to stick around and help Geoff."

"No law says you can't do something else parttime."

"If I pursue my ideas about auditorium acoustics, I'll need someone to provide the sound. How about you give those concerts for me?"

Her brows lifted. "What an intriguing idea."

"I like it too." As usual, Paige had shown up long before she made her presence known. "Paige, now that we both agree you're a young adult," her mother said, "it's time for you to stop listening in on other people's conversations. Only kids do that."

"Gram does."

Jenna raised a brow. "Which makes my point."

Paige hung her head for a beat. "Okay." Then she brightened. "So, we're going back to Burlington—to live?"

"You okay with that?" Gray asked. "You'd have to leave your life and friends here in California behind?"

"Sure! But I'll need a new coat and boots come winter."

Clothes now topped off her daughter's list of priorities. The years ahead were going to be quite the challenge, but one she was ready to face. Still, Paige had to accept Gray. Although the two of them seemed to be getting along better since Paige returned to California, their initial meeting hadn't gone well. "Gray and I have become, uh, more than friends during our trip, Paige."

Paige returned an eye roll. "Well, duh! You think I didn't see that happening? You've got to give me more credit, Mom. I keep telling you, I am not a child anymore."

Jenna pulled Paige into her arms, then Gray embraced them both. "You sure aren't," Jenna chuckled.

Gray turned to Jenna, "This sounds corny and unoriginal, but with you playing the piano in an auditorium I design, we could make great music together."

The biggest smile she'd given anyone for quite some time lit her face. "Corny, maybe, but I can't wait for the music to begin."

Dear Reader

Don't miss the next book in the series, *Keeping It Casual*. Read on for an excerpt.

Thank you for reading this book. If you liked it, won't you please take a minute to leave a review?

To learn more about the eleven contemporary romances and two novellas I've written, sign up for my newsletter at https://www.subscribepage.com/BBContempRom.

I've also written two cozy mystery series, the Mah Jongg Mysteries and Nailed It Home Reno Mysteries. You can learn more about them on my website, www.barbarabarrettbooks.com.

Follow me on Facebook: http://bit.ly/2aXZvG9
Follow me on Twitter: https://twitter.com/bbarrettbooks

Sneak Peek

Here's an excerpt from Book 3 in the Matchmaking Motor Coach trilogy, *Keeping It Casual.*

The woman interested him, no doubt about that. Not only was she fantastic looking in an exotic sort of way, but here she was proposing he do her a favor for which so far he'd seen no advantage to himself. Yet if he agreed to help her and screwed up, he could offend his brother's woman and thus his brother as well.

The lady had gall. Though she'd explained why she'd asked him and why it was necessary, it still didn't ring true. But he was curious. And attracted.

Plus, he had his own agenda. She might be just the answer to his dilemma with Eileen. She'd laid her cards on the table, and now it was his turn. "As it happens, I could use your help also."

"Really?" She flipped her bangs away from her eyes. "Do tell."

"You met my girlfriend, Eileen, the other day?"

"Miss Warm Personality?"

"That's her. I need your help breaking up with her."

She gulped, retreated a step. "Me? I'm supposed to come between the two of you? Surely, you don't think—"

"No, of course not! I just want it to look like we've got a thing going." Although now that he'd denied the idea, it lingered in the back of his brain.

"I got the impression the two of you were serious. She was a bit territorial when she met me, but that's natural for someone who thinks she's got a right to her claim."

"Yeah, well, I'm not ready to be claimed."

"Oh."

"But I, uh, feel I owe her. She was the first woman I've seen on a serious basis since being diagnosed with MS. She helped me see I can live a nearly normal life, even with my disorder. She gave me back my self-confidence. But now it's just not working out between us."

"So just end things."

"I want this to be her idea, not mine."

"You think she'll break things off if she finds me sitting there holding hands with you in front of her? Why not find her another man?"

"Might have done just that, except you came along with this other proposition. Thought I could parlay it into a mutual deal."

"Surely you don't expect me to move in with you and, uh, other things?"

She'd done it again, planted an image in his head that wouldn't easily go away. "You mean sex? No. Although it would help if everyone else believed there was something going on."

She backed up a few inches, shook her head. "I don't know, Geoff. This will make me look like the 'other woman.' My relationship with my stepsisters is shaky enough."

"Might be your chance to get closer, if they come to your defense." He'd been banking on her initial negative reaction to Eileen to gain her agreement. Apparently her desire to make nice with her stepsisters was stronger than he'd realized.

Her phone interrupted their negotiation. When she checked the screen, her expression changed to one of forced tolerance, as if she had to deal with a pesky telemarketer. She stepped away to take the call.

"Yes, I'm working on it, but it's even more complicated than I imagined." For the rest of the call, Alex listened, although she opened her mouth a couple of times to say something, then didn't. He couldn't hear the other party. She pressed her lips together and glared.

Within minutes, it was over. Alex blew out a breath, then put her cell away.

"Client?" Geoff asked as she returned to where he had perched once again.

"Recognized the look, huh? If I didn't know better, I'd say you were in cahoots with said client."

"Tightened the screws?"

"Nice way of putting it." She stuck out a hand. "Looks like we have a deal."

Learn more at BarbaraBarrettBooks.com.

Acknowledgments

Thank you to The Wild Rose Press, who first published this book in 2015. I learned so much about the publishing process from them before recently regaining my rights to this book. In all, they handled the original publication of eight of my contemporary romances.

In order for this book to take on new life, it needed a brand new, snappy cover suggesting the loving relationship that develops between Jenna and Graham. My grateful thanks to my cover artist, Chris Kridler of Sky Diary Productions, for taking the few snippets of ideas I fed her about this story and bringing this lovely cover to life. I also have her to thank for the formatting.

Thank you, Bernadine Marsis, for proofing the reedited version of this manuscript. Although many pairs of eyes have reviewed the book over its lifetime, the updates required one more look.

Thanks always to my husband, Veryl, for his continuing support of my writing career. He has seen me through more typewriters, tabletop computers and laptops than I can recall.

Books by Barbara Barrett

Cozy Mysteries

The Mah Jongg Mystery Series

Craks in a Marriage

Bamboozled

Connect the Dots

Beware the East Wind

Flower Power

Jokers Wild

The Charleston Challenge

The Dragon Lady Gets Her Due

Courtesy Call

also available in paperback

Nailed It Home Reno Mysteries

Measure Twice, Murder Once

Loose Screw

Death by Drywall

Homicide by Hammer

Nuts and Bolts

Snared by the Snake

A LITTLE ABOUT
BARBARA BARRETT

Barbara Barrett skipped a midlife crisis by writing romance novels at night when she wasn't at her day job as human resources analyst for Iowa State Government. The first took longer to complete than she likes to admit and remains unpublished. But after that, the words flowed, especially after she joined the local chapter of Romance Writers of America.

Her first book was published in 2012. She has now published eleven full-length contemporary romance novels and two novellas. More recently, she has published nine cozy mysteries in her Mah Jongg Mystery series and six in her Nailed It Home Reno Mysteries series. This book is the second in "The Matchmaking Motor Coach" trilogy, which she wrote as a love letter to her hometown of Burlington, Iowa. The motor coach in this book is the linchpin of this series as it unites three sisters with the McKenna brothers.

Barbara is married to the man she met her senior year at college. They have two grown children, eight grandchildren and two great-grandchildren.

Now retired, she spends her time in Florida, Iowa and Minnesota. She earned her B.A. degree in history from the University of Iowa and her master's degree in history from Drake University.

When not in front of her laptop creating her next story, she plays Mah Jongg, is learning to paint with acrylics and enjoys lunches with friends.